Michael Rousell

Enjoy

NINE

9/11: OFFICIAL COMPLICITY

… connecting the dots

A Novel

BY MICHAEL ROWLAND

AuthorHouse™ UK Ltd.
500 Avebury Boulevard
Central Milton Keynes, MK9 2BE
www.authorhouse.co.uk
Phone: 08001974150

First published by AuthorHouse 1/8/2010

ISBN: 978-1-4343-7884-2 (sc)
ISBN: 978-1-4343-7885-9 (hc)

Printed in the United States of America
Bloomington, Indiana

This book is printed on acid-free paper.

NINE

9/11: OFFICIAL COMPLICITY

… connecting the dots

Official complicity: Construction of a false account?

A Novel

BY MICHAEL ROWLAND

A conspiracy theory, according to the Concise Oxford Dictionary, is:
"A belief that some covert but influential agency or organization is
responsible for an unexplained event".

This novel is a work of fiction, and the imagination of the author, yet the detailed facts and events relating to 9/11 in this novel are:
'ALLEGEDLY TRUE'

All characters, organizations and events portrayed in this publication are either the product of the author's imagination or are used fictitiously.

This work is intended to inform all those among us (the interested public) who desire to know the truth behind a truly horrific event.

To the memory of all the innocent victims who lost their lives, and the many injured on 9/11 and 7/7; also dedicated to the emergency services in both the United States of America and Great Britain

LEST WE EVER FORGET

****

This novel is not meant to offend or upset the families of the victims of 9/11 and 7/7.
If I have, I am truly sorry. MR

The American people have the right to know the TRUTH.
I hope by writing this novel I may have helped in some way.

"We have not heard from Osama bin Laden in a long time, I truly am not that concerned about him."

President George W. Bush at
a news conference on 13 March 2002

"Let me be very clear about this. Had we had the information that was necessary to stop an attack, I would have stopped the attack ..."
"... If we had known that the enemy was going to fly airplanes into our buildings, we would have done everything in our power to stop it."

President George W. Bush, to reporters, 5 April 2004

OSAMA bin LADEN: "... I was not involved in the September 11 attacks on the United States, nor did I have knowledge of the attacks ..."

September 11 2001

TIMELINE FACTS (according to the U.S. Department of State, 2002)

08.47 a.m. Plane crashes into the North Tower of the World Trade Center

09.03 a.m. Plane crashes into the South Tower of the World Trade Center

09.17 a.m. The Federal Aviation Administration (F.A.A.) shuts down all New York City area airports

09.21 a.m. The Federal Aviation Administration (F.A.A.) halts all flights at U.S. airports. It is the first time in history that air traffic has been halted nationwide

09.38 a.m. Plane crashes into the Pentagon. Evacuation begins immediately

09.43 a.m. The White House evacuates

09.59 a.m. The South Tower of the World Trade Center collapses

10.10 a.m. A portion of the Pentagon collapses

10.10 a.m. Plane crashes in Somerset County, Pennsylvania

10.22 a.m. The State and Justice Departments, as well as the World Bank, are evacuated

10.28 a.m. The World Trade Center's North Tower collapses

10.45 a.m. All federal office buildings in Washington, DC, are evacuated

01.44 p.m. Five warships and two aircraft carriers are ordered to leave the U.S. naval station in Norfolk, Virginia, to protect the East Coast

04.10 p.m. Building 7 of the World Trade Center collapses

The Flights

American Airlines Flight 11

From: Boston, Massachusetts (Logan Airport)

To: Los Angeles, California

Lives: 92 people on board

Crashed into the North Tower of the World Trade Center at 08.47 a.m.

United Airlines Flight 175

From: Boston, Massachusetts (Logan Airport)

To: Los Angeles, California

Lives: 65 people on board

Crashed into the South Tower of the World Trade Center at 09.03 a.m.

American Airlines Flight 77

From: Washington, DC (Dulles Airport)

To: Los Angeles, California

Lives: 64 people on board

Crashed into the Pentagon at 09.38 a.m.

United Airlines Flight 93

From: Newark, New Jersey

To: San Francisco, California

Lives: 44 people on board

Crashed in rural Pennsylvania (south-east of Pittsburgh) at 10.10 a.m.

VICTIMS

Victims came from more than ninety countries around the world.
World Trade Center: 2,823 (includes airline passengers)
Pentagon: 125 (not including plane victims)

'THE PLANE FACTS'

The Project for a New American Century, which wrote of the need for a 'catastrophic and catalyzing event, like a new Pearl Harbor', had members from throughout top government echelons, including Cheney, Rumsfeld, Perle, Wolfowitz, Feith, Bolton, Armitage, Abrams and Wurmser, as well as Bush's brother Jeb, the governor of Florida.

'America's top military leaders drafted plans to kill innocent people and commit acts of terrorism in US cities to trick the public into supporting a war against Cuba in the early 1960s. Approved in writing by the Pentagon Joint Chiefs.'

'Operation Northwoods even proposed blowing up a U.S. ship and hijacking planes as a false pretext for war.' (ABC News, 1/5/01; Pentagon documents)

1980s: Osama bin Laden runs a front organization for the mujahedin/ Islamic freedom fighters rebelling against Soviet occupation of Afghanistan. The CIA secretly backs the mujahedin. Pakistan's President Benazir Bhutto, understanding the ferocity of Islamic extremism, tells the then President Bush:
'You are creating a Frankenstein.' (MSNBC, 24/8/98; Newsweek, 1/10/01; more)

Chapter One

'The tongue is but three inches long, yet it can kill a man six feet high.'

Japanese proverb

SEPTEMBER 12 2007 (a.m.), Central Park, New York

Frightened, cold, hungry, exhausted, and a fugitive in a foreign country!

'Well, I can't imagine it getting any worse than this,' thought Alex, trying to come to terms with the predicament he currently found himself in.

'Or could it?' he wondered.

While on vacation in New York, on the sixth anniversary of 9/11, fifty-eight-year-old Alex Monroe unwittingly becomes involved with a 'group' calling themselves 'The Plane Facts'.

Over the last six years the group have been peacefully demonstrating in the area bordering Ground Zero, handing out leaflets, detailing some of the available facts and incidents surrounding 9/11.

They are totally convinced, along with millions of other people around the world, that the President of the United States, together with his trusted senior advisers, was somehow involved with the tragic events on that fateful day.

Sleep!

That's what Alex longed for right now. He wouldn't have said no to a little food and a hot drink, but they would have to wait a while, given that there were government agents out there searching for him, and his accomplice Larry Underwood and, if caught, what would become of them?

Alex and Larry had been outside most of the night, in the cold, owing to the fact that they had to hastily escape from their pursuers, or, to be more precise, one determined secret government agent, whose sole purpose was to relieve them of incriminating evidence, which, if it ended up in the wrong hands, could ultimately topple the American government. There was yet another reason for this particular agent to apprehend them. The evidence which Alex had unsuspectingly found in his possession pointed to this agent's involvement in one of the worst acts of terrorism on the American mainland.

Deciding to move around to keep warm, Alex, slowly and cautiously, lifted himself off the cold floor, trying to avoid the damp newspapers and fetid stain-soaked blankets which were scattered around their hideout, located beneath one of the many bridges dotted around the grounds of Central Park.

Gingerly, he started to pace the area, stamping his feet on the ground, at the same time rubbing the cold from his arms, his breath pluming before him in the crisp morning air. The blood in Alex's veins felt like ice water. He couldn't ever remember being so cold.

Larry, likewise, began to stir, stretching his arms, flexing his back, trying to circulate some warmth around his chilled body.

Now feeling considerably warmer, Alex made his way back to their makeshift shelter, avoiding the pools of water which had accumulated from the previous day's rain. Satisfied they were protected from the elements, he then began to arrange his backpack – which contained a handful of his hastily packed possessions, into a crudely made pillow. Then wrapping his coat snugly around his shivering body, trapping whatever heat there was, he began to stare at the rippling image of the fading moon in the black, filthy puddles through the gap in their crude shelter. As Alex was slowly falling asleep, his thoughts began to drift back to the weeks and months since he'd received the tragic news about his wife.

The day that changed his life ...

July 7 2005 LONDON BOMBINGS

Location: London, England
Targets: London Underground and a double-decker bus
Date: 7 July 2005
08.50 a.m.–09.47 a.m.
Attack: Suicide bombings
Deaths: 52
Injured: Approximately 700

TIMELINE FACTS

08.50 a.m. Initial reports of an incident between
Liverpool Street and Aldgate
Tube stations, either an explosion or a collision between trains. The
reports from the two stations were initially thought to relate to two
separate incidents.

08.50 a.m. Explosion on a train between King's Cross and Russell Square
Tube stations. Eyewitnesses report that the explosion appeared to come
from outside the train (this explosion was initially reported to have
happened at 08.56).

08.50 a.m. Explosion on a train at Edgware
Road Tube station (this explosion
was initially reported to have happened at 09.17).

09.28 a.m. Tube operator Metronet says the incident was caused by some
sort of power surge.

09.33 a.m. Reports of an incident at Edgware
Road Tube station. Reports that
passengers on a train hit by an explosion attempted to break windows
with umbrellas in order to escape.

09.46 a.m. British Transport Police announce there have been more
explosions at King's Cross and Russell Square.

09.47 a.m. Explosion on a number 30 bus
traveling between Marble Arch and
Hackney Wick at Upper Woburn Place/Tavistock Square.

09.49 a.m. Entire London Underground system shut down.

July 21 2005 SECOND LONDON BOMBINGS

12.26 p.m. Small explosions occur at Shepherd's Bush Tube station
(Hammersmith and City Line), Warren Street Tube station
and Oval Tube station.

13.30 p.m. A backpack is reported as exploding in East London on the
number 26 bus traveling from Waterloo to Hackney Wick.

14.30 p.m. University College Hospital is cordoned off by police; it is
feared that the bomber from Warren Street Tube station,
opposite, ran into the building.

14.45 p.m. Whitehall, which was previously
sealed off after the explosions, is
reopened.

15.25 p.m. A major security alert again closes Whitehall.

15.30 p.m. A man carrying a backpack is arrested by armed police outside
the Ministry of Defence in Whitehall, approximately twenty metres from
Downing Street.

16.00 p.m. Sir Ian Blair, the Metropolitan Police Commissioner,
now describes the situation as 'firmly under control'.

JULY 22 2005

10.00 a.m. Jean Charles de Menezes is shot dead by plainclothes police
at Stockwell Tube station.

Chapter Two

'For the word "terrorist" substitute the word "government" and everything makes sense.'

Graffito

Alex Monroe was born on May 17 1949, in London, to an American father and a British mother. His parents had met at the end of the Second World War, when his father, Earl Monroe, was stationed at Martlesham Heath airfield as a volunteer pilot with the RAF. His mother, Elizabeth (or Lizzie as she preferred to be known), was just beginning her career in nursing on the base.

They were married following a six-month whirlwind courtship.

Shortly after Alex's eighteenth birthday, his father was tragically knocked down and killed by a drunk driver who had been out celebrating the birth of his first child. During the months following the funeral, Alex's mother found it difficult living away from her family in Leeds. So after consulting Alex, she decided it would be best for them to move north, to Yorkshire.

From an early age, Alex had always been an outgoing, pleasant young man, therefore it didn't come as any surprise to his mother when, within a month of them moving into their new home, Alex had joined the local youth club, then after a further six months; met his future wife, Marie. They were living proof that opposites not only attract, they also complement each other, and in this case it was undoubtedly true.

By the age of eighteen, Alex had grown to well over six feet, his slim frame likened that of a marathon runner. He had dark brown hair, which he always kept neat and tidy. This was something he'd copied from his father since an early age.

Marie, on the other hand, was the opposite. She was five foot two (in her stocking feet), had long blonde hair which, invariably, she kept tied back in a ponytail. Her physique would be best described as 'petite'. Alex used to tease her by introducing her to his friends as his 'cute little Barbie doll'. Much to Marie's constant annoyance. They experienced a few unpleasant comments and strange looks when they first started dating, but it never bothered them in the slightest.

Alex and Marie were married on 14 February 1970 (Valentine's Day), at the local register office. After trying for a family for two years, their first son, Michael, came into the world. Andrew soon followed, eighteen months later. They lived a comfortable life, ensuring they had enough money saved to go on at least one holiday each year with the boys. After leaving school, Michael went to Sheffield University to study Japanese; Andrew gained a place at Leeds University, studying IT, both successfully graduating, then returning to the Leeds area, living only a few miles from their parents.

At the age of fifty-five, Alex decided to retire. They had managed to save enough money over the years, so he felt it was time for them to enjoy life, together. Marie likewise finished her full-time job, yet decided after a few weeks to work part time, in the kitchens at the local village primary school for two hours a day, during the lunch period. 'For a little female company,' she said.

They were both happy and contented with life.

Unfortunately for Marie, it wasn't to last for long …

JULY 7 2005

Marie had gone on a day's shopping trip to London with her sister, Ruth. They'd always enjoyed each other's company, spending most summers visiting local towns and villages, searching out car boot sales, only to return home with shopping bags full of what Alex would describe as 'other people's rubbish'.

Arriving in London on the morning of 7 July 2005, at 8.30 a.m., after catching the early train from Leeds, they decided to split up, arranging to meet later for lunch at the Cheers bar in Piccadilly. Ruth made her way out through the main exit of King's Cross station to the taxi stand, hoping she wouldn't have to wait too long for one, whilst Marie cheerfully strolled towards the Tube station, to catch the next train for Oxford Circus …

It was shortly after 11.30 a.m. that day, whilst listening to the local radio station, when Alex heard the devastating news of the terrorist bombings in London. Never in his wildest dreams could he imagine Marie would be somehow caught up in the horrors of the events developing before him, but he did expect her to phone him, once she was aware of the bombings, just to put his mind at ease. After two agonizing hours, pacing the floor, constantly trying to contact her on her mobile phone, only to be continually diverted to her voicemail, Alex started to become frightened.

'Why won't she answer the phone, what's the point of having one if you haven't got the fucking thing switched on?' screamed Alex, his face twisted in anguish.

As each passing hour went by, Alex became more concerned for her welfare.

It was just after 3 p.m. when the phone in the hall rang. He raced across the room to answer it, expecting to hear Marie's apologetic voice coming down the line.

'Alex, it's Ruth, have you heard what's been happening down here? Has Marie been in touch? We ...'

'Yes, I have ... I thought she was with you?' interrupted Alex, panicking.

'We'd arranged to meet up for lunch, but she hasn't arrived ... Oh God! Alex, I'm worried ... when we decided to split up this morning, she said she was going shopping down Oxford Street, and I'm certain she made her way down to the Tube, the one that ...'

Alex's mind was in turmoil. No, not Marie, he thought, she wouldn't hurt a fly, never having a bad word for anyone, always accepting other people's views and beliefs ... It was Ruth's incessant, hysterical voice screaming down the phone line that eventually brought Alex out of his stupor.

'Please be quiet, Ruth, I need time to think this through.'

Eventually composing himself, he put the phone back to his ear.

'Ruth ... I think the best thing for me to do is to catch the next train down to London, and in the meantime, will you try and find out where the casualties are being taken ...' implored Alex, '... and if you do hear of anything, anything at all, please don't hesitate to get in touch with me.'

'Alex! ... don't be so damn stupid. You're not thinking straight. King's Cross station has been shut down, and the rest of the rail network down here is in absolute chaos ... I've also heard that the Underground systems have all been closed, and don't even think about driving down, as you will only get caught up in all the traffic that's heading out of London ... wait there, just in case Marie calls.

You never know, she may be trying to get through to you right now. It's taken me over two hours to reach you. I can well imagine all the telephone lines and mobile phone networks being constantly busy, no doubt with other worried families trying to contact loved ones.'

'I can't just wait around here, not knowing what's happened to her, I need to be down there, looking for her,' pleaded Alex.

'Leave it a few hours will you Alex, just in case either of us hears anything.'

'Ruth, I could be down there in just over four hours' time if I leave now. Just listen to me will you, and don't argue. As I see it, the best thing for me to do is drive down to Milton Keynes, and catch the first train going into London. There must to be some trains going into the city. I can't imagine all the mainline stations being closed; some must still be in operation?'

'Well, it seems you've made your mind up, so I suppose there's no point in arguing with you,' responded Ruth.

'No there isn't. Where were you meeting for lunch?' snapped Alex.

'The Cheers bar in Piccadilly Circus. Do you know where it is?'

'Yes, I've been there a few times. Hopefully I will see you in about four hours time, and Ruth, I know I'm repeating myself, but if you do hear anything, anything at all, please try and get in touch with me, and I will do the same.'

'Alex, keep faith, see you later.'

'See you later Ruth. Oh, and I'm sorry for losing it back there. It's just that I'm eager to get down as soon as I can.'

'You don't have to apologize Alex; you must be beside yourself with worry. Take care.' Ruth then ended the call, wiping away the tears she couldn't hold back any longer.

Placing the phone back in its cradle, glancing over towards the wedding pictures on the mantelpiece, Alex slid his back down the wall until he sat on the floor. He pulled his knees up with his arms around them, put his face against them, and cried as he had never cried before.

It was 10 p.m. by the time Alex eventually arrived at the bar. Owing to the vast majority of London being on a high terrorist alert, the security at most bars and restaurants had been increased as a precaution. The Cheers bar was no exception, with male customers being politely frisked, and ladies asked to open their handbags for a cursory inspection. After being patted down, and ushered in with a sweeping hand gesture from the doorman, Alex cautiously made his way into the packed bar, hoping to see Marie rushing towards him, arms open wide, a big happy smile on her face. But there was no Marie.

Elbowing his way towards the centre of the room, nervously running his eyes over the faces of those around him, searching for Ruth, he eventually spotted her waving, noticing that she had managed to find a table under one of the many television screens situated around the room, showing scenes of the day's devastation.

Acknowledging that he'd seen her, he made his way through the crowd of drinkers. The bar's atmosphere was laden with a sense of bewilderment and shock, with everyone shouting over one another, voicing their feelings and opinions about the day's tragic events.

Standing up to greet Alex, Ruth hugged him, rubbing his back with genuine concern, hoping it would give him some comfort.

'Sorry I'm late, and you were correct, the traffic on the motorway was horrendous, then to make matters worse I had to wait nearly two hours for a train. I thought I'd never get here. I take it you haven't heard from Marie?' enquired Alex, despairingly.

'No, I'm sorry, and I've been here most of the time since we last spoke.' Ruth informed him. 'Have you?'

'No, nothing, I've just kept pressing the redial button on my mobile every few minutes,' replied Alex. 'I feel the worst may have happened to her. It's not like her not to ring; she must surely know the torment I must be going through.'

'Alex, don't think like that, we must always have hope,' responded Ruth, her eyes beginning to mist over.

'Right,' he replied, without any conviction.

Ruth decided to move her chair around the table to be closer to Alex so she could be heard over the noise in the room. 'The police have issued an emergency number to call. I've been trying it for the last four hours, but it's constantly engaged, and there's no point in going down to King's Cross. The police have already appealed to the public not to venture down there.'

'It's understandable when you think about it – the last thing the emergency services need right now is dozens of hysterical relatives and friends hampering their search,' shouted Alex.

'We've also no idea where any of the victims and survivors have been taken …' replied Ruth. 'Alex, I've managed, luckily, to book two rooms for tonight at a hotel just around the corner. So I suggest we go there now, try and get some sleep, then first thing in the morning we can call into the nearest police station for some help. There is no way we will be able to find out anything tonight.'

'Ruth, do you think I'm going to be able to sleep, not knowing what's happened to Marie? I need to be out there, walking the streets, looking for her. She may be in a state of shock, wandering around, frightened,' pleaded Alex.

15

'Alex, you're exhausted. Just listen, there's bound to be hundreds of other worried people with the same idea as you. You need to get some rest, then in the morning we can concentrate on finding Marie, together.'

Gradually the stress, and emotions, caused by the day's catastrophic events crept up on him.

'I suppose you're right,' replied Alex, 'but there's no way I'm going to be able to rest easy, and sleeping will be totally out of the question.'

Smiling, Ruth placed her hand on top of his, acknowledging the anguish Alex must be going through.

Once they had decided to leave the noise, and the smell of stale, spilt beer, they set off searching for the hotel, which they quickly found, as it was fortunately only a ten-minute walk from the bar. After signing in, and once again hugging each other, reassuring one another that everything would be fine in the morning, they made their way to their respective rooms.

Collapsing down onto the bed, Alex laid his head on the pillow, deciding not to get undressed, just in case Marie rang, as he wanted to be ready to rush out of the hotel as quickly as possible. His eyes started to wander around the room, eventually ending up at the ceiling. He started to think back to the good times, also silently praying to any God that would listen to him to watch over his Marie.

Not realizing how exhausted he was, within a few minutes he was fast asleep.

July 8 2007

After a restless sleep, Alex woke up with a start, after having had a bad dream.

Suddenly he realized where he was, and the reason why he was lying on top of a bed, in unfamiliar surroundings, fully dressed. Lifting himself from the bed, he hurriedly picked up his phone, checking to see if he'd missed any calls or messages whilst he'd been asleep. Nothing! He glanced at his watch to check on the time: 6 a.m. He knew he wouldn't be able to go back to sleep again, so he popped into the bathroom, returning to make himself a cup of black coffee from the hotel's complimentary tray, before switching on the television for the news. All the news channels had on-the-spot reporters, each assigned to the various sites, interviewing witnesses, along with exhausted-looking emergency personnel who were still frantically organizing the search-and-rescue.

Alex started to scan the television screen, hoping to catch a glimpse of Marie in the concerned-looking faces in the crowd. There was no one resembling her at all. He was now starting to feel desperate, and lonely.

It was the knock at the door that brought him out of his hypnotic state.

'Alex, Alex, it's Ruth, are you up?' Came the voice from the corridor.

Walking away from the TV towards the door, continually looking back over his shoulder, praying he would catch a glimpse of Marie's face on the television, he opened the door, inviting Ruth into the room.

'Morning, come in, I've got the news on … I assume you haven't heard from Marie? I haven't,' said Alex.

'No, nothing and I've been trying the emergency number most of the night, without any joy,' answered Ruth.

Moving over to the bed, they sat down, concentrating on the reports and images being televised.

'Come on Ruth, we won't find Marie sitting around here. I think the best thing for us to do is make our way over towards King's Cross station. That's where you saw her last, there's bound to be someone there we can ask,' suggested Alex.

After quickly draining off his cup of cold coffee, and switching off the TV, they made their way out of the hotel, stepping out into the early morning sunshine.

Alex had already accepted the fact that Marie wouldn't be found alive, as he could already sense his loss.

Alex and Ruth were given the devastating news about Marie after enquiring at police stations and hospitals, in and around the King's Cross area.

An exhausted and sympathetic doctor at the Royal London Hospital informed them that Marie had died on the King's Cross train.

They had identified Marie by her driving license, and passport.

She had been confirmed dead at the scene by the paramedics.

'If there is any consolation, Mr. Monroe ...' the doctor said, '... she wouldn't have suffered ...'

Marie had caught the southbound number 311 train, which left King's Cross station at approximately 8.50 a.m. The train had travelled only five hundred yards when the bomb exploded at the rear of the first carriage.

Six months later

During the first few months after the tragedy Alex dropped out of sight, hiding away from family and friends, not even replying to the many cards and letters of condolence, sometimes not even bothering to answer the telephone. He just wanted to be left alone with his fond memories of Marie. They had just recently returned from holidaying in France a week before the tragedy. Whilst there, they had both said that someday they would like to visit America.

Little did Alex know at the time that he would be visiting America, alone.

Alex's two grown-up sons still lived close by. Michael, the eldest, had only been married six months before he lost his mother. He was currently teaching Japanese at Leeds University. Alex's youngest son, Andrew, was working at the printing company Alex used to work for, before his retirement.

They were still a close-knit family, his sons making certain that one of them visited their father at least once a week to check on his welfare, ensuring he was eating properly.

Over the course of a number of weeks, they noticed a deterioration in Alex's appearance. It was at this agonizing stage that they made up their minds to have a serious talk with him.

So one sunny Sunday morning they arrived at their father's house with the sole purpose of putting across their concerns about his state of health and mind.

After lunch (which was prepared by the boys), they sat down, whereupon they slowly and compassionately made him aware of their feelings, and fears, pleading with him to snap out of his self-pity, and to get on with his life, pointing out to him that 'Mum would have wanted him to enjoy life, and get out more'. After they had expressed their concerns, Alex eased back in his chair, considering what had been said.

They had purposely not tidied up any of the downstairs rooms, hoping that their father would become aware of the state he had been living in; the startled look on Alex's face proved that it had worked; thankfully.

Surveying the room, Alex was horrified by the sight before him. There was old newspapers scattered all over the lounge floor, plus at least half a dozen dirty coffee cups which had been left on any available space throughout the room. Glancing over towards the kitchen, he saw to his disgust at least a dozen of what looked like half-empty, discarded, mouldy pizza boxes lying around on the kitchen work surfaces were he'd dropped them.

'What's become of me?' Alex whispered to himself. He now knew the boys were right in what they'd been saying and he did need to look after himself more, and stop ignoring the people around him, who had only his best interests at heart. Alex thanked them for making him come to his senses, promising them he would take their advice. His sons were relieved, and happy that they had achieved in what they had set out to do. So after a much-missed family hug, they left Alex to clear up the mess, and ordered him to have a hot bath, followed, hopefully, by a decent night's sleep, which he acted on as soon as they had closed the front door.

The following morning he woke up feeling refreshed.

'Alex,' he said to himself out loud, 'this is the first day of your new life. Respect and enjoy it.' Slipping on his dressing gown, he made his way downstairs to the kitchen to make himself a full English breakfast of eggs, bacon, sausages, mushrooms, and a large mug of strong tea, conscious of the fact that the food had been stored in the refrigerator the day before by Andrew and Michael. After finishing his breakfast, he carefully washed all the dirty plates and cutlery, stacking them neatly so they could drain. He spent the next few minutes having a wash and shave, followed by a desperate search through his wardrobes, looking for the 'best' of his creased, dirty clothes.

Satisfied that he at last looked somewhat respectable, he ambled down the stairs, collected his car keys from the hall table, jumped in his car, and happily drove into town, with the aim of purchasing some new clothes.

When he had finished trying on numerous coats and trousers, he ended up buying himself four pairs of trousers, half a dozen shirts, and a couple of dark blue blazers, plus some underwear. All he needed now was a pair of soft, comfortable walking shoes. After paying the assistant for the garments, he sneakily slipped back to the fitting rooms to change into his new clothes. Rolling up his old ones, he stuffed them in the waste bin by the entrance to the store. Walking out into the morning sunlight, feeling like a new man, he stopped to admire his reflection in the shop window. Giving himself a smile of approval, he ventured out into his new world.

If either of my sons or any of my friends walk past me right now, they wouldn't recognize me, he thought, smiling to himself.

Alex started visiting his sons and friends on a regular basis, also occasionally going out for dinner with his old workmates whom he had lost touch with. He found it difficult at first, as he was the only single person at the dinner table, yet everyone made him feel welcome, making sure he was never left out of the conversations.

Now that Alex had a new lease of life he decided to renew his membership at the local gym, starting to go at least twice a week, attempting to get rid of the 'flab' he had gained over the months he had spent lazing about.

'THE PLANE FACTS'

1996–2001: Federal authorities have known for years that suspected terrorists with ties to bin Laden were receiving flight training at schools in the US and abroad. One convicted terrorist confessed that his planned role in a terror attack was to crash a plane into CIA headquarters. (Washington Post, 23/9/01; more)

2000–2001: Fifteen of the nineteen hijackers fail to fill in visa documents properly in Saudi Arabia. Only six are interviewed. All fifteen should have been denied entry to the US.
If the State Department personnel had merely followed the law, 9/11 would not have happened. (AP, 18/12/02; more)

2000–2001: The military conducts exercises simulating hijacked airliners used as weapons to crash into targets, causing mass casualties. One target is the World Trade Center (WTC), another the Pentagon. Yet after 9/11, over and over the White House and security officials say they're shocked that terrorists hijacked airliners and crashed them into landmark buildings. (USA Today, 19/4/04, Military District of Washington, 3/11/00; *New York Times*, 3/10/01; more)

Chapter Three

'America will never be destroyed from the outside. If we falter, and lose our freedoms, it will be because we destroyed ourselves.'

Abraham Lincoln

JUNE 2006

Throughout the course of the following months, slowly adjusting to being single once again, Alex contemplated whether to visit the site where Marie had been murdered, yet knowing full well that it would be harrowing, and stressful. But he knew that once he had been to the site, he would feel more at ease and contented.

So, after finally plucking up the courage, Alex booked the train tickets online, making sure he would be in London on the first anniversary of that tragic day.

On the morning of 7 July 2006, Alex caught the train from Leeds to London, imagining Marie making the same trip twelve months ago. Standing on the platform in Leeds, he wondered whether his decision to go on the pilgrimage had been a good idea. After a few minutes of deliberating, he realized he had to go, so at least he would feel that Marie was with him for a short while at least.

Arriving at King's Cross station, he fought his way through the throng of people who were congregating within the main concourse. Most of them were attending a memorial service which was being held beneath the large electronic timetable, whilst others just simply wandered aimlessly around in a dream like state, soaking up the calming atmosphere. No doubt most of them were family and friends of the victims of 7/7, Alex presumed. He nervously headed down the escalators towards the tube station, asking himself over and over again, 'Am I doing the right thing?' 'Yes, I am, I have to do it for the boys as well as myself,' he kept on reminding himself, continually wiping away the sweat from his brow with a handkerchief.

Minutes later he ended up on the platform; then he froze. He just stood there, taking no notice of the dozens of commuters who were bumping and pushing him aside. The next thing Alex sensed was the sudden rush of warm stale air coming down the tunnel. He knew it was a sign that a train was approaching. Once the train had stopped, the doors automatically opened, and as usual there was a sudden stampede of commuters elbowing their way off and on. As Alex wasn't in any hurry to get on, he gradually eased himself back towards the wall, leaving the milling crowd to get on with their daily routine. Three trains had arrived and departed before Alex had the nerve to catch one. Making his way slowly down the aisle, he found a spare seat. After a few nervous minutes, he decided he couldn't stay any longer; he had managed to do what he had set out to do, which made him feel slightly better. So jumping off at the next station, he ran up the escalator, taking two steps at a time, and barged his way through the crowds towards the exit. He needed to be on the outside, in the fresh air, quickly. Exiting the station, he stood for a moment, composing himself, releasing a long-pent-up breath. He observed he'd been sweating: stains were evident on the front of his shirt, also in the armpits of his jacket. Now feeling somewhat thirsty, and jaded, he made his way towards the nearest Starbucks for a coffee, and a bite to eat.

It didn't take him long to find one. After collecting his order he sat down, and picked up a morning newspaper which had been left on the chair next to him. He somberly began to read the articles on the front page which highlighted the events of that dreadful day twelve months ago, which came as no surprise to him. He didn't have the heart to read any more, so he put the paper back down, relaxed, and appreciated the strong coffee. When he'd finished, leaving the comfort of the air-conditioned surroundings, only to come out into the humid July heat, he began strolling around the streets, sightseeing along with the hundreds of other tourists, and occasionally, stepping into shop doorways for some welcoming shade from the blistering sun. After window-shopping for an hour, he felt the need to visit Tavistock Square, to pay his respects to those who had perished on the bus. He had no idea where it was located, so the best thing, he thought, was to catch a cab.

Alighting from the cab, the first thing Alex noticed was how busy the area was, with what seemed to him to be dozens of solemn-looking people. Some were laying cellophane-wrapped flowers by the side of lamp-posts, whilst others carefully leant them against garden walls. As he was slowly walking down the road, stopping now and again to read the messages on some of the many cards of condolence, he thought he heard the characteristic sounds of American accents. Alex was right in his assumption, as only a few feet away a small number of American tourists were laying flowers outside The British Medical Association building; then recalling that the Number 10 bus had exploded whilst it was passing by the building. Out of curiosity, he tentatively moved across to talk to them. During their engaging conversation Alex mentioned that his wife had been a victim on the King's Cross tube. They were deeply moved and upset hearing about Alex's loss, saying that they had also lost friends in the Twin Towers on 9/11, and they were still grieving. They also intimated to him that they weren't at all confident in the 9/11 Commission's findings and they were hoping that in the none too distant future, an unbiased public inquiry may be set in motion, especially if the Democrat's were elected in 2008.

After the initial shock of hearing their beliefs about the Commission's findings, Alex informed them that he had hoped to visit America with his late wife, Marie, and because of the kindness they had shown him, he said he would organise a trip as soon as he could, to pay his respects to all the victims of 9/11.

Making it safely home at the end of a long and emotional day, Alex poured himself a large JD with Diet Coke and ice, collapsed onto the sofa, and excitedly phoned his sons, reciting the conversation he'd had with the American tourists, also enthusing over his decision to visit New York.

Both his sons said they were thrilled with his news, adding that it would do him good, but insisted that he either rang or emailed them whilst he was over there. Alex readily agreed to their demands, saying he would attempt to contact them every day, if at all possible, only to put their minds at ease, reminding them, however, how inadequate he was when it came to computers, and strange overseas telephone systems.

Michael had always been interested in conspiracies – Pearl Harbor, the assassination of JFK, and the supposed Apollo Moon landings. He was currently reading about the events surrounding 9/11, and the so-called cover-up, which prompted him to suggest to his father that he might want to read one of his books, then at least he'd have some understanding of the events.

Alex had always enjoyed reading, mostly science fiction and horror, he would never have considered reading about conspiracies, but he excitedly went to Michael's house, collecting two books Michael recommended, promising him he would look after them. On his return home, Alex made himself a mug of strong coffee, stretched out his long legs on the sofa, relaxed, and started to pore over the detailed information in one of the books. He was instantly absorbed, wanting to know more; yet little did he know that his obsession would eventually put him in a precarious position, which could ultimately expose him to danger.

There had been times when he was sitting alone at home, reading about the tragic events, when he felt like quitting. It was the thought of all those innocent men, women and children who perished in those planes and buildings that upset him.

It certainly puts life in perspective, he thought, and recalling the amazing statement from the American tourists he'd met in London, expressing their doubts and concerns about the 9/11 Commission's findings.

He now wanted to know more than ever about what really happened on that fateful day. Was it 'an inside job', or were all the accusations about the American government's involvement false and misleading?

He had to know the truth – not for his sake, but for the sake of the thousands who lost their lives on 9/11.

It was at this point when Alex decided he would organize a trip to New York on the sixth anniversary of 9/11, in 2007.

'THE PLANE FACTS'

December 1998: A Time magazine cover story entitled 'The Hunt for Osama' reports that bin Laden may be planning his boldest move yet – a strike on Washington or possibly New York City. (Time, 21/12/98)

Late 1998–early 2000: On at least three occasions, spies in Afghanistan report bin Laden's location. Each time, the President approves an attack. Each time, the CIA Director says the information is not reliable enough and the attack cannot go forward. (*New York Times*, 30/12/01; more)

January 2001: After the November 2000 elections, US intelligence are told to 'back off' investigating the bin Ladens and Saudi royals. There have always been constraints on investigating Saudi Arabians. (BBC, 6/11/01; more)

May 2001: For the third time, US security chiefs reject Sudan's offer of thick files on bin Laden and al-Qaeda. A senior CIA source calls it 'the worst single intelligence failure in the business'. (Guardian, 30/9/01; more)

Spring 2001: A series of military and governmental policy documents are released that seek to legitimize the use of US military force in the pursuit of oil and gas. One advocates presidential subterfuge and hiding the reasons for warfare 'as a necessity for mobilizing public support'. (Sydney Morning Herald, 26/12/02; more)

Chapter Four

'If you believe everything you read, better not read.'

Japanese proverb

SEPTEMBER 10 2007 – Leeds, United Kingdom

The morning of Alex's trip had finally arrived.

He hadn't had too much sleep, as he was both nervous, and excited to be going at last.

After studying himself in the wardrobe mirror, making certain he looked presentable, he made his way downstairs. Placing his shoulder bag and suitcase on the floor by the front door, he eagerly waited for his lift to the airport. Glancing out of the window, scanning the road, he noticed that it was still dark and it had just started to rain, which made the street lights reflect in the small puddles forming on the road. He suddenly had an awful thought; what if it's foggy at the airport – the flight may be delayed or, heaven forbid, cancelled.

After anxiously wandering around for ten minutes, constantly peering through the hall curtains, he noticed a set of car headlights coming down the road. He instantly recognized the car as being Michael's. Michael had insisted on taking his father to the airport, as he wanted to be certain Alex arrived safely, and in plenty of time.

So leaving at 7 a.m., on a cold, wet Monday morning, they drove across the Pennines towards Manchester Airport. During the course of the journey, Michael kept reminding his father about keeping in touch, also to be aware that there were certain areas in New York which were unsafe for both residents and tourists alike. Alex knew that Michael had only his best interests at heart, which deeply moved him.

After a monotonous hour's drive in the pouring rain, they finally arrived at the airport, with Michael deciding to park the car in the long-stay car park, as he had no idea how long he would be hanging about. As they entered the terminal building, the first thing they observed was how busy it was with excited passengers queuing for their boarding passes, or just simply wandering around, patiently waiting for their flights to be shown on the countless screens which were dotted around. After ten minutes of searching for the check-in desk, they eventually found it, and, like the rest of the other passengers, Alex stood in line, waiting nervously for his turn. He was once again becoming excited, knowing that in only a few hours' time, he would be in New York. Realizing he was at the front of the line, he made his way across to the counter, the young lady assistant asking him the normal questions: 'Did you pack your suitcase? Have you left it unattended whilst at the airport?' Alex answering her with a confident 'yes' and 'no'. Aware that everything was in order, he started to relax, a little. He politely asked her if it would be at all possible for a seat with extra legroom (suggesting the emergency exit), as no doubt she could see that he was well over six foot, and 'he didn't feel like being cramped up for seven hours'. Checking the seating availability, she happily informed him that one of the emergency exit seats was free, also stating that passengers seated there were responsible for the opening of the emergency doors, if an emergency did occur, but this would be explained to him when the cabin crew went over the 'on-board emergency procedures'. Alex already knew the procedures, as he had sat by the emergency exit before when he had flown to Finland on business, and with Marie and the boys to Spain. Thanking the young lady for her help and kindness, he gathered up his boarding pass and slipped it into his passport for safe-keeping. As all this was going on, Michael had been waiting patiently by the wall.

'Is everything OK Dad?' And with a cheeky grin all over his face, he added, 'Are they going to let you in?'

'Cheeky bugger, of course they are,' responded Alex, playfully clipping Michael on the side of the head.

Chuckling, and tapping each other like big kids, they made their way across to Departures.

'Look after yourself, Dad, won't you? I've noted which hotel you're staying at, and I'll come and collect you on the nineteenth, and don't worry, I've copied all the times, and the flight number, so I'll check with the airline the day before I collect you to make sure there are no delays over there, OK? See you later.'

'See you later son. I know how concerned you are for me, but I can assure you, I'll be fine, and I promise I will keep in touch with you. I might even buy you both a present, something "tacky",' he said, with his usual cheeky grin on his face.

After saying their final goodbyes, Alex picked up his shoulder bag, turned, and made his way through to Departures and ultimately passport control. After clearing passport control, Alex made his way towards the duty-free shops. He always enjoyed wandering around the counters, checking out the prices, but rarely buying anything. As far as he was concerned, most of the items could be found cheaper on the high street. He followed his normal pattern of examining the aftershaves, always trying the most expensive ones, but not necessarily the best, he thought. When he'd had enough, he called into the Gents to wash off the mixed aromas, as he didn't want the plane's cabin smelling like a perfumery. He checked his watch to see how long he had to wait. Two hours. 'That's enough time to buy a decent novel at the bookshop,' he muttered to himself (he hadn't read many novels lately, due to the fact he'd been reading so much about 9/11). Spotting a nice cozy bar next to the bookshop, he decided he would call in there for a drink, after purchasing his book. Alex usually had a few drinks when he flew, mainly for courage, but it also helped him relax.

After scanning the shelves, feeling like a child in a sweet shop, he decided to buy the new Lee Child paperback, along with an assortment of newly released horror novels, much to his delight. So, with his newly purchased books, having strolled next door to the bar, he ordered a large Jack Daniel's with Diet Coke and ice, his favorite drink at the moment. He paid for his drink, instructing the waiter to have another one ready, as he would be back shortly. Carrying his drink outside, he looked around for somewhere to sit. Making his way to a free table, gazing over towards the large viewing window, he noticed that the weather outside had deteriorated; a blanket of white fog was creeping across runway. Checking the information screen, he observed that a few of the flights had been delayed. He wondered how long it would be before his flight would depart. Thankfully it was still indicating that it would be leaving on time, plus the gate number had now been entered. Given this good news, he decided not to have another drink, as he would wait until he was on board the plane. Quickly finishing off his drink, and returning the empty glass to the bar, thanking the waiter, saying, 'One large one was enough, thank you,' he made his way over to the departure gate, which by this time was busy with nervous looking passengers.

'Christ, we'll never all board in time,' he moaned to himself.

But as always the cabin crew was well organized, with everyone shown to their seats and made comfortable, ready for the flight. Alex was pleased that he'd asked for the emergency exit, as he had glimpsed, as he was walking down the aisle, that the other seats had very little legroom.

As the plane slowly taxied, Alex strapped himself in, brought his seat to the upright position, like a good boy, and began to relax, ready for the journey across the Pond.

Once the plane was at cruising altitude the stewardess came with the complimentary drinks trolley. Alex politely asked for his preferred drink of Jack Daniel's with Diet Coke and ice. After rummaging through his bag for one of his books, he sat back and relaxed, enjoying the drink, the book and the flight.

The vibration of the plane, combined with the drink, eventually caused Alex to drift off to sleep. He always used to say to Marie when he was tired, 'I could sleep on a washing line,' with which, giggling, she agreed.

Alex had only been asleep for a short while before he was abruptly woken up by the sudden turbulence they were experiencing, and just for a split second he was momentarily disorientated. He knew the past months had been a constant strain, which had resulted in him being exhausted and drained, but he hadn't realized how bad he had become; also aware that the drink he'd consumed at the airport, plus the one on the plane hadn't helped; so he decided to cut out the alcohol, for the rest of the flight at any rate, and just stick to the coffee. Over the course of the next few hours, Alex kept nodding off, only to be constantly woken up by the turbulence. Out of the blue, the captain announced that they would be shortly descending, and were expected to arrive at JFK airport at 7.30 p.m., local time. Alex was now feeling relaxed, although hoping he wouldn't have to wait around too long for his luggage in the arrivals hall. It was the stewardess, gently shaking his shoulder, who brought him out of his daydream.

'Sorry to disturb you sir, but you need to fill out these before you are allowed on American soil,' she said, handing Alex two official-looking documents.

It was at this point; the man sitting next to Alex leant over, whispering in his ear, chuckling, 'Make sure you answer all the questions correctly buddy. If you don't, you'll be hanging around passport control for hours – we are very particular about whom we let in the U.S. of A.'

Alex suddenly became anxious. Filling in forms was his pet hate. The reason for this was because he invariably missed something. After spending an agonizing fifteen minutes, making sure he had completed both forms correctly, he slipped them in his passport. He then put away his tray and sat back, now expecting a long delay at passport control.

Because Alex's father was an American, he was entitled to an American passport, but he preferred to hold a British one

The flight landed on time, with the plane gracefully taxiing towards the main terminal building. The cabin signs pinged, indicating that they could now unfasten their seat belts. Glancing out of the window, Alex cheerfully noticed that the weather was bright and sunny. He packed his book in his bag, slipped his shoes back on, having removed them before take-off, in the hope of avoiding any swelling during the flight, which thankfully he had. He stood up, made his way down the aisle, emptying his litter in the bin by the exit on the way, and proceeded to follow his fellow passengers towards the terminal building.

Approaching the arrivals hall, Alex observed that it was as busy as it had been in Manchester, if not more so, which wasn't surprising in such a large airport as this, he thought.

He made his way over to the passport control counter, nervously handing over his passport, along with the two forms for inspection, expecting the forms to be handed back for not having been filled out correctly.

Thankfully, that didn't happen, which meant he wasn't hanging about too long. They took his fingerprints, and scanned one of his eyes. He found out later that this checking procedure was added after 9/11. When asked the reason for his visit, Alex said, 'It's a long-promised vacation.' The immigration officer handed the passport back to Alex, gesturing with a wave of his hand for him to proceed through the gate. Alex turned back to thank him, wishing him a nice day. 'Bloody hell,' he chuckled to himself, 'I'm already talking like them.'

He waited patiently, along with the rest of the other passengers, next to the carousel, looking out for his luggage. It wasn't long before he noticed his light blue case coming towards him around the bend of the conveyer belt. Well, he thought, at least I won't have to hang around with the rest of them, watching dozens of cases going round and round in circles.

'A good start to the holiday,' he said to himself, 'let's hope the rest of the stay is as good.' Gathering up his bag, he made his way through customs, thankfully without being stopped, and hurriedly made his way across the terminal building towards the exit. Once outside, he noticed that it had started to rain. Fortunately for him the cab line wasn't too long, and within minutes he was at the front. Climbing into the cab, he instructed the driver to take him to the Chelsea Hotel at 222 West 23rd Street.

Sitting back in his seat, Alex began to listen to the cab's wipers beating relentlessly backwards and forwards, swish, swish, swish, which eventually, after ten minutes, lulled him to sleep.

He woke up just as the cab pulled up in front of the hotel, noticing that it was still raining. The driver opened the divider slot, notifying him that they had arrived. As Alex was carefully counting out the crisp new dollar bills, he unexpectantly became aware that all the dominations were the same size.

I never noticed that before, I'm going to have to be careful paying for anything whilst I'm over here, or I'll end up with no money left after two days, he thought, feeling concerned.

After sliding his case from the cab onto the sidewalk, and closing the door, he stopped to look up to admire the outside of the building. The frontage is magnificent, he thought. He was, without doubt, impressed with his choice of hotel; and noticing that the front of the hotel had wrought-iron balconies, which were delicately decorated with sunflower motifs.

'I hope one of those is mine,' he said to himself.

Not wanting to stand out in the rain too long, he dragged his case to the entrance and stepped inside. To his astonishment the lobby resembled an art gallery with oil paintings, and odd-looking objects hanging from the ceiling. The reception desk looked as if it had come straight out of an old black-and-white movie. Making his way across the lobby, he felt as though he was walking through a film set. If this is the entrance, he thought, what are the rooms going to be like? After checking in, he headed straight to his room on the second floor, using one of the slowest and noisiest lifts he'd ever used. Getting out of the lift, he was surprised to see that the walls in the corridor were also decorated with framed paintings. (He found out later from the desk clerk that the objects in the lobby were kept by the hotel management in lieu of payment for a long-overdue rent; the man also added that the hotel had been the tallest building in New York until 1899).

Once inside his room, he stopped to admire his surroundings. Again he was impressed by what he saw before him: it was a spacious layout, consisting of what he considered reproduction furnishings; there was a high ceiling and a large bed over by the window, and, to his delight, a balcony, which overlooked the main street. The amenities were as he had expected from an old-established hotel such as this: air conditioning, the standard cable/satellite TV, and a laundry service. He went to investigate the bathroom and he was pleasantly surprised to see a shower/tub combination like the one he had back home.

Alex had booked the hotel direct over the Internet at the same time as he had booked his flight, promising himself that he would stay in a hotel with some character and history, and after some research he eventually came across the Chelsea Hotel. The hotel became famous as a haunt for writers, painters and composers. Celebrities who had stayed there included Bob Dylan and Jimi Hendrix, which really excited Alex, as they were two of his favorite musicians.

Lying on top of the bed with his arms outstretched, taking in the scene around him, he shouted out for everyone to hear, 'Welcome to the Big Apple, Alex Monroe.' When he was putting together his trip, he had checked through his many travel guides, looking for any clue as to how New York ended up with this nickname, and according to one source it stated that it came from the jazz musicians of the 1920s and 1930s, who apparently used to say: 'The tree of success has many apples on it, but when you pick New York, you pick the biggest of them all; the Big Apple.'

Once he'd unpacked his case, he sneaked a look in the minibar, helping himself to a bottle of Dr Pepper's and a large packet of peanuts. He laid on the bed, once again admiring his room. The bed was soft and large, with four big fluffy pillows, propped up against an ornate brass headboard. The bathroom, he'd noticed, was big enough to hold a dance in and the view from his bedroom window was admirable. Feeling pleased with himself, he decided to freshen up with a shave and a hot shower.

A few days before his holiday he'd bought the Lonely Planet book which recommended some of the sights to see in New York, and he had written down some of the places he would like to visit apart from Ground Zero. There were a number of places he wanted to visit, but the main reason for his trip was to visit Ground Zero on the anniversary of 9/11, and, as he had promised the American tourists in London, pay his respects. Also, during the time he was researching 9/11, he had read that for the first time, this year, 2007, 9/11 fell on a Tuesday, the same day the terrible events took place.

After quickly dressing after his shower, now excited about being in New York, he decided he would go for a leisurely stroll around the local area, making sure he didn't wander too far away from the vicinity of the hotel, when suddenly he become conscious of the fact that he hadn't eaten since the bland meal on the plane. Never mind, he thought, I'm sure I will find somewhere open, offering meals packed with thousands of calories. On his way out of reception he picked up a leaflet from the desk, detailing more of the history of the hotel.

He read that the hotel's most ignominious night came in 1978, when punk rocker Sid Vicious stabbed his girlfriend to death in their suite. He hoped it wasn't his room. (He later found out from the chambermaid that it was Room 100, which to his relief wasn't his. The maid also revealed to him that some of the survivors from the Titanic had stayed at the hotel, after being rescued. He never did find out whether that was true or not).

As he exited the hotel he was delighted to see that it had stopped raining, making the night feel warm and still. After wandering the streets for twenty minutes, all the time being aware of his surroundings, ensuring he was never too far away from the hotel, he came across an old restored silver Pullman car with what looked like a small version of the Empire State Building perched on top of the shiny stainless-steel roof. The lights inside were still on, which suggested it was open. The illuminated sign above the door informed him that the restaurant was called 'The Empire Diner', and judging by the menu fixed to the window, it was a typical American diner, serving enormous burgers with a vast choice of relishes, and every American's favorite, 'home-made apple pie'. To his delight the diner was open twenty-four hours, so he made his way in, and was instantly escorted to an empty booth by one of the windows. Studying the long list of meals on the menu, casually observing the lively crowd seated around him, the waitress came over. He played safe, and ordered a fat omelette with a side salad, plus his usual large cup of coffee.

While he was eating his meal, Alex noticed that the diner was constantly busy with late-night partiers, and a few old-timers, which made him realize he had picked a creditable establishment. He was now becoming tired, so he politely asked the waitress for the bill, which he paid by the entrance, requesting that they pass on his compliments to the chef for an excellent meal.

Leaving the diner he realized that it had begun to rain heavily whilst he'd been inside. So buttoning up his coat, and turning up his collar, he quickly headed back to the hotel, avoiding the many puddles and scurrying pedestrians on the way. Arriving in the hotel's reception, he looked down to see that his coat and trousers had become soaked from the sudden downpour. Walking cautiously over to the desk, he noticed that he was leaving a trail of water on the tiles, and rugs from his dripping clothes and wet shoes. Apologizing to the desk clerk for the mess, feeling slightly embarrassed, he hastily collected his key, and went straight to his room. Once inside, he swiftly undressed, showered, called housekeeping to have his laundry picked up, asking that, if at all possible, they be ready in the morning. Which they ensured him they would. He began to stuff balls of toilet paper inside his shoes, hoping they would soak up some of the moisture from them overnight. Feeling clean, and refreshed, and all wrapped up in the hotel's fluffy dressing gown, he decided he would relax and watch some TV before retiring to bed. Flicking through the dozens of channels, which he had heard about from family and friends who had visited America, he came across a local news channel which caught his attention. It was highlighting all the events that were to be held in and around Ground Zero, listing the dignitaries who would be attending. The newscaster also mentioned that there was a likelihood that a group calling themselves the Plane Facts would appear, stating that the group normally frequented Zeccotti Park, which was adjacent to the site, and always made a point of showing up at the anniversary ceremonies each year, implying that they invariably ended up causing a disturbance. Alex had read that there were a number of groups throughout America voicing their strong opinions about the events surrounding 9/11, accusing the American government of a cover-up, demanding an 'independent and unbiased public inquiry'. After all the information Alex had pored over during the past months, this was the opinion he had finally come to hold too.

'The visit to Ground Zero is going to be very interesting,' reflected Alex.

By the time the program had finished, Alex's eyes had started to droop. Feeling exhausted and drained, he decided it was time for him to go to bed. Satisfied his shoes were drying out, he made his way over to the bed, collapsing on top.

Quickly covering himself with the blankets, he curled up into a ball, and was fast asleep within seconds.

He ran his hand along her smooth, naked back, to her waist, then down the back of her leg. His body was pressed against hers, her head resting on his chest. As he slowly moved his finger up and down her leg, she started to shiver and cry out with delight. 'Oh, Alex stop it! It's time I got up and dressed. Ruth will be here soon, and I need to shower.'

Creeping out of bed, Marie piled all the blankets on top of him.

He suddenly felt trapped, and began to panic.

'Marie, Marie, stop it, I can't breathe. It's like a furnace under here … ' Pulling at the blankets to free himself, Alex suddenly woke up, and for a brief moment he became confused, trying to remember where he was. 'Yes, now I remember,' he mumbled to himself. The dream had felt so real. 'If only Marie could be here with me, enjoying all the sights, smells, visiting all those designer shops, spending all our money,' he said, feeling downhearted. Reaching over to check the time on his watch, he realized that he had only been asleep for a couple of hours. Rolling over towards the edge of the bed, he leant over to collect the covers lying on the floor. Once he was comfortable, he slowly fell back into a deep restless sleep.

'THE PLANE FACTS'

July 4–14 2001: Bin Laden reportedly receives kidney treatment from Canadian-trained Dr Callaway at the American Hospital in Dubai. Dr Callaway declines to comment. During his stay, bin Laden is allegedly visited by one or two CIA agents. (Guardian, 1/11/01; Sydney Morning Herald, 31/10/01; The Times, London, 1/11/01; UPI, 1/11/01; more)

June–August 2001: German intelligence warns the CIA that Middle Eastern terrorists are training for hijackings and targeting American interests. Russian president Vladimir Putin alerts the US to suicide pilots training for attacks on US targets. In late July, a Taliban emissary warns the US that bin Laden is planning a huge attack on American soil. In August, Israel warns of an imminent al-Qaeda attack. (Fox News, 17/5/02, 7/9/02; CNN, 12/9/02; more)

July 22 2004, The 9/11 Commission Report is published. It fails to mention that a year before the 9/11 attacks a secret Pentagon project named 'Able Danger' had identified four 9/11 hijackers, including leader Mohamed Atta. The Commission spokesperson initially stated members were not informed of this, but later acknowledged they were. (*New York Times*, 11/8/05; more)
The report also fails to investigate the collapse of WTC7.

2004–2005: A growing number of top government officials and public leaders express disbelief over the official story of 9/11. One hundred prominent leaders and forty 9/11 family members sign a statement calling for an unbiased inquiry into evidence suggesting that high-level government officials may have deliberately allowed the attacks to occur. (Various publications)

August 9 2006: A book by 9/11 Commission chairmen Kean and Hamilton outlines repeated deceptions by the Pentagon and FAA, including the timelines of Flight 77 and Flight 93. CNN News: 'The fact that the government would perpetuate the lie suggests that we need a full investigation of what is going on.' (CNN, 9/8/06; MSNBC/AP, 4/8/06; more)

Chapter Five

'The cruelest lies are often told in silence.'

Robert Louis Stevenson (1850–94)

29 AUGUST 2001, 10.00 a.m., World Trade Center, New York

Tony Rider was oblivious to the mass of people close by making their way to work at the Twin Towers, owing to the fact he was nervously waiting for the result of the New York Yankees' game with the Boston Red Sox on his portable radio. He had placed a $200 bet on the Sox to win; the result was just coming through. They had lost 3–2.

'Oh fuck! I'm right up shit creek now,' cried Tony, staring down at the radio, fraught with panic.

Tony Rider was employed as a security guard, overseeing the thousands of employees and sightseers at the Twin Towers.

He was twenty-five years old, tall and solid, with blond hair, which was always 'US Marine buzz-cut short', which he hoped would give any prospective troublemakers the impression he wasn't to be messed with. It also enhanced his boyish features, making people think he was a much younger guy, which he happily played along with their assumptions.

Whilst Tony was anxiously waiting for the outcome of the game, he wouldn't have spotted the bald, smartly groomed, well-built man in a buttoned-up black overcoat, leaning against a tree, over to his left. Anyone glancing at the stranger would have assumed he was just some tired businessman taking time out from his busy work load, relaxing in the shade.

In reality, he was a senior member of a clandestine American government department, who, along with his associates, were in the process of putting together a series of events that would ultimately cause the loss of thousands of innocent lives in various locations throughout America.

The stranger, who wasn't too pleased with the fact that Tony was creating a scene, resulting in a number of people in the vicinity to stop and stare, discreetly made his way towards him, shaking his head, tut-tutting to himself.

'Hi Tony, how's it hanging? And take it easy will you? People are starting to stare. You're acting as though you are some kind of mad dumb ass.'

'Some dead dumb ass you ...' snapped Tony, stopping midsentence, realizing the stranger knew his name. 'Who the hell are you, and how come you know my name?' His eyes narrowed with suspicion. The stranger moved closer to Tony, so he wouldn't have to shout.

'I know a great deal about you Tony, especially your gambling addiction, along with your growing debts. I can't imagine your cute little reporter sister being impressed if she found out. Now would she?'

Tony was the brother of Sally Rider, crime reporter for the *New York Times*.

'You keep her out of this you shit, or I am going to kick your butt,' shouted Tony, pointing his finger at the man in anger.

The stranger stealthily closed the gap between them, and in a blink of an eye, he had Tony's arm twisted up around his back, with him lying on the floor, the side of Tony's face being pushed down against the concrete sidewalk.

'Tony, Tony, Tony, let's not be stupid, eh! … Just listen to what I have to say, and then you can carry on with the rest of your sorry-assed life.'

Realizing he was no match for this guy, Tony stopped resisting, which resulted in him being helped to his feet. Such was the speed, and professionalism of the whole incident, anyone witnessing the event would have thought that the young man had accidentally slipped, with a kind, smartly dressed gentleman assisting him. This being the stranger's intention from the start.

Once composed, after brushing himself down, wiping away the dust from the side of his face, Tony moved a safe distance from the stranger, yet ensuring he was within earshot of anything he had to say.

'OK, I will listen, but it had better be good, and next time you won't be so lucky, you just caught me off guard,' mocked Tony.

The stranger inched his way towards Tony, wiping the sweat from his tanned bald head with a white handkerchief he'd produced from his breast pocket, glaring at Tony, with the meanest eyes he had ever seen, causing Tony to shiver.

'Right Tony, button your lip and listen to what I have to say. As I understand, you're up to your neck in debt. The last I heard, it was a hundred grand; correct?'

'Who's counting?' retorted Tony, smirking.

'I am, so don't start acting like a moron. The guys you owe money too won't just force your arm up your back. If you don't pay up, and soon, they will break off both your arms, and stick them where the sun don't shine, so wipe that stupid grin off your face, got it?'

Aware that he had no choice in the matter but to listen to what the stranger had to say, Tony nodded, followed with a nervous 'Yes'.

'Tony, we are willing to pay you two hundred thousand dollars for certain items you have in your possession,' stated the stranger.

'In my possession? The only thing I have is twenty dollars in loose change, a worthless betting slip, plus the keys to the Towers. Oh! And yes, the keys to my mom's apartment … Just hold on, who the hell is this we?' queried Tony.

The stranger held out a card for him to read, which Tony hesitantly took from him.

'Special Agent Tyler Nash. Doesn't say which government department you work for – is it a secret or what?' Tony grinned.

'No, it's no secret, but we are very particular about who we confide in. Let's just say it's a powerful department in the government that's going to get you out of trouble,' remarked Nash, sneering.

'Can I keep hold of the card, just in case I need to get in touch with you for any reason?' asked Tony.

'There shouldn't be any reason why you should need to contact me, but if it makes you feel better, yes, but make sure you keep it safe, and don't show it to anyone, it's our little secret, OK?' answered Nash, with a keep-your-mouth-shut look.

Nodding his agreement, secreting the card safely in his pocket, Tony realized what the agent wanted from him.

'Oh no! You want the keys to the Towers, don't you?' he cried, nervously shuffling his feet.

'Calm down, and be quiet will you?' replied Nash, looking around, checking to see if anyone had witnessed Tony's outburst. Satisfied no one had, he proceeded to tell him the rest of his agenda.

'Let's just say we want to borrow them for a few weeks, that's all. You don't have to do anything. I know what you can do, call in sick. Spend some of your ill gained money ... Oh, and one more thing. I wouldn't return to work for at least a couple of weeks if I was you. After that, you can decide what to do with your sad, good-for-nothing life. Oh yes, I nearly forgot in all the excitement, I will also need the security codes for the alarm systems throughout the two buildings as well.'

Sounds too good to be true, thought Tony.

'Why do you need my keys? I would have thought you could get a set from the Towers' management company. Also, if you are legit, they would willingly give you the codes,' Tony inferred, looking away from the agent's piercing stare.

'Tony, Tony, Tony, you're asking too many questions, which isn't very healthy for you, under the circumstances. Listen; let's just say that we are examining the security procedures and fire alarms throughout the two buildings. And in the next two weeks we will be reporting back to the owners the response times of your fellow workers, informing the owners if anything needs to be updated or improved. Does that make you feel any better?'

Looking slightly puzzled, Tony nodded. Come on, he thought to himself, $200,000, plus the added bonus of time off work, and all this for doing diddly-squat.

Nash asked Tony for the codes, along with the keys to the Towers. Tony hesitated at first, but the thought of all that money got the better of him. When he had finished, Tony handed the paper containing the codes, together with his set of keys, minus his mom's, to Nash.

Nash discreetly handed a large padded envelope to Tony, who hastily opened it, carefully examining the contents. Pleased that all the money seemed to be there, Tony slyly slid the envelope in his inside coat pocket.

'So long Tony, and I hope we don't meet again. Oh! One more thing before you disappear, and spend all that dough on booze and broads. If you breathe a word of this conversation to anyone, I will find you … and kill you. Understand?'

Gulp! Tony was now becoming scared.

'Don't worry, I won't tell a soul, I'm not that stupid,' replied Tony, wiping the sweat from the palm's of his hands down the front of his shirt.

After their frank exchange of words, they went their separate ways, with Nash; now feeling pleased with himself that he'd managed to get hold of what he'd come for, made his way to his parked car – yet stopping occasionally to glance back over his shoulder at Tony, wondering whether he could be trusted or not to say anything, then quickly coming to the conclusion that someone like Tony Rider may be useful to him, in the future. In the meantime, Tony had nervously made his way down towards the basement of the South Tower to inform his colleagues that he wasn't feeling well, adding that he was going home to bed for a few days. After collecting his change of clothes from his locker, he hurriedly made his way across town to his mother's apartment, constantly trying to work out why Nash would want the keys, and codes.

'Never mind, eh,' he said to himself, thinking about all that money he had to spend.

Over the course of the next few days, government agents, along with a number of foreign-looking gentlemen, were assigned to each Tower, all on a secret mission. Unbeknown to the men and women who worked at the Twin Towers, controlled explosives were being planted throughout both buildings; also specialized teams were brought in to place 'super-thermite' in strategic positions on the main supporting pillars in the basement.

These were the controlled explosives hundreds of eyewitnesses heard and reported on the day of the terrorist attacks on 9/11.

After paying off his debts, Tony began to reflect back to the meeting with Special Agent Nash.

He kept on asking himself; why had Nash said not to return to work for a few weeks, and then decide on his future? Both his mother and sister were getting suspicious about the time he was taking off. His explanation was that he'd had a good win on the Yankees game. Also he hadn't been feeling well – too much stress with the job was his main excuse. Yet he also informed them that he was thinking of returning to work soon anyway. 'So quit pestering me will you?' he quipped.

Tony's sister Sally had noticed a change in his moods lately; she also became aware of his excessive spending. 'I hope, while you've been out spending all your new-found wealth, you've remembered to keep some back for your rent for the coming months? You know what you're like with money. It burns a hole in your pocket.'

'Get off my back, will you, Sis? I'll make sure all my bills are paid. I may even throw in a little extra for Mum, so she can go out and buy something nice for herself.'

Tony had always been jealous of his older sister. Sally had worked hard through college; he'd just played around most of the time. But with a little help from his friends, he finally landed a job, which was a big surprise to all the family. Sally had applied for a number of journalistic positions when she'd left college, spending the first few years working her way up the ladder with the local newspapers. Her aim was to land a job with one of the big city tabloids, so when she was offered a post reporting for the *New York Times* crime section, she was blown away. Sally was a very ambitious girl, making certain no one got in her way; always sniffing around for a good story.

After continuously being bored, also becoming aware he was slowly running out of money, Tony decided to get back to work. So on the morning of 9/11, he jumped out of bed, quickly washed and dressed, collected his bag with his change of clothes from the bottom of the bed, and was out of the door by 6 a.m.

The morning air was fresh and clean with a warm breeze coming in from the coast. The sun was just starting to creep through the clouds. Little did he know that it would be the last day for thousands of innocent people.

Approaching the Twin Towers he started to become nervous, and a little agitated, once again recalling the conversation he'd had with Agent Nash.

Well, I'll see soon enough if anything has changed with the security and alarms, he thought.

Arriving at 7 a.m., he made his way across to the South Tower's side entrance, only to stop a few feet from the door.

'I need some caffeine to calm my nerves,' he mumbled to himself, sweat beading on his face, his shirt sticking to his skin. So off he strode down the road to the nearest coffee bar, hoping the caffeine would give him enough courage to return to work. After collecting his steamy latte, with a touch of caramel, he sat over by the window, enjoying the view of the many commuters strolling innocently to work …

… And, unbeknown to them, in just over two hours' time, hundreds of those innocent, trusting employees, and visitors of the Twin

Towers would be the victims of the most ungodly attack inflicted on American soil.

Draining the last of his drink, Tony buttoned up his coat and made his way apprehensively back towards the South Tower. Once he was at the side door, he didn't hesitate this time, but went straight inside to the main office, informing his colleagues that he'd returned to work, and was fit and ready for duty. He was welcomed back without any question and within minutes he had started to delegate duties to his workforce. The one job that he hadn't assigned to be carried out was the checking of the fire alarms and emergency exit doors. This he would do himself.

'This is going to take me most of the day,' he moaned. 'I wonder what I'm going to discover.' Once again he felt the tension encircling his whole body.

As Tony was changing into his uniform in the locker room, he was alarmed to find out from one of his colleagues that over the last weekend there had been a 'power down' condition lasting thirty-six hours from Floor 50 upwards.

When Tony enquired why, he was told that the cabling in the Towers had been upgraded, which slightly unnerved him. After accepting the man's explanation, he proceeded to carry on changing into his work clothes.

By 8.30 a.m. Tony had started his inspection of the South Tower.

At 8.47 a.m., American Airlines Flight 11, a Boeing 767 en route from Boston to Los Angeles, struck the north face of the 110-story North Tower of the World Trade Center, between the 95th and 103rd floors. Tony had heard the explosion, but hadn't realized what had happened until someone cried out that a plane had flown into the building. It was at this stage that he, along with his colleagues, started to evacuate the workers from the South Tower, worried that the falling debris and burning fuel might land on them. Word had got back to him that the staff in the North Tower were doing exactly the same, but with more urgency. Tony decided to leave his colleagues, so he could go across and assist with the evacuation of the North Tower.

At 9.03 a.m., with the evacuation under way in the North Tower, a second Boeing 767, United Airlines Flight 175, also flying from Boston to Los Angeles, ploughed into the south-east corner of the South Tower, at the 80th floor, sending a massive ball of burning fuel into the air over lower New York City. Tony was in the foyer of the North Tower when he heard the explosion.

'What the hell!' he shouted. 'Listen up everyone, just get the hell out of here as quickly as possible, and head over towards the exit over to your left, it looks to be clear of rubble. I think the damn building's going to collapse.' How he'd come to the conclusion that the building was going to collapse was beyond him. He just had this dreadful awareness, as though he were in a nightmare, of which he already knew the ending. Also, for some unknown reason, he had a gut feeling that his meeting with Agent Nash had something to do with what was happening around him. He also had a hunch that it was going to get a whole lot worse.

He began issuing orders to the terrified people coming down the stairs, and to those who, to his amazement, were coming out of the lifts. Herding as many people as possible towards the exits, he looked up at the clock by the reception desk. It read 9.05 a.m.

It was at this point that he heard small explosions coming from the South Tower.

Oh Christ, he thought, I need to get these men and women out of here as fast as possible, and I don't want to be hanging around this place too long.

Directing the walking wounded down the stairs towards the exit, through the thick dust floating in the air, Tony instructed them to place a hand on the shoulder of the person in front and to call out if they hit an obstacle so others would know to avoid it; hoping that this may prevent anyone from wandering off. As he was organizing the evacuation, he heard another explosion, but this one was from above him in the North Tower, the force blowing the elevator doors out, knocking Tony off his feet, landing him heavily on his back. After carefully clearing his eyes with his shirt-tails, he noticed that the elevator doors had buckled outwards, causing thick smoke and scorched paper to pour out. It was now becoming more difficult for Tony to see what was happening around him, also the thick soot and ash swirling in the air was making it hard for him to breathe.

He suddenly stopped what he was doing as he became aware of the distinct smell of cordite drifting through the deformed opening of the buckled elevator doors.

'They weren't checking the alarms, they were planting explosives,' raged Tony, through gritted teeth. 'That's why Nash wanted the keys.'

It was at this crucial point when Tony came to the awful realization about the events occurring around him.

'Oh no,' he whispered. 'If Nash is working for the government, that means they must have been aware that the two planes were going to be flown into the Towers …'

He knew he didn't have time to work out the whys and where-fores, but he did know he had to find some way of capturing some of the evidence before it was destroyed, if at all possible. He came up with an idea of how to do just that. I have to find a way of getting to my office, and let's hope my camera is still there, he thought.

Stumbling around, looking for the door to his office, he bumped into a number of injured people lying on the floor. One of them was a young boy whose skin was hanging off his arms and face. Tony didn't have time to see to him, relying on the emergency services. He came across dozens of other bruised and blood-streaked people, all blindly wandering around the foyer, searching for any sign of light; a beacon they could head for.

Eventually managing to reach his office, Tony started to rummage through his set of drawers, scattering paper and pens all over the floor. Thankfully he found the camera lodged at the back. Feeling angry, and consumed with remorse, he quickly and carefully manoeuvred his way around the prone bodies and injured survivors up the stairs, looking for any signs of hidden explosives, knowing that if there were any in his vicinity they could go off; but the way he was feeling at the moment, he didn't care. He just wanted to take some pictures as evidence of the involvement by the American government. Fighting his way upstairs through the vast number of people who were coming down, trying to escape, Tony was grabbed by the arm, and forcefully shoved up against the wall. It was Brad Gilbert, one of his drinking buddies.

'What the hell are you doing Tony? You should be going down the stairs with the rest of us, not going up.'

Seizing Brad by his elbow, Tony steered them both closer to the wall, securing a safe passage for the hordes of people who were desperately trying to make their escape.

Dragging Brad closer to him, Tony shouted into his ear, 'Can you hear me? … Good. I heard a number of explosions going off above us, just a few minutes ago. I'm going to see if there are any more, and hopefully take some pictures; so get out of my way and get the fuck out of here.'

'Tony, listen, as I was making my way out of the door to my office on the fifty-sixth floor, I heard a small discharge, something similar to a detonator going off. It was near to the fire hose, by the elevators – maybe it was one that hadn't worked. Tony, please be careful.'

By the time Tony had reached the 56th floor the power had shut off, making it almost impossible to see where he was going; he was also gasping for breath, black sweat was running down his face. Whilst collecting his camera, he'd had the foresight to pocket his flashlight, but unfortunately the beam was only strong enough to penetrate a few inches through the thick, swirling soot and ash drifting around in the air, which caused the beam to reflect back at him. Adjusting his eyes to the dark, wafting away the dust with his free hand, hoping to get a clearer sight of where he was going, he slowly and cautiously made his way over towards the elevator doors. Pointing the beam at the walls, he successfully managed to locate the devices hidden behind the fire hose, and to his relief observed that the wires around the outside were scorched.

'Lucky for those on the stairs – if these had exploded, those people would have surely died,' he mumbled to himself.

Quickly switching his camera to flash mode, he started to take as many pictures at close quarters as he could in the time he had allowed himself, hoping the light from the flash was good enough to capture the evidence. Satisfied he'd taken enough, he promptly slipped the camera back in its case, heading for the stairs, praying he would manage to get out of the building before anything drastic happened. Making sure he wasn't going to fall over anyone in his haste, he started running down the stairs, taking two to three steps at a time, constantly grabbing hold of the handrail for additional support. Oblivious to the noise enveloping him, he was suddenly aware that the dust that had settled on the stairs was nearly a foot thick. His eyes were beginning to sting, making them water and once again he was having difficulty breathing; his throat was parched, making it feel like sandpaper. Stopping on the fourth floor to catch his breath, he managed to break a window with his flashlight, letting in some welcome fresh air. Having got his breath back, he decided to take his shirt off, before cleaning as much of the sticky black sweat from his face as possible, then wrapping it around his mouth and nose, leaving just enough space for him to see where he was going.

Finally making it down to the main entrance, he became aware of the vibrations of the building, along with the whimpering and cries for help, coming from the dark recesses. Mindful of the dangerous predicament he was in, he realized he needed to find a way out of the building, and fast. Appraising the scene in front of him, he noticed that most of the roof was missing; electrical shots from power cables fizzed and spat amidst the demolished charred plaster and broken ceiling tiles; also the water pipes had ruptured, causing polluted water to gush like a river over the floor and down the corridors. He glanced across at the clock in the foyer: it read 09.59 a.m. It was the noise from the South Tower, plus further vibrations coming from the building, which caused Tony to realize what was happening. The South Tower was starting to collapse. Tony realized that this meant that the North Tower was sure to follow. The thunderous noise, plus the dust and debris coming in through the doors and openings caused by the explosions in the foyer, made it difficult for Tony or anyone else close by to breathe and see where they were going. They all waited helplessly, hoping the subsidence would soon end, praying that the visibility would improve. Tony kept on looking for any kind of light to head for. After a few frightening minutes of constantly scanning through the dust and soot, he thankfully spotted one of the exits which had a small amount of light seeping through it. Dashing over, the floor seemingly clear of bricks and concrete, he literally ran for his life, clutching the camera close to his chest, never stopping to look back at the carnage which he knew he had been party too. He also knew that the cries of human suffering he'd heard would haunt him for the rest of his life, along with the gruesome images he'd witnessed, which would constantly reappear before him as if they had somehow been seared onto the back of his eyelids.

Wandering the streets for two days, disoriented, feeling totally ashamed of himself, Tony decided he would phone Nash. After searching through the accumulation of rubbish in his pockets, he finally came across Nash's ID card. The phone was picked up on the second ring.

'Nash, how can I help?'

'You fuck shit, you set me up,' screamed Tony.

'Who the hell is this?'

'Don't play the bloody innocent with me, you piece of shit. You wanted the keys and me out of the way so you could plant the explosives in the Towers. If I'd known that, I would have preferred to have had my bones broken … And one other important matter – if what you say is true, and you are working for the government, involved with the planting of those explosives, it can only mean one thing. The American government must be somehow implicated in the hijacking of those planes. Am I correct in my assumption, Nash, you SON-OF-A-BITCH?'

'Calm down, will you, Tony. Get a grip of yourself, you're becoming hysterical and we can't afford that. You got what you wanted, we got what we wanted … Tony, there are always casualties in war.'

'What fucking war are you talking about, Nash? I wasn't aware we were at war. Those victims who perished were on our side, you murdering bastard … Anyway Nash, I've got something you, and your so-called American government buddies may be interested in. You see, I didn't listen to your advice. I went back to work on the morning of 9/11. I was in the foyer of the South Tower when the first plane struck the North Tower, then I heard explosions going off above me, and you know what Nash? I decided to investigate, and guess what? I found two of your devices which hadn't gone off. And the best is yet to come. I managed to take at least a dozen damning pictures of them.'

There was total silence at the other end of the phone.

'Cat got your tongue, Nash?'

'Tony, listen, don't do anything rash. Let's meet up somewhere, you decide, and we can have a little chat. You never know, there could be a small gesture of gratitude, for the pictures. What do you say?'

'What do I say Nash? GO TO HELL! That's what I say.' Tony slammed the phone down, tears streaming down his cheeks, his whole body shaking with rage.

Following Tony's shocking revelation, Nash didn't move, but just stared out of his office window in a state of shock, panic evident on his face; the phone slowly slipping through his sweaty fingers onto the desk, now regretting that he hadn't wasted Tony Rider when he had the opportunity.

From that day, Tony Rider was never seen again, until …

At 9.59 a.m. the South Tower collapsed in its own footprint.

At 10.28 a.m. the North Tower also collapsed in its own footprint.

A total of 2,823 people died in the Towers (including the airline passengers)

Here are just a few of the hundreds of eyewitness reports of 'explosions' in the Twin Towers on 9/11.

These are from credible sources, such as New York firefighters and law enforcement officers.

Firefighters, law enforcement officers and other extremely credible witnesses have also discredited the administration's version of why the World Trade Center buildings collapsed on 9/11:

A reporter for USA Today stated that the FBI believed that bombs in the buildings brought the buildings down.

A firefighter said, 'There was just an explosion. It seemed like on television [when] they blow up these buildings. It seemed like it was going all the way around like a belt, all these explosions.'

A police officer noted, 'People were saying, there's another one and another one. I heard reports of secondary bomb explosions.'

A British newspaper stated, 'some eyewitness reported hearing another explosion just before the structure crumbled. Police said that it looked almost like a planned implosion.'

A maintenance worker who worked in the basement of the North Tower witnessed an explosion in the basement at around the same time the plane hit far above.

Two other eyewitnesses working in the Twin Towers witnessed explosions in the basement at about the same time the second plane hit.

A highly reputable astrophysicist wrote in an email that, immediately before the collapse of each Twin Tower, he heard explosions and low-frequency rumbles (he also uses the phrase 'demolition-style implosion').

A detective for the Port Authority reported, long before the collapse of the tower, 'When we reached the fifteenth floor, the building began to vibrate and shake. I heard loud explosions and rumblings in the background. The stairwell shifted and gave out a large metal-on-metal groan. The stairwell then twisted back into place with another loud groan. The lights went out. At that point the stairwell became filled with smoke and dust.'

A police officer stated: 'You would hear a loud boom go off at the top of Tower One … the building continued to burn and emergency equipment kept on responding, stirring up the dust and debris in the streets. After approximately fifteen minutes suddenly there was another loud boom at the upper floors, and then there was a series of smaller explosions which appeared to go completely around the building at the upper floors. And another loud earth-shattering blast with a large fireball which blew out more debris and at that point everyone began to run north on West Broad Street.'

'THE PLANE FACTS'
Bush's Reaction On 9/11

Why did George Bush go into a meaningless photo shoot at an elementary school, after hearing that an airliner had crashed into the World Trade Center? He was briefed by National Security Adviser Condoleezza Rice before entering the classroom. She must have told him that the plane had been hijacked for forty-five minutes by this point. She also must have told him that another plane had been hijacked, since it had been known for twenty minutes by this point. Finally, while listening to second-graders read, why does Bush merely nod calmly when told about the second plane smashing into the WTC? He gazes off into space for whole minutes while the Towers burn, looking conflicted and worried.

(Internet/Fahrenheit 9/11)

September 11 2002: the story of Bush's 9/11 conduct changes for 9/11 anniversary

President Bush states, 'I was sitting outside the classroom and I saw an airplane hit the tower. The TV was on.' (CNN, 4/12/01) 'When we walked into the classroom, I had seen this plane fly into the first building.' (White House, 5/1/02) There was no live coverage of the first crash on TV and President Bush was in a classroom reading with children at the time of the second crash. How could he forget this?

On the first anniversary of the 9/11 attacks, the story of what Bush did on that day is significantly rewritten. In actual fact, when Chief of Staff Andrew Card told Bush about the second plane crash into the WTC, Bush continued to sit in a Florida elementary school classroom and hear a story about a pet goat for at least seven more minutes, as video footage later broadcast in the 2004 movie Fahrenheit 9/11 shows. But one year later, Card claimed that after he told Bush about the second WTC crash, 'It was only a matter of seconds before Bush excused himself very politely to the teacher and to the students, and he left the Florida classroom.' (San Francisco Chronicle, 11/9/02) Paul Thompson, The Terror Timeline

September 12 2002: Major paper first to give room for 9/11 skeptics

For the first time, a mainstream US newspaper looks at the people who believe there was government complicity in or criminal incompetence on 9/11 and does not immediately dismiss them. The San Francisco Examiner quotes a number of 9/11 skeptics and lets them speak for themselves. 'While different theorists focus on different aspects of the attacks, what they seem to have in common is they would like an independent investigation into 9/11.'
(San Francisco Examiner, 12/9/02)
Paul Thompson, The Terror Timeline

Chapter Six

'My mother used to say that there are no strangers, only friends you haven't met yet.'

Dame Edna Everage (1934–)

SEPTEMBER 11 2007, 8.00a.m., Chelsea Hotel, New York

It was the noise of the traffic, combined with the sweet sounds of birdsong on the balcony, which finally woke Alex up. Once he was fully awake, he made his way to the bathroom, showered and shaved. When glancing at his reflection in the mirror, he was alarmed to see how much he'd aged; there was evidence of small crow's-feet by the corners of his eyes, along with a few worry lines across his forehead, which was to be expected, he thought, especially after all the distress he'd been through over the past couple of years. Alex was never one to stop to admire himself. He'd always been shy in that respect, never understanding how someone as beautiful as Marie could have chosen him.

Checking in the hallway to see if his damp clothes had been returned; he wasn't surprised to see that they were ready for him by the door.

'What excellent service, you wouldn't get this back in the UK,' he commented.

He quickly dressed, pulled out the soggy toilet paper from his shoes, checking inside, making sure they were dry enough to wear. Thankfully, they were, although he was aware that he may have to do the same again that night. He began sorting through the additional set of clothes he'd brought with him, making sure he chose sombre colors, rather than bright, loud ones.

'The day requires some dignity,' he said to himself.

He ended up wearing an open-neck crisp white shirt, neatly pressed chinos (ones that had been laundered at the hotel), and one of his dark blue blazers. He also decided to take his overcoat, which he draped over his arm, knowing it would be cold once he was at the site.

Pleased with his overall appearance, he nervously left his room, not knowing what to expect of the coming day, or how he would react. He decided to walk down the stairs for a change, and once again stopping to admire the many framed pictures on the walls in the corridor, wishing he had the talent for painting something as stunning. Stepping through the exit door, he unexpectantly came across a cast-iron staircase, which immediately reminded him of a Second World War film – where he could imagine Clint Eastwood leaning over the banister, randomly firing his machine gun down at the advancing German soldiers as they tried to take him prisoner. The hotel was full of unexpected surprises, he thought.

Exiting from the hotel, the first thing he noticed was the clouds, gradually dispersing, leaving the sun to warm up the chilly, early morning air. He'd only walked a short distance when, unexpectedly, he heard the pealing of church bells in the distance. Checking the time, he understood the significance of the bells: 8.47 a.m. It was at this moment the first plane struck the North Tower. People near by, also mindful of the significance, stopped what they were doing, and where possible cars were carefully pulling up by the side of the kerb. In unison, the gathered masses encompassing him, solemnly bowed their heads in silence, paying their respects to the victims. A warm glow cloaked Alex's whole body, raising the hairs on the back of his neck.

After a few minutes the bells ceased, with everyone beginning to carry on with their business; the cars easing out into the slow moving traffic. Wiping the moisture from his eyes, Alex sombrely made his way downtown.

Alex had already made up his mind that he would aim to arrive at Ground Zero by early afternoon, but first, on the way, he was hoping he'd have time to visit the WTC Memorial Annual Floating Lanterns Ceremony at the New York Buddhist Church, which had been advertised in the hotel's lobby. The poster stated that the event would be ongoing throughout most of the day, and into the early evening. Ever since his eldest son Michael had started studying Japanese, Alex had taken an avid interest in their history and culture; and it would be something to report when sending his email, he thought. The poster claimed that the event was an ancient Japanese custom of floating small lanterns on water, a symbolic representation of respect for the lives that had gone before, also representing a light of hope, peace and harmony.

After searching around for half an hour, he finally arrived at the church, detecting that most of the spectators were congregated around what looked like a small stream adjacent to the church, so he went over to investigate. The atmosphere encompassing him was soothing and peaceful, which no doubt the organizers had been hoping for. Alex quietly roamed around the scene, soaking up the atmosphere, taking in the aroma of the burning incense sticks drifting in the morning air. Realizing there wasn't a lot more to see or do, he decided to head towards Ground Zero, hoping that by the time he arrived most of the dignitaries and family and friends of the victims would have already left the ceremony. This would enable Alex to sit quietly by himself, reflecting over the past months.

But to his disappointment the streets in the vicinity were crowded with hundreds of visitors, making their way towards the vast area of the site. Alex knew he was close, as he could see in the distance two two-mile-high laser beams illuminating the sky, commemorating this special day, which had been mentioned on the news.

The 'Tribute in Light', he remembered, also recalling that this year the surviving firefighters and other emergency workers on duty on 9/11 were to read out the names of all the victims.

Ground Zero

Making his way around the corner, close to the office buildings overlooking the site, Alex observed a number of families; most of them sitting quietly at the foot of the steps, clutching framed pictures close to their chests. No doubt family and friends of the innocent victims of 9/11, he presumed. Stopping to take in the scene before him, Alex was stunned by the sheer size of the area where the Towers had stood, detecting that the perimeter had been cordoned off with high heavy-duty fencing and boarding on which pictures of the devastation were hung alongside historical photos of the area. The process of laying the foundations for the 'Freedom Tower' (the chosen design for the World Trade Center memorial) was now under way at the site. Dotted at random around the periphery of the site were the Stars and Stripes, fluttering in the light breeze, all at half-mast. Despite being over six foot, Alex was finding it difficult seeing over the top of the solid wooden fencing. After numerous attempts, he finally gave up, and made his way towards where he observed most of the people were congregating, which was Zeccotti Park, on Liberty Street. The mood was calm, and tranquil. He stopped to look towards the heavens, noticing dreary grey skies, creating a grim backdrop, which was a sharp contrast to the clear skies of that morning in 2001, he thought. Casually roaming round the park, he came across what looked like new-laid grass and recently planted shrubs, and throughout the gardens there was also fluorescent lighting, set into the marble-tiled pavement.

Alex was surprised to see that there were still a number of television crews packing their gear into the many high-sided trailers parked by the side of the road. No doubt, he thought, editors would be in the process of cutting and pasting together the day's events for that evening's news channels, plus the numerous talk shows aired around the world. Wandering around, soaking up the atmosphere, he unexpectedly came upon a life-sized bronze figure of a man, which looked to be covered in dust, seated on one of the granite benches by the corner of the park. The figure was gazing down into his briefcase, which was resting on his knees.

'How poignant,' he whispered to himself, holding back the lump forming in his throat. He found out later, during a conversation with some of the other visitors, that the sculpture was called 'Double Check'. It had sat in the original park for nearly twenty years, and had been relocated to the new park after 9/11.

A number of granite benches had been erected inside the park, where relatives and friends could sit, and be left alone with their thoughts. Alex needed to be alone, to collect his, so he headed over to one of them. The whole place felt so surreal, with the enormous expanse of land where the Towers had stood looking forlorn and desolate. Yet the many high-rise glass-and-concrete buildings surrounding the site made him feel as though he were looking at 'sentinels protecting some sacred site, waiting for their long-lost friend's return'.

What other way would I describe the scene around me? he pondered. After mulling it over for a while, he whispered to himself: 'A wound that would never heal.' Light rain was beginning to fall once more, with the gloom among the surrounding buildings deepening.

'Tears of a thousand souls falling down towards their loved ones ...' he said, then scanning the sky, continued with, '... mixed with the many tears which have been shed down here today.'

He was then lost for words.

It wasn't long before he realized the weather had turned cold, also becoming aware that it had stopped raining as quickly as it had started.

So, along with the rest of the crowd who were drifting around the park, he began to survey his surroundings; and to his amazement, he observed at the top of the park a large six-pronged red sculpture, which reminded him of a big red X.

He recollected reading about it. The seventy-foot sculpture had been designed and constructed by Mark di Suveros, and was named 'Joie de Vivre'.

'No doubt Big Red X in French,' commented Alex, chuckling to himself. Moving slowly towards the sculpture, Alex could sense an aura encircling him which made the hairs on the back of his head once again stand up. It was almost as if the inside of his skull was being gently stroked. The atmosphere had once again started to become peaceful and tranquil. Surprisingly, he heard raised voices in the distance, close to the sculpture. Cautiously, he started to make his way towards the commotion, checking out what the fuss was all about. Suddenly he found himself surrounded by a candlelit vigil, also noticing a few groups scattered around the sculpture; some were quietly singing gospel songs, whilst others were talking in hushed tones, which drifted in the afternoon air. Yet over in the top left-hand corner of the park, he detected a group of what he presumed were protesters, waving placards, and above the noise of the traffic he could hear them shouting, but from this distance he couldn't make out what was being said. Alex, being nosy, decided to go across to see what the disturbance was all about. It was clear to him that most of the protesters were circulating around the crowds of people, handing out leaflets, which Alex obligingly took one from a pretty young blonde girl, who reminded him of Marie when she was in her early thirties. So young and innocent, he recalled. Gingerly moving away, Alex decided to find a bench, to read the information printed on the leaflet. The material listed was just a small proportion of the information he'd already come across over the past few months in the many books he'd amassed. He was now suddenly becoming excited by the fact that he'd met a group of people who, he surmised, were strenuously trying to attempt to inform the American public about the damning facts behind 9/11, and to his delight it was the group that had been referred to on the news the other day: The Plane Facts.

9/11 – 'The Plane Facts'
Letter to the President and the Commission

Some of the distortions and omissions from the report that STILL need answering:

No mention of the fact that several credible sources stated that at least six of the alleged hijackers are still alive, including Waleed al-Shehri, accused of stabbing a flight attendant on Flight 11 before it crashed into the WTC North Tower.

No mention of the role of the Pakistani ISI, a pivotal element with reported ties to both the 9/11 hijackers and the CIA.

No mention of how it was possible that the South Tower collapsed first, even though it had been burning for a much shorter time than the North Tower, and also had less fire.

The omission of the fact that the publicly released flight manifests contain no Arab names.

Absolutely no mention of fatal anthrax attacks in the days following 9/11, which involved weapons-grade pathogens obtainable only through the US military, and were directed against leading Democrats who might have balked at the anti-terrorist measures within the Patriot Act.

No mention of all the various testimony that has been used to cast doubt on whether remains of a Boeing 757 were visible either inside or outside the Pentagon.
Omission of the fact that there have been no photos released of the reconstructed debris of Flight 77 although this has been standard procedure in past airline disasters.

Omission of Mayor Giuliani's statement that he had evacuated his temporary command center because he had received word that the World Trade Center Towers were about to collapse.

After digesting the contents of the leaflet, Alex found the nerve to go over and have a chat with the group, in the hope of finding out more about them.

The first member Alex came across was a large man, dressed in jeans and a tired-looking brown leather jacket, his slicked-back hair gleaming in the glow of the recessed lights. He guessed the guy was in his early thirties, and roughly the same height as himself. Not someone to mess with, thought Alex; so he decided to be polite, as always. Alex approached the man, stopping three strides away so as not to appear a threat. Once he was certain he wasn't going to ignore him and walk away, Alex offered him his hand, which the stranger took, hesitantly.

'I'm sorry to bother you, but would you mind if I have a word with you? I've just been wandering around the site …' Alex paused, checking out the guy's reaction to his intrusion. '… and this has been my first holiday since my wife was murdered in London on the Underground in 2005 …' Alex could see from the stranger's expression that he didn't know whether to trust him or not, but once again he carried on, regardless. '… I've been sat over there reading through one of your leaflets, and I would be interested to know more about your group, if at all possible. Oh! I'm sorry, I haven't introduced myself properly. My name's Alex Monroe, I'm from England, if you haven't already guessed by my accent.'

Alex decided to move back a couple of steps from the stranger, not knowing what to expect from this big guy. On closer inspection, he noticed moisture appearing from the stranger's eyes, which he kept wiping away with a tissue, whilst studying Alex. Unexpectedly, and with a big smile across his face, he put out his hand for Alex to shake. Alex responded, noticing that he had a firm but gentle grip.

'Sorry if I seemed rude just then, but you never know who are the bad guys and who are the good guys these days. Larry Underwood's the name, ex-firefighter. I've been here most days with these other guys and gals since 9/11, protesting to the masses, urging them to write to their senators, up there on Capitol Hill, demanding an independent public inquiry about the true facts surrounding 9/11; Alex Monroe, welcome to the Plane Facts group, also I'm really sorry to hear about your wife.' Alex smiled and whispered 'Thanks,' under his breath.

After an awkward few seconds, Larry wrapped his arm around his shoulder, recognizing the fact that Alex wasn't a threat, before guiding him across to the rest of the group.

'Let me introduce you to the rest of the gang, there's only a few of us here tonight. Sally Rider, a crime reporter for the *New York Times*, Guido, he's a cab driver, and lastly Moon – no one knows what he does, I bumped into him on 9/11, he just appears, but don't worry about him, he's harmless. The others you can see handing out leaflets help out when they can.' So, the blonde girl's name's Sally Rider, and she's a crime reporter to boot. Interesting, thought Alex. He couldn't help but notice that most of the group looked clean and well dressed. Well, at least I'm not getting mixed up with vagrants, thankfully, he reflected. As they approached the group, Larry stopped, asking Alex if he wouldn't mind waiting a minute, whilst he conferred with the rest of them. Alex said it wouldn't be a problem.

Alex couldn't make out what was being said, but he did hear a few raised voices, and the shaking of heads. After a few tense minutes, Larry turned back towards Alex, indicating for him to come over and meet the rest of the team. As he approached the waiting group, the young blonde woman let out a high-pitched scream. Suddenly, she dashed across to a tall, bedraggled looking figure, emerging from behind the red sculpture.

'What the . . .' exclaimed Larry, . . . 'that guy looks like Sally's brother, Tony. He was working as a security guard at the Twin Towers when they were attacked. Sadly, Sally said that he was officially declared dead, yet his body was never recovered at either of the two sites.' There was a moment of stunned silence. Alex and Larry stared at each other, while the rest of them seemed lost for words, unsure what to do. Cautiously approaching the shadowy figure, Sally abruptly stopped, making sure that it was her brother. Certain it was, she ran the last few feet, jumped straight into his open arms, both of them sobbing uncontrollably.

'Where do you think he's been all this time?' questioned Alex.

'Beats me,' answered Larry, looking slightly bemused. 'Yet Sally did mention to me that a few days prior to 9/11, Tony suddenly came into a great deal of money … started acting a little strange, taking time off work, spending it mostly at home. Then, unexpectedly, he announced he was going to go back to work: a bit of a coincidence, really, it was on the morning of 9/11.'

Larry walked across to make sure everything was fine. By the time he had reached them, Sally had separated from her brother.

'Is everything all right Sally?' Larry asked, tentatively.

Sally glanced over her shoulder to see who had spoken.

'Yes thanks, Larry, it isn't every day a ghost appears before you,' replied Sally, keeping hold of Tony's hand for reassurance.

'I think you've some explaining to do young man,' remarked Larry. 'Six years ago your family and friends mourned your death. They were all mindful of the fact that your body was never found, they just all presumed you'd died when the Towers collapsed.'

'Can you trust these guys Sis?' asked Tony, scanning the faces before him.

'Yes, why, what's wrong?' Sally enquired, panicking.

'I've done something terrible, something so bad that you'll never forgive me.'

'Don't be such a moron Tony, you can't have done anything that bad, can you?' queried Sally, her hand slowly slipping away from Tony's grasp.

'We need to move away from here, somewhere where we won't be overheard,' replied Tony, nervously examining the crowd around him.

'I'm not going anywhere until you tell me what you have to say,' demanded Sally, 'you're starting to frighten me now.'

'You'd better bring the rest of your friends along as well,' mumbled Tony. 'I want them to know all the sordid details. I've carried it around with me for the last six years; I need to bring it all out in the open.'

Larry indicated to Alex and the rest of them to move closer to Tony, so they could hear what he had to say, which took Alex by surprise, as he had only been in their presence a few minutes. Once Tony was certain there was no one else in hearing distance, he started to relay his story, up to and surrounding the events of 9/11 …

When Tony had finished his graphic account, the group just stood there, speechless, paralyzed, feeling both angry and appalled at his confession. It was Tony who eventually broke the stony silence.

'Now you know why I couldn't show my face, or come home. For the last six years I've kept well away from you, living like a hobo; working in bars, washing up, taking out the garbage for a pittance of a wage.'

'Tony, how could you have done such an atrocious thing?' asked Sally, 'I hope you're not expecting me to feel sorry for you, because I fucking well don't?' She screamed. 'The only key part about your involvement and subsequent actions is that you somehow managed to find evidence, pointing to this governments involvement in the planting of the explosives; and I don't know if you are aware? . . . It's what this group's been claiming over the past six years . . .'

'Look guys, I'm not begging for forgiveness. I just want to make amends that's all, if I can,' pleaded Tony. 'The pictures of the explosives ... I have them here, on me. I've also had to stay well clear of Nash over these past six years. I don't know if he's still around, but I couldn't take the risk of him finding me, especially with what I know about him, and have in my possession.'

Alex began to scan the faces of the rest of the group, checking their reaction to Tony's shocking revelation. He'd only spoken to Larry; the others were strangers as far as he was concerned, so he didn't know what to expect from any of them.

Alex was now frightened and concerned about his welfare; his mind was becoming confused, which was understandable under the circumstances, he reasoned, especially after what he'd just heard.

Christ almighty, he thought. If all that damning information, plus those pictures ended up in the wrong hands, it could ultimately bring down the current American government. Slowly walking away from the rest of the group, wondering what to do next, Alex's concentration was abruptly broken by nearby movement. He became aware that they had been surrounded by six imposing-looking men, all dressed identically in dark overcoats, the expressions on their faces giving nothing away. As they made their way closer to the group, Alex caught sight of the wired transparent earpieces each of them were wearing, but owing to the fading light, he couldn't see any telltale bulges indicating that they might be concealing weapons. This was some relief, he thought, yet he deduced that they might be government agents, and that he was in some serious trouble.

One of the six, a serious-looking bald-headed guy, who looked to be in charge, sauntered over in the direction of Tony.

'Oh no!' roared Tony.

'Tony what's the matter, do you know this guy?' cried Sally.

'Nothing's the matter, just stay calm Sis, everything will be fine,' replied Tony, his voice quivering with fear.

Unbeknown to Sally, and the rest of the group, the serious-looking bald-headed guy heading towards Tony was Special Agent Nash.

'Tony, Tony, Tony,' said Nash, smirking, 'what can I say? You've been one hell of a guy to find over these last six years.'

Tony started to shuffle around, looking for an escape route. But they had all the bases covered, and they knew he knew he was trapped.

'The rest of you can go, we've no reason to detain you, it's this one we want to have a quiet little chat with,' Nash said, pointing towards Tony, his other hand waving his badge around for them to examine, if they were quick enough, which none of them were.

'You know what Tony, for some unknown reason, I don't know why, I had an idea you'd appear this year, and I was correct wasn't I?' sneered Nash.

Looking towards the other agents, he barked out his orders. 'Take him away, and let's get the hell out of here, we have the one we came for.'

Without any warning, Sally bulldozed her way through to Tony, grabbing his arm, heading away from the park. Along with the rest of the group Alex reacted instinctively, but the agents were wise to them all; they had left a couple of agents in the street to block off any escape. Tony and Sally were dragged back towards the group, kicking and shouting. Sally wasn't going to give up her brother to these men that easily, not after seeing him again for the first time in six years. Alex could see that, besides Tony being manhandled,

Sally was also being roughed up, and it seemed the agents weren't bothered that it was a woman they were doing it to either, and with this in mind, Alex quickly leapt to her aid. The brawl that followed was frantic, with fists flying, shins being kicked, and bodies falling all over the damp grass. Alex was in the thick of it, strenuously trying to free Sally and Tony from the agents who had them both pinned to the ground.

Knowing he had no chance of escaping from his captors, Tony struggled to slip one of his hands inside his coat pocket for the envelope containing the pictures. Confident no one was watching, he sneakily dropped it into Alex's coat pocket, hoping he hadn't felt anything untoward.

When everything had all calmed down, with them all separated from one another, Sally noticed Tony lying motionless on the floor. Blood was starting to trickle from his nose and ears, and the swelling to the side of his head made the damage to his face look worse.

'Oh no, Tony!' shrieked Sally. 'What have you done to him?'

Kneeling down beside him, cradling his head in her lap, stroking his forehead, she started to whisper in his ear. 'Tony, please don't die on me again, wake up, please.' Her voice trembling with emotion.

Realizing the situation had suddenly become serious, Nash quickly called for an ambulance on his cell phone.

Alex, along with the rest of the group, began to slowly circle Sally and Tony, protecting them from the cold wind which had suddenly just sprung up. Nash knew he had to search Tony's pockets at some stage to relieve him of the pictures; that's if he had them on him, yet he didn't want to make it too obvious, as he wasn't sure if Tony had said anything about them, or his involvement.

After ten awkward and anxious minutes, during which time Moon and Guido had casually drifted away from the scene, it was the squeal of the ambulance's tires that brought everyone out of their disturbed thoughts.

Once the paramedics had safely strapped Tony to the stretcher, they wheeled him to the waiting ambulance, carefully sliding the gurney into place. Before they left, Nash called over to ask the paramedics which hospital they were taking him to.

'St Vincent's Catholic Medical Center at 170 West 12th Street,' they replied. Nash acknowledged with a nod of his head. Sally had insisted on going along with Tony in the ambulance, which Nash agreed to with the proviso that she wouldn't try to escape, with Tony in tow, which she accepted grudgingly.

After sorting the situation out with these two guys, he would go to the hospital and retrieve the pictures, Nash hoped. Standing firm, legs apart in a defensive stance, arms folded across his chest, Nash started to stare menacingly at them.

'Now listen up, especially you…' glaring towards Alex with his piercing eyes. '…it's your lucky day, you've caught me in a good mood, especially now that I have that scumbag, so you can both go home. But it doesn't alter the fact that you are all just a bunch of annoying wise asses, upsetting everyone with your lies and accusations. I would strongly advise you to stop now, or you may end up in more trouble than you can handle, and don't worry too much about Tony, we'll look after him.'

'That's what we're worried about. I don't think we will be seeing Tony alive again if you have anything to do with it,' Larry pointed out.

'Yes, you're all the same,' interrupted Alex. 'What's one more statistic? Human lives mean nothing to you lot.'

'Oh, I should have guessed, we have a Brit in our midst,' barked Nash. 'A knight in shining armour, rescuing the damsel in distress from the nasty villains. *Thank you, kind sir, for helping me,'* mimicked Nash, in a woman's voice, chuckling to himself.

'Yes you have, and it's arse-holes like you that are giving Americans a bad name,' roared Alex.

'Right, that's it,' shouted Nash, glancing over towards a suited gentleman who had appeared by his side. 'Detective, take them both down to the station. Keep them there all night if you have to, let them mix with the lowlife of New York for a while – that will teach them a lesson for getting mixed up with the likes of Tony Rider.'

The detective began to escort Alex and Larry towards the squad car that had been parked by the side of the road. Once they were safely locked inside, they pulled out into the traffic and headed towards the local police station. In the meantime Nash had walked over to his waiting car, which he had left down a side street. He buckled his seat belt, and drove to the hospital, hoping to have a quiet chat with Tony. But more importantly he had to get his hands on the pictures, if he had them.

Throughout the time the ambulance was making its way to the hospital, Tony had been floating in and out of consciousness, mumbling lucidly about the pictures, plus indistinct words Sally couldn't make out; then unexpectedly he grabbed hold of her arm, pulling her down so he could whisper in her ear.

'Sis-s-s, that guy … the guy … at the p-p-park … it was N-N-Nash, d-d-don't let … don't … let … pictures … d-d-don't …' Tony then lost consciousness once more.

'Oh shit,' cried Sally, 'what the hell do I do now?' Now knowing who the bald-headed guy at the park was, she decided to search Tony's pockets whilst no one was watching, hoping to find the pictures. But to her dismay his pockets contained only dirty tissues, some loose change and a YMCA meal voucher.

'What's happened to them?' she asked herself, panicking. 'I wonder if they fell out of his coat pocket during the fight. But I don't recall seeing any scattered about on the floor.'

Tony was eventually taken into a side ward to be examined by the doctors. Sally was asked to leave whilst they prepared him, and wait in the visitors' room until someone came to inform her of his condition.

Trying to come to terms with Tony's sudden appearance, Sally realized she'd have to let her mother know that her son had just returned from the dead. The news would kill her, she thought. She decided to hold off for a while, and wait and see if Tony pulled through; if not, she wouldn't say anything.

It was the creaking of the door that brought Sally out of her distressed state of mind. Straightening herself in the uncomfortable chair, wiping away the dried-up tears she had shed, looking up to see who had entered, she came face to face with the bald-headed agent from the park, who was sat on the chair directly opposite her.

'I wondered when you'd show up,' snapped Sally.

'Now, now, I've only got your brother's best interests at heart, especially with him being a friend of mine,' sneered Nash.

'I don't think you have any friends, so get lost and leave me alone,' shouted Sally. 'Also, you didn't have the good manners to introduce yourself properly. You barge into the park, arrest my brother, for what reason, I have no idea? Then thanks to your heavy-handed goon's, Tony's ended up in surgery. So who are you? Or are you a member of some government secret department?'

'No, it's not a secret, let me introduce myself. My name's Nash, Special Agent Nash. You don't need to know which part of the government I work for. Let's just say I am looking after all our interests, and as to why we arrested your brother, that's classified; also you have only yourself to blame for Tony's condition. If you hadn't tried to make a run for it, he wouldn't be here. Now would he?' he said, flashing his badge under her nose, leering at Sally with his piercing eyes; causing her to shiver.

Whilst Nash was introducing himself to Sally, he was carefully scrutinizing her eyes, searching for any telltale signs that she may already be aware of his association with her brother. If she had anything to hide, she was hiding it well, he thought, feeling slightly relaxed, under the circumstances.

Sally also concentrated hard, making sure she didn't give Nash any reason to think that she already knew his name, plus his connection with Tony. Feeling slightly guilty from her outburst, she thought she would be pleasanter to him.

'What time is it please? I broke my watch in the fight, and the hands on the clock on the wall over there have been frozen in that position since I arrived.'

'It's nine p.m.,' answered Nash.

'He's been in theatre two hours,' observed Sally, 'and no one's been in to update me on his progress.'

'They'll come once they have some news, don't worry,' said Nash, with a hint of concern in his voice.

'Be careful Nash, you're showing the delicate side to your nature …'

She suddenly stopped talking, as she could make out the sounds of squeaking shoes coming down the corridor, hopefully towards her room. The door was opened by a young doctor, who looked as though he'd been working all day and night.

'Are you the sister of the patient with the head injury that was brought in a few hours ago?' he asked, looking towards her. Sally's hands were beginning to sweat, and her heart was beating fast, as she expected to hear the worse.

'Yes, Sally Rider. How is he doctor, will he pull through?' Her voice was cracking up.

The doctor picked up an empty chair, placing it next to Sally's.

'He's in a critical condition; the next twenty-four hours are going to be crucial. If he can manage to hold on that long, he has a fifty-fifty chance of surviving.'

'If he does survive, what chances are there of him being brain damaged? The injury to his head appeared to be serious,' said Sally, frightened.

'I can't assess that at the moment, but the early signs emanating from the brain scan look fine. Don't worry; he's in safe hands now.'

'Can I see him, just for a minute?' mumbled Sally, trying to hold back the tears. The doctor agreed she could stay with him for a short while. Leaving Nash by himself, Sally nervously walked down the corridor, escorted by the doctor. Tony had been taken into a side ward. Slowly and quietly opening the door, she nearly fainted when she saw the depressing hospital apparatus around his bed. He was hooked up to a bank of monitors, which indicated to Sally, to her relief, that he was still alive, and breathing, unaided. There was an IV line leading into his arm, a tube up his nose and his face was heavily bandaged.

'It looks worse than it is,' remarked the doctor, realizing the sight had upset her.

'The tubes are to keep him sedated, and fed – without them he would be in a great deal of pain, also he would start to dehydrate.'

Moving nervously over to the side of the bed, Sally placed her hands on Tony's, slowly stroking them.

'Tony, if you can hear me, I forgive you, please get better,' she pleaded, tears now forming in her eyes. Wiping them away with the back of her hand, she bent over to gently kiss his bandaged forehead, before leaving the cold, sterile room.

Whilst Sally was making her way towards Tony's room, Nash unexpectedly spied her pocket book leaning against one of the chair legs. He quickly leapt up from his chair, and cautiously opened the door, checking outside in the corridor, ensuring no one was likely to disturb him. Satisfied, he securely closed the door, and went across to search through her pocket book, hoping to find the pictures. 'Nothing! Well, that's one less suspect to worry about,' remarked Nash, carefully placing the contents back in their correct place, before quickly returning to his chair before anyone came into the room.

Suddenly becoming aware that she had left her pocket book back in the visitors room, Sally called in to collect it on her way out of the hospital. She quickly moved across the room to pick it up, saying nothing to Nash, not even acknowledging him, then made her way to the exit, hoping to grab a cab, thousands of questions swirling around her head.

Feeling certain Sally wasn't likely to return, Nash headed towards Tony's room, stopping at the nurses' station on the way to show the nurse his credentials, saying that he was going to check that his patient was comfortable before he left for the night, also informing her that there would be an officer positioned outside the door all night, watching over the prisoner … 'sorry, patient.' Reluctantly, the nurse acceded to his request, stating that he wasn't to disturb the patient, or try in any way to wake him up. Nash nodded his understanding, and proceeded towards the room. Quickly taking in the surroundings, he started to search around for Tony's clothes, especially his coat, eventually finding it hanging up in the closet. After ferreting around in all of the pockets, he ended up empty handed.

'Fuck, where are they, I have to find them? He could have handed them over to the big guy or the Brit at the park before we arrived. There's also a possibility they could have fallen out of his pocket during the fight,' he muttered, totally dejected. 'Well, there's no alternative but to check out the park first, and if they're not there, I'll just have to question the two guys. Let's see what they have to say on the matter,' he said feeling downhearted. Slowly easing the door shut behind him, he quickly made his way down the corridor towards the exit.

'Once I'm certain I've got the pictures, I'll do what I should have done six years ago - I'll make damn sure Mr Tony Rider doesn't cause me any further trouble,' said Nash, grinning to himself.

It hadn't taken them long to reach the station, and once Alex had been attended too by the first-aider, Alex and Larry were escorted through a busy squad room that led to a number of rooms at the back of the building. It was at this stage they were separated, with Alex being ushered into one of the interview rooms. Checking out the sparsely furnished surroundings, Alex spotted the detective who had escorted them to the station perched on the edge of the table, concern evident on his face. After asking Alex for some formal identification, he began to politely introduce himself.

'First things first, my name is Detective Harry Pinchpeck, and just in case your wondering, you've not been arrested. What you and your friend said to that agent in the park wasn't serious enough for you to be locked away for the night, we'll just keep you here for a short while, yet your heroic attempts in helping the young lady was admirable, but I would suggest you not doing it again, as you may not have an understanding detective next time.'

Alex's eyes began to wander around the room, expecting to see hidden cameras and microphones. He thought he would be cautious to start with, as he didn't want to make matters worse for himself.

Collecting a chair from the other side of the room, the detective pulled it up close to the table, silently weighing Alex up. Can I trust him or not? he wondered.

'What's on your mind, Detective? You look more worried than I do,' asked Alex.

Harry began to inform Alex that he had always agreed with what the group were trying to achieve and he honestly believed in what they were saying; also, for the last few years, he needed to talk to someone about his beliefs and more importantly his suspicions about certain events that had affected him deeply.

'First of all, why don't you take your coat off,' suggested Harry. 'You're going to be here for a while, so you might as well make yourself comfortable. I can't let you go just yet, so sit back and take it easy.'

Alex declined, saying he felt more comfortable with it on.

He could sense that the detective was a genuine kind of guy, so he began to relax a little, noting that Harry was a large man, not fat, but beefy. He had a Roman nose, and his face was tanned, probably from sitting under a sunlamp, he thought, or from the expensive moisture creams now available on the market.

'Before I pour out my beliefs, I'd be interested to know how you managed to get yourself involved with the group?' said Harry. Alex had been thinking a great deal about that whilst he was being driven to the station. Easing himself forward in his chair, resting his arms on the top of the desk, Alex launched himself into a short version of his story. 'On the seventh of July 2005, in London, terrorists murdered my wife. She was on the Tube that was traveling between King's Cross and Russell Square when it was blown up. I went down to London on the first anniversary, and it was while I was down there I met a few American tourists, paying their respects to our dead. They mentioned that they had lost family and friends in the Towers, so I decided I would visit New York, to pay my respects to your dead. When I arrived at Ground Zero this afternoon, I noticed the group. I just happened to go across to see what they were doing – unfortunately I got too involved with them. But I have to say, the agent who was talking to Tony, Sally's brother, was a total ass, he had no manners, and the way his men were treating them was barbaric, to say the least.' Alex then gave Harry his opinion of the facts surrounding 9/11.

'Also I have to agree in all honesty that the information in the leaflets is damning and frightening. How can so much information be available to the American public, yet nothing is being done about it, to seek out the truth?'

Well, I've made it known how I feel; let's see what happens now, thought Alex, deciding not to say anything just yet about Tony's damning confession. He would wait and see what the detective had to say.

Harry didn't say anything at first. He just sat there, studying Alex, trying to work out if this Englishman sitting in front of him was genuine or some plant, working with the FBI, tracking down sympathizers for the group. Deciding Alex could be trusted, he started telling him his suspicions.

'First off all Alex, I'd just like to say how sorry I am to hear about the loss of your wife. I never got around to getting married, maybe because I like my own space too much. Anyway, what I'm going to tell you is most definitely off the record, and if you breathe a word of it to any of my superiors I will vehemently deny it, and that will mean you will have just lost the only friend you have at this moment in time, OK?'

Alex nodded his agreement, also acknowledging Harry's kind sentiments about Marie.

'I won't mind if you let the rest of the group know. They may be able to come up with some ideas to check out my theory,' said Harry.

Alex once again nodded that he understood what he was saying, adding that if he came across the group, he would let them know the information was to be kept between them.

'I don't know why I'm confiding in you Alex, a total stranger, but someone like yourself who is, to a certain extent, impartial, may be more open minded. Anyway, I've decided, I'm going to trust you.' Harry began to convey his theory. 'A few weeks before 9/11, I was in Washington investigating sightings of known terrorists in the area. I had a partner of six years with me, Nathan Ford, a big guy, quietly spoken – the scum in the area respected him, and he definitely wasn't one to run away from a fight. We had drawn a blank with the sightings, so Nathan, or Nat as he liked to be known, decided to go for a few days' vacation. He'd booked himself on American Airlines Flight 77 from Dulles airport to Los Angeles, and as you are no doubt aware, this was the flight that supposedly crashed into the west wall of the Pentagon.' Harry took a few seconds to compose himself before carrying on. 'Nat was not afraid of a fight or confrontation. If we are led to believe that terrorists had taken over the plane, there is no way that Nat would have just sat there and left them to fly the plane into the side of the building without doing anything. He would have organized the rest of the passengers and crew to help him … My theory is that a missile or a small plane hit the Pentagon, and Flight 77, along with its crew and passengers, were whisked away to a secret government facility, probably somewhere in the desert, and they are being held captive.'

Alex was shocked by Harry's assumptions, but they did make some sense as the pictures Alex had seen in the books he'd acquired didn't seem right somehow. The hole in the Pentagon should have been much wider to allow for the aircraft's wings, yet the impact hole was small in comparison to the width of the wings of a 757.

'Harry, if what you think is correct, you have to find a way of notifying the citizens of American. It's the government who are the terrorists in this case.'

Harry knew that he shouldn't have said anything, especially to a stranger, but he had been losing sleep over the past months; plus the nagging feeling that Nat was still alive made him want to get it off his chest, and see what response he received from someone else, someone not involved in the events. They had been in the room for a while now, so Harry decided to let Alex get on his way.

'Alex, I want you to go back to your hotel. Get washed and changed, find a cozy bar, have a few drinks, and forget about what you've just heard. I shouldn't have put you in this awkward position. I just needed to talk to someone that's all, so I could check out their reaction to my theory.' Alex had decided he was involved; he wanted more than ever to get to the truth about the events surrounding 9/11. 'Sorry Harry, I'm hooked. Your theory seems plausible, and once I've left here, as you've suggested, I will have a wash and visit a bar for a few drinks, but don't worry, I won't tell your superiors about our conversation. But I'd like to convey your story to the group – that's if I do manage to come across them again. You know what Harry? I think their background knowledge could be an asset to your case. Don't you think you should start your own investigation about the possibility of the people on Flight 77 being kept captive …?'

The door suddenly opened, surprising them both, and in walked Detective Jordan Holmes, the chief of detectives and Harry's boss.

'Haven't you finished in here yet? The other guy has gone and left you. Some friend you've got there.' He was laughing as he closed the door behind him.

'We'll wait a few minutes, and you can be on your way,' said Harry. 'I hope you've learnt your lesson,' he shouted for the benefit of anyone listening outside, 'and in future don't get involved with issues that don't concern you.' Alex could see Harry was smiling as he was giving him the stern warning. As Harry was slowly opening the door to the interview room, Alex began to fasten his coat, only to feel an unexpected bulkiness in one of his pockets. He slowly eased out the object, and to his amazement he had in his hand an envelope with 'Sis' scrawled on the front, quickly coming to the conclusion that it may have the pictures inside; the one's Tony had mentioned to them all in the park. Alex began to wonder how they had managed to end up in his coat pocket, then figuring out that Tony must have somehow slipped them inside his pocket during the struggle with the agents.

Alex waited for Harry to turn round, as he didn't want to alarm him and cause him to shout out in surprise. Looking back over his shoulder towards Alex, Harry noticed that he had put his fingers up to his lips, indicating for him to be silent.

It was at this stage Alex confided in Harry about Tony's involvement in the planting of the explosives at the Twin Towers, but forgetting in his excitement to mention the agent's name. Ensuring the door was secure, they made their way back to the table, cautiously opening the sealed envelope, sliding the contents out onto the table. Lying in front of them were a series of cloudy photographs, of what looked like explosives hidden behind a fire-hose, plus a handwritten note. Carefully unfolding the note, they both read the damning contents. It was addressed to Sally, and contained the timeline details of Tony's involvement up to and including the day he had returned to the Twin Towers on 9/11. It also mentioned Special Agent Nash's association with Tony. It was Harry who broke the silence.

'Who would have believed it? Special Agent Tyler Nash. I wondered why he was so insistent on being at the park tonight, and now I know.'

'So the obnoxious bald-headed agent at the park was Nash? I'm not surprised Sally's brother was shocked and frightened when he saw him coming towards him,' said Alex. 'This information is sensational, and in the wrong hands it could cause mayhem. There would be riots in the streets,' stated Alex, panicking.

'Just calm down Alex, we need to seriously think about what to do next,' responded Harry. 'What will become of Tony?' asked Alex. 'Also, I can imagine Nash moving heaven and earth for these pictures. Let's hope he doesn't think one of the group has them – if he does, we will be in some serious trouble.' Alex was now becoming frightened.

Harry came up with an idea. 'The first thing we must do is to keep quiet and not panic. Put the pictures and note back in the envelope, and make sure they're kept well hidden. In the meantime I suggest you go straight back to your hotel for a good night's sleep.

Let's meet up again tomorrow with the rest of the group, if you can find them. You'd be best looking in the area around Ground Zero; they seem to be hanging around there most days. Then, hopefully, try and work out a plan of action. The best place I can think of right now to meet is inside the Grand Central terminal. If we can all make our way there for, say, four p.m. It's so large we can lose ourselves in the crowd. Also, it will be easy for you to find – if you happen to get lost, you can always ask a policeman.' Alex noticed a cheeky smile on Harry's face, relieving some of the tension in the room.

'Where are you staying, just in case I need to reach you?' asked Harry.

Alex lifted his head and told him the Chelsea Hotel. Harry handed Alex his card, just in case he needed to reach him in an emergency. Getting up from his chair, Harry moved over to the door. Having opened it, he glanced up and down the squad room, making sure Nash wasn't hovering around.

Stealthily they advanced down towards the main exit door, and with a gentle push from Harry, Alex found himself outside, alone, in the cold.

In the meantime, Harry headed back to his office to finish off some tedious paperwork that needed to be completed before he left for the night, which he knew would take him the rest of the evening to finish. 'Hours of typing, and forms to complete. Great,' he complained.

After a gruelling few hours of pen-pushing, Harry prised himself from his chair, stretched his back, releasing the stiffness that had set in, and was just about to switch off the remaining lights in his office when Detective Holmes walked in.

'Has the Brit gone?' asked Holmes.

'Yes, there was no reason to hold him any longer, so I gave him a caution, advised him to keep away from the group,' responded Harry.

'He was trouble Harry, I could feel it. You just watch. I have a nasty feeling we will be hearing from that guy again, and sooner than you might think. You mark my words.'

'Chief, the Brit, Alex Monroe, he was only visiting Ground Zero, paying his respects to the victims – what harm is there in that? He also mentioned to me that he'd lost his wife in the July bombings in London in 2005, so don't come down too hard on him if we do happen to run into him again.'

'I'm sorry to hear about his wife, but it doesn't alter the fact that he found himself involved with that goddamned group,' Holmes said. 'The Plane Facts – stupid name. You know what? The publicity and support they are now receiving from the media concerns me. The mayor's now on my case. He's been on the phone a number of times this evening already, asking awkward questions. We need to be extremely careful next time we come into contact with them. Try and find a sound reason to arrest them. Put them away for a few weeks, let things cool down a bit.'

'Chief, we are always going on about living in a democratic society, free speech and all that. You can't just lock up innocent people for their views. May I remind you of the term habeas corpus, which isn't a fancy term, may I add. It protects against being thrown in prison illegally, with no help and no end in sight. No one, especially the President, should ever be given the power to call someone an enemy, wave his hand and lock them away indefinitely, which this administration seem to be good at. The Founders made the President subject to the rule of law, rejecting dungeons, and chose due process. We all know the difference between fairness and persecution.

If we do not act immediately to restore our constitutional rights, basic protections like habeas corpus would be lost for ever, and our country would become unrecognizable.'

'Jesus Harry, I thought you were never going to stop. You need to change your night-time reading, you're becoming boring. Anyway, it doesn't alter the fact that if I come across them again I will lock them up,' exclaimed Holmes, shaking his head, trying to clear it of Harry's dreary monologue.

'Come on Harry, it's getting late, we both have homes to go to. Switch the rest of the lights off as you go out. We'll carry on with this discussion in the morning; unless we hear from them again to-night.'

After leaving the hospital, Nash immediately returned to the park to search the area where the scuffle had taken place, hoping to find the pictures. After a fruitless fifteen minutes of grovelling around on his hands and knees, finding nothing, he finally came to the conclusion that the only ones who could possibly have them was either the tall American guy, or the Brit. Slowly easing himself of the ground, wiping away the dirt from his hands on his handkerchief, he headed back to his car.

As Harry and Holmes were making their way out of the building, Nash came barging through the dividing doors from the main entrance, elbowing his way amongst the police officers and their detainees.

'Holmes, what the hell are you playing at?' he screamed. 'I've just heard from the sergeant at the front desk that you've released the two scum-bags that I ordered to be held here over night.'

Holmes turned away, sniggering, hoping Nash wouldn't notice. There'd always been friction between them, ever since Holmes had busted a drug syndicate Nash had had under surveillance for over twelve months.

'Do you know what you've done, both of you? I needed to take them both down to headquarters for questioning, in securer sur- roundings. I have reason to believe that they may have taken some- thing of importance from Tony Rider and I need to get hold of it right away. Listen guys, I'm not too happy about this, but I'm going to have to confide in you both. Over the last six years, we've had this group under surveillance. Unfortunately I'm not at liberty to tell you all the relevant details; all I can say is that it's a matter of national security. That's all you need to know for now.'

Nash started to pace around, nervously shaking his head, growl- ing under his breath, finally ending up facing both detectives.

'I need to talk to the Brit first. Where's he staying? You must have checked his passport and place of residence whilst in New York? Also his sidekick, Larry Underwood, and don't go giving me any bullshit addresses,' snarled Nash. Reluctantly Harry wrote down Alex's details Nash asked for, and handed them over. Nash in turn checked them out to make sure Harry hadn't written down some stupid address, like 'Disney World'. Satisfied it looked kosher, Nash folded the piece of paper and slipped it into his pocket.

'Well, do you have this other guy's address or not?' asked Nash.

'No we haven't,' answered Harry. 'There was no reason to ask for it, he wasn't under arrest, so if you want it, find it yourself . . . just hold on a minute Nash, I thought you said you've had this group under surveillance. Are you saying in all that time you never found out where this Larry Underwood guy lived?'

Nash grunted something incomprehensible under his breath, before turning on his heels, leaving the station, an embarrassed and worried man.

'Christ Harry, look at the time, my old lady is going to kill me when I get home.'

'No she won't, she's a pussycat,' replied Harry.

'Cats have claws Harry, don't you forget that. Goodnight.'

Exiting the police station, Alex started to make his way down the street, with the intention of taking a cab back to the hotel, his mind mulling over what Harry had said, speculating whether he was correct in his assumptions about Flight 77. He had only walked a short distance when he heard the sound of someone approaching him from behind. Careful not to be caught off guard, he suddenly spun around with his hands balled into fists, ready for a fight, and the mood he was in at the moment, he was ready for one.

Quickly adjusting his eyes to the gloomy surroundings, Alex soon realized that the person following him was Larry.

'For crying out loud Larry, you scared the shit out of me then. What the hell are you still doing here? I thought you would be miles away from here by now.'

'I just couldn't leave you behind, not after getting you involved in the first place with our little group of warriors.'

Alex's heart started to slow down after his fright.

'I'm on my way back to the hotel. Do you fancy a quick drink before you go home?' asked Alex.

'I'd love to thanks,' replied Larry. 'Which hotel are you staying at?'

'The Chelsea Hotel between Seventh and Eighth Avenues. Do you know it?'

'Know it? My sister has an apartment there, and at the moment I'm apartment-sitting for her – what a coincidence. Come on, let's have that drink.'

'There's a bar a few doors from the hotel we can call in at, Jake's Saloon, no doubt you frequent that establishment,' remarked Alex in his posh British accent, giggling. Larry turned round to face Alex, and he too was laughing. They had both been through a harrowing few hours, and the adrenalin rush was now slowly wearing off. Larry gave out a high-pitched whistle, which resulted in a yellow cab pulling up beside the kerb.

'Christ Larry, you'll have all the dogs in the area coming after you with that whistle of yours,' laughed Alex.

'Comes in handy, don't you think?' smiled Larry.

As the cab was making its way towards the bar, they started to discuss what had been said while they were being questioned. Alex was inclined not to say anything at first; worried he might land Harry in trouble. Once Larry had finished his account, Alex said he would prefer to inform him of what had been said to him when they were safely inside the bar, away from prying eyes and ears, but he did say he was glad Larry had stayed back as he required the group's help; adding that the news was earth shattering, and it would blow his mind. Larry said he was very eager to hear what he had to say. Once again Alex observed Larry wiping the moisture away from his eyes whilst he was talking. He didn't want to raise it with him, as he really didn't know him that well.

Arriving at the bar, checking out the room, looking for any familiar faces they didn't want to bump into, like the obnoxious agent at the park, they ordered their drinks and proceeded to sit at a table in the corner, well away from the rest of the crowd and the sound of the TVs.

'Before I start,' said Alex, 'how come your sister lives in the hotel?'

'Most people won't be aware, but only one hundred of the four hundred units are available to paying guests, the rest are occupied by permanent residents, and my sister is one of them.'

'That's fantastic,' enthused Alex, 'where is your sister now?'

'She's on holiday for a few months. Her husband, the shit, left her for his boss, and she needed some time to chill out.'

'Typical. A younger woman, I guess?' remarked Alex.

'No actually, an older man. I'd always thought he was a little queer.'

Alex spilt his drink over his shirt and trousers after what Larry had said registered.

'Right, now it's your turn Alex, what's so earth shattering that it's going to blow my mind?'

After mopping the spilt beer from the front of his shirt and trousers, Alex started to relay Harry's suspicions about Flight 77, finishing off by pulling out the envelope and placing the photos and note in front of Larry on the table.

'For Christ's sake Alex, put them away before someone sees them. Are you sure they're genuine? You know, Tony could be setting us up. The guy goes missing, presumed dead for six years, and suddenly he turns up with incriminating pictures, which could ultimately destroy the whole government.'

Alex quickly hid the contents, safely sliding the envelope back in his jacket pocket.

'So, the agent at the park tonight was this Nash guy – interesting. I wonder what Sally will say when she finds out he was the one behind Tony's involvement and his subsequent disappearance,' said Larry.

'Look Larry, I think we should do as Harry suggested. Get a good night's sleep, then decide what our next step should be. Have you any way of contacting the rest of the group? I think they should be told what's been said, let them have a say in what we need to do about Harry's assumptions, plus the pictures. He suggested we should all meet at the Grand Central terminal at four p.m. tomorrow. Do you think we can trust him?' asked Alex.

'You've spoken to him, I haven't. If you think he can be trusted, that's fine by me. Anyway, what do we have to lose? Also I'd be interested to hear more of his gut feelings about his partner. It's too late now to get in touch with the rest of the group, and I suspect Sally will still be at the hospital. First thing in the morning I'll get in touch with her paper to see if she's called in for work; if not, I have her home and cell numbers. I can reach Guido through his cab company, and as far as Moon is concerned, it's anybody's guess where he will be. And you're right, a good night's sleep will do us both good. What room are you in, just in case I need to get hold of you? I'm in Room Forty on the fourth floor if you need me,' said Larry, 'and don't forget, we number our floors differently to you lot in the UK, our ground floor is the first floor, so remember that, if for some reason you start looking for me, OK?'

'Room Ten on the second floor, just by the emergency exit, and thanks for the advice,' answered Alex.

After taking their empty glasses back to the bar, they proceeded to make their way back to the hotel. Reaching reception, Larry picked up his mail, and Alex collected his keys; then they both headed for the lift.

As Alex was exiting the lift on the second floor, Larry wished him goodnight, to which Alex responded with, 'See you later Larry,' causing Larry to suddenly look up, and ask him what the phrase meant.

'It's a term of endearment where I live in the UK,' answered Alex. 'It means I hope to see you again, soon.'

Larry smiled, calling out as the door was closing, 'See you later Alex,' giggling away to himself.

Once inside his room, Alex suddenly felt relieved, safe and totally exhausted. It was the rumbling of his stomach which alerted him to the fact that he hadn't had anything to eat for nearly twenty-four hours; so he quickly grabbed the menu from the bedside table, dialled reception, and ordered a large club sandwich with a pot of hot coffee. Carefully easing out of his shirt, he made his way over to the bathroom to examine the damage that had been inflicted on his fifty-eight-year-old body during the skirmish. There appeared to be a few blue-and-yellow bruises forming, but nothing too serious. The last few hours had been traumatic, but interesting, he thought. Sitting on the bed, with his head cupped in his hands, he started to contemplate what the group should do with the pictures and note, also Harry's theories. It was the knock at the door that brought him out of his reverie. Discreetly opening it, peering around the edge, he spied the waiter holding a large tray of food, which looked, and smelt delightful.

Thanking him, and taking the tray, he quickly closed the door, making sure it was locked, and sat by the window. The view and the food were excellent.

Due to all the excitement and turmoil of the past few hours, he had completely forgotten about sending an email to his sons. When booking the hotel, Alex had made sure that it had email facilities; so picking up the hotel's information pack from the bedside table, he looked through the directory, searching for the floor housing the computers. It didn't take him long to find that they were located in the lobby. He tentatively slipped on his shirt; collected his coat from behind the chair, and made his way downstairs. When entering the lobby, he spotted a notice attached to one of the doors, informing everyone that the complimentary wireless Internet accesses, and local newspapers, were available to guests twenty-four hours a day. Feeling somewhat relieved, he opened the door, and walked over to the nearest vacant computer; perching himself on the seat in front of it. Because of his height, and long legs, Alex sat awkwardly at the keyboard. He started to put together all the details he could remember about his visit to Ground Zero and his observations. He decided not to divulge anything about his arrest and subsequent involvement with the group as he didn't want them to worry about him. Finishing off his story, he ended it by saying he would email them again, soon. After closing down the computer, he made his way back to his room. He got undressed and collapsed onto his large, comfortable bed. Making certain the envelope was safely tucked under his pillow, he finally started to relax, and within minutes he was fast asleep, snoring.

'THE PLANE FACTS'

September 11 2001: In what the government describes as a bizarre coincidence, a US intelligence agency (the National Reconnaissance Office or NRO) was all set for an exercise at 9 a.m. on 11 September in which an aircraft would crash into one of its buildings near Washington, DC. (AP, 22/8/02) Four war games were also in progress at the time of the attacks. (C-SPAN Congressional Testimony, 11/3/05; more)

September 11 2001: Hours after the attacks, a 'shadow government' is formed. Key congressional leaders say they didn't know this government-in-waiting had been established. (CBS, 12/3/02; Washington Post, 2/3/02; more)

September 11 2001: Six air traffic controllers who dealt with the two of the hijacked airliners make a tape recording describing the events within hours of the attacks. The tape is never turned over to the FBI. It is later illegally destroyed by a supervisor without anyone making a transcript or even listening to it. (Washington Post, 6/5/04; *New York Times*, 6/5/04; more)

FLIGHT 77 AND THE PENTAGON
What really happened?

8.20 a.m: 20 miles from the Pentagon. Flight 77 departs from Dulles Airport.

8.50 a.m: 260 miles from the Pentagon. Last radio communication with Flight 77

8.55 a.m: 300 miles from the Pentagon. Flight 77 turns while over southern Ohio.

8.58 a.m: 299 miles from the Pentagon. Transponder/radar contact lost.

9.38 a.m: 0 miles from the Pentagon. Flight 77 crashes into the Pentagon.

Dulles Airport is nearly twenty miles from the Pentagon. So it is insane to believe that the 'hijackers', who started from Dulles Airport, waited until they were 300 miles away from their target, the Pentagon, before hijacking the aircraft, turning it around and retracing their path back to the Pentagon. This would give the US Air Force over forty minutes to investigate and, if necessary, shoot them down.
guardian.150mcom/pentagon/small/9/11-flights.htm-18k

Chapter Seven

'When war enters a country, it produces lies like sand.'

Anonymous

LANGLEY AIR FORCE BASE, WASHINGTON

The facility, the oldest continuously active air force base in the United States, is the headquarters of the air command and contains air-defence missile units. NASA'S 'Langley Research Center' is adjacent. The base is located some 130 miles from Washington.

From the latter part of 2001, to the present day, American air force pilots Gary Sawer and Ray Marsden have relaxed in the bar at the base on numerous occasions whilst off duty, both reflecting over the past events that changed their lives.

Unbeknown to the rest of the servicemen on the base, these two pilots played a major role on 9/11.

Gary Sawer had always wanted to be a pilot from an early age. Especially in planes that flew 'really fast', as he used to say to his father when he was a small boy.

Gary was a twenty-eight-year-old single man, who was currently in a steady relationship with a new recruit on the base. At six foot four, with close-cropped black hair, he was not easy to miss as he strode around. He always found time to stop and have a chat with his fellow servicemen.

The reason for this was because he was frightened. Frightened that when, and if, the truth came out about his involvement on 9/11, his colleagues on the base might not forgive him.

But I was only following orders, he kept reminding himself.

Gary was twenty-two years of age when he was ordered to scramble from Langley Air Force Base at approximately 9.00 a.m. local time on 9/11.

He was ordered to locate United Airlines Flight 93, which had left Newark Airport at 8.42, and confirm reports that it was flying erratically, and immediately report back to air traffic control.

It didn't take long for Gary to have the aircraft in his sights, and from the way it was being flown, it looked as though there was a serious problem inside the cockpit.

He instantly radioed back his findings. In reply they informed him that the flight had been hijacked, and for the time being he was to closely monitor the aircraft.

After Gary had been trailing the aircraft for a few minutes, air traffic control came over the radio ordering him to shoot it out of the sky. Under no circumstances should he let Flight 93 fly any farther, as it was heading towards the White House.

'This order is coming from the highest authority,' he was told.

Gary couldn't believe what he had been ordered to do.

'Shoot down a commercial aircraft over American soil?' he cried.

He was suddenly returned to reality by his radio coming back to life; instantly recognizing the Vice-President's voice.

'Pilot, this is the Vice-President speaking, do you read …? Son, you cannot, I repeat cannot, let that aircraft fly any farther. It's a matter of life and death. If you do …' Once again, Gary couldn't believe what he was hearing. What was so major that the Vice-President was involved, giving him orders to fire on an innocent commercial aircraft...?

'... Son! Son, can you hear me? I am giving you a direct order, take it down!'

Gary had signed up to follow orders. He knew he had to make the most important decision of his life. He couldn't just sit there, hoping for a change of orders.

So without any further hesitation, he locked on to Flight 93, releasing one of his heat-seeking air-to-air missiles. Within seconds the aircraft erupted in a massive fireball, which covered a wide area with twisted, blazing debris. Gary knew no one could have survived the explosion. Looking back over his shoulder, he made certain the directive had been carried out successfully. He headed back to base, before activating his radio.

'Mr Vice-President this is Delta One. I would like it to be known that I have followed your orders to the letter. I can also confirm that Flight 93 has been destroyed – Over and out.'

Switching off his radio, he broke down in tears. The last time he had cried like this was when his mother had died of cancer five years earlier.

'How do I live with this for the rest of my life?' he wailed. He was stunned and numb at the thought of what he had just carried out.

Suddenly coming out of his reverie, he noticed the landing strip of the base from his cockpit window.

'What do I say to my buddies back at base when they ask me what happened out there?' he asked himself. He had a fair idea what his answer would be when he observed a large black limousine with darkened windows waiting next to the hangar doors. He parked, climbed out of the cockpit and made his way over to the car. The back door was already open for him to enter, so, bending his large frame, he climbed inside. It took him a few seconds for his eyes to adjust to the darkness. When they did, there was someone sitting in the back, waiting for him. It was the Vice-President. The VP moved closer to Gary, offering his hand, which Gary declined.

'On behalf of the American people, and its government, we are indebted to you for your bravery, also avoiding a monumental catastrophe. I couldn't divulge too many details over the radio as it is classified, but now that you are here I can inform you of the reason for the order to take down the aircraft. The pilot of Flight 93 had managed to inform us that they had been hijacked, and the hijackers were getting ready to set off a "dirty bomb". They were about to fly the aircraft into the White House … So now you see, son, there was no way we could let Flight 93 come anywhere near Washington … by destroying it, you also destroyed the deadly bacteria the bomb was carrying,' explained the Vice-President.

Gary sat there, speechless. At least, he thought, by shooting down the aircraft, I may have saved thousands of other lives on the ground. Accepting the explanation, he felt slightly better. But it was still hard to take in.

'Son, just listen to what I have to say. As I stated earlier, what you have been told is highly classified, and it must be kept that way. So for your own good, when you leave this car, you will be taken to a secret location where you can spend a few weeks' leave. This will give you time to get over the trauma. Once we are satisfied that you are ready to proceed with your duties, we will arrange for your return back to the base.'

That had been six years ago. Six years of remorse, regretting that he had followed the Vice-President's orders. It was when he eventually returned from his secret location (a prison more like) that he found out the full facts about the events surrounding 9/11. He was constantly reminded by his base commander not to breathe a word to anyone about the incident. But the more he read and heard, the more he thought he had been used. Yet he knew he had to keep quiet, for his and his family's well-being.

Ray was different in many ways to Gary. Where Gary was quietly spoken, Ray had a bullhorn voice which caused people to move away from him as they felt threatened. Yet he was a calm, responsible person, short and stocky, and maybe, people remarked, his voice compensated for his small stature. He was a single man, who liked his freedom to do what he liked doing best: playing golf.

On 11 September 2001 at 9.00 a.m., twenty-four-year-old Ray Marsden was ordered to scramble and head towards the Pentagon. A Boeing 757, American Airlines Flight 77, which had left Dulles Airport, Washington, destined for Los Angeles, was reported to have been hijacked.

When Ray acknowledged he was ten miles away from the Pentagon, he was ordered simply to confirm visual contact with the cockpit, and monitor the aircraft, but not to take any further action, unless ordered to do so. After flying for five more minutes, Ray spotted the Boeing, which to his alarm was heading straight for the west wall of the Pentagon. All of a sudden, to his amazement, the aircraft took evasive action, cleverly manoeuvring away from the building. Ray relayed the events back to air traffic control, and within seconds he was ordered to fire at the west wall of the Pentagon. Not having the time to think of the consequences, he complied, firing one of his ASTRA BVRAAM missiles. Seconds later, the west wall had exploded, causing that section of the building to collapse before his eyes. Whilst all that was happening, Ray had manoeuvred away from the area. He reported back immediately that the missile launch had been successful. He was ordered to escort the Boeing 757 on a heading of: 31° 50′ 58′′ north, 106° 24′ 47′′ west. Ray obeyed without question, yet he couldn't make out any sense at all of what had just occurred, and he didn't want to. 'Not just yet, anyway', he thought. But he did note down the coordinates for future reference.

Ray's F-16, along with American Airlines Flight 77, flew across the vast American countryside, with barely a cloud in the sky, also with no other aircraft in sight, which alarmed him. 'There is at least some evidence of vapor trials on the horizon,' he said to himself, feeling anxious.

As he was nearing the coordinates which he had programmed into his flight computer, it was the crackle of his radio which brought him out of his musing.

He was ordered to keep Flight 77 in clear sight, and to report back immediately when it had touched down safely. Which he obeyed, without further comment.

The next voice he heard ordered him to return as soon as possible to base, stating that under no circumstances should he make radio contact until he had landed.

What was that all about? Ray thought. First of all it's a hijacked aircraft I'm told to monitor, then I'm responsible for destroying a section of America's Military Command Center, and to cap it all, I'm ordered to escort the allegedly hijacked aircraft to a deserted airfield, or what I thought was deserted.

There must have been a large number of casualties at the Pentagon, he reflected.

During his return trip, Ray began to go through the horrendous events of the morning, but not really coming up with any logical conclusions. Suddenly recognizing the landscape of the base around him, he began to slowly descend.

He taxied his F-16 towards the corner of the field as instructed, and climbed down from the cockpit, only to be greeted by a welcoming committee of two large gentlemen, both wearing identical black overcoats and matching shades.

'Pilot,' one of them said, with authority, 'will you please come with us. We just want to have a little chat with you, which I am sure you will find beneficial.'

Both men moved swiftly over to Ray; forcefully guiding him towards the hangar which was next to his parked jet. He noticed that the building couldn't have been used for a long time, as most of the roof was missing, and what furniture was lying around inside was broken and rusty.

If I wasn't in serious trouble, Ray thought, I might believe I'd interrupted a scene in the making of Men in Black 3.

The guy who Ray thought was the senior of the two men motioned for him to sit down on the only chair that wasn't broken.

'There isn't any reason for you to know our names, or which government department we work for, but what we can say is, we're batting for the same team.'

Ray couldn't think straight. He had just realized the extent of his actions, and more importantly, he'd been ordered to do them. He was starting to shake, and on top of that he was well and truly pissed off. As far as he was concerned he wanted some answers, now.

'I signed up to defend this fine nation of ours. Instead I am ordered to fire on the Pentagon, no doubt killing hundreds of innocent civilians inside, and you stand there and say we are batting for the same team. There's no fucking way I'm on your team, mister, whoever the hell you are.' Ray was in his element. His booming voice, which echoed all over the building, caused the men to shuffle around, clearly agitated.

'First of all, pilot, calm down, we can't have a constructive conversation if you are upset. Once you've cooled down, we can talk.'

Ray started to ease up a little, knowing he needed to get a grip, or he could be here all day. Slowly, he started to take long, deep breaths, easing the tension out of his taut body. He nodded, indicating he was ready for their explanation.

'Pilot, what you are about to hear is highly confidential, and you must not repeat it to anyone, not even your family. If we find out that you have, we will not be responsible for the actions of this government. Have I made myself clear?'

'Crystal,' replied Ray, with some venom.

'The reason you were ordered to fire on the Pentagon was that we were reliably informed that a number of terrorists had taken civilian hostages inside the building. They were keeping them in an office close to the west wall, demanding the release of their comrades we are holding in US prisons. So now you can see the reason why you were ordered to fire the missile at the Pentagon ... They also threatened to murder the hostages along with themselves for their beliefs. It was also rumoured that they had somehow managed to smuggle in a "dirty bomb" into the Pentagon ... We as a nation will not be held to ransom by some towel-heads who are basically fanatics and terrorists, also I would strongly advise that you don't disclose the whereabouts of Flight 77 to anyone. So, as far as we, the government, and the American people are concerned, you did a damn fine job.'

Ray was speechless. Why was the aircraft heading for the Pentagon in the first place? He was thinking. Perhaps the aircraft had been hijacked by terrorists, and the crew somehow, managed to tackle them, regaining control, and the terrorists, along with the passengers and crew were to be interrogated at the base I escorted them too? Christ almighty, I don't want to know.

'Gentlemen, the secret is safe with me. I am not going to tell anyone about my actions of today. I don't think my mates would believe me anyway.'

Satisfied, Ray reluctantly shook their hands and moved to the door, leaving the two agents to slowly make their way to their waiting car.

'Don't forget what we said,' one of them shouted over to Ray, 'let's keep it our little secret, all right?'

Ray just nodded and walked away from them as quickly as possible, as he didn't want to be in their presence any longer than he had to.

Over the course of the next few days Ray found out about the other atrocities that had befallen America on 9/11. He was also intrigued by the story of Flight 93 over Pennsylvania. The more he read, the more he realized that he had been used as a patsy by the American government.

He knew he couldn't say anything, as he was worried about what would happen to himself and his family if he did.

There was one thing he couldn't fathom out.

'Whatever happened to the passengers and crew of American Airlines Flight 77?'

Michael Rowland

'THE PLANE FACTS'

September 13–19 2001: Bin Laden's family is taken under FBI supervision to a secret assembly point. They leave the country by private plane when airports reopen days after the attacks. (*New York Times*, 30/9/01; Boston Globe, 20/9/01; more)

September 15–16 2001: Several of the 9/11 hijackers, including lead hijacker Mohamed Atta, may have had training at secure US military installations. (Newsweek, 15/9/01; Washington Post, 16/9/01; *New York Times*, 15/9/01; more)

September 20 2001: Several hijackers later mentioned in the 9/11 Commission Report turn up alive. 'Five of the alleged hijackers have emerged, alive, innocent and astonished to see their names and photographs appearing on satellite television … The hijackers were using stolen identities.' (Chicago Tribune, 18/3/02; more)

Chapter Eight

'The tree of liberty must be refreshed from time to time with the blood of patriots and tyrants. It is its natural manure.'

Thomas Jefferson (1743–1826)

SEPTEMBER 12 2007, THE WHITE HOUSE – the Oval Office

The Oval Office is the President's formal workspace, where he confers with heads of state, diplomats, his staff, and other dignitaries; and also where he often addresses the American public and the world on television or radio; plus where he deals with the issues of the day.

Shafts of morning sunlight shone across the Oval Office, dappling the thick rug with light and shade as the President viewed the Rose Garden. He was seated by the famous Resolute desk, which had been constructed with timber from an abandoned British ship.

The desk was given to President Rutherford in 1880 as a token of friendship from Queen Victoria. Most Presidents since have used the desk during their term in office.

It was the polite rustle of papers, followed by a muffled cough, which brought the president out of his reverie. He looked round to see his Secretary of Defense standing by the open door.

'Good morning, I never heard you entering the room,' remarked the president, drawing his eyes away from the White House lawn.

'Good morning Mr President, I did knock, but when you didn't answer, I thought you may have been on the phone.'

'No, I was just daydreaming, as usual,' answered the president.

'Mr President, I think you should read this from this morning's edition of the *New York Times*. It seems there was another protest last evening, in the park adjacent to Ground Zero. It was our friends again. The ones calling themselves the Plane Facts. The article states that they were taken away, and subsequently released, without being charged. I've found out since from official sources that there was a heated argument between some members of the group and our own agents ...' The SoD hesitated as he handed the newspaper over to the president.

'I'm sorry to report that one of their group was seriously injured when he tried to make a run for it. The guy was quickly rushed to hospital; he's at the moment in intensive care, and the doctors can't say if he will pull through or not.

'Mr President, I'm becoming very concerned about the coverage this group's receiving from the press. If we're not careful, the American public may start to become sympathetic to their cause. The more press coverage they receive, the more difficult it will be for us to try and calm the waters.'

The president laid the newspaper out on top of the desk, quickly scanning its contents.

'Sorry again to be the bringer of more bad news, but Special Agent Nash was one of the agents at the gathering last night – he's just sent a report of the incident through special channels. It was thrust into my hands as I was making my way over here, and I've just had time to quickly glance through it. It doesn't bode well. Do you want me to read it out?'

'God dammit,' shouted the president, crunching the newspaper up in a ball and tossing it across the room in anger. 'When are you going to stop throwing problem after problem at me? You haven't come up for breath yet. What does it say in layman's terms? I don't want all that security jargon bullshit.'

Nervously, the Secretary of Defense made his way to the chair closest to the president, and sat down, without an invitation.

'To be brief, sir, the report states that the guy who was rushed to hospital was a security guard at the Towers, the one Nash bribed for the keys and security codes before 9/11. Nash paid off this guy's gambling debts, plus some extra for his silence … If you cast your mind back, sir, Nash was the agent we chose to organize the planting of the explosives in the Towers.'

'Of course I remember Nash, he's the egotistical little shit who creamed a million dollars out of us to keep his mouth shut. I thought Nash said this security guy had died when the Towers collapsed?' The president's temper was now bubbling under the surface.

'You're correct, he did say that, but it seems he's been hiding out all this time …'

'Come on, come on, I can see you have some other bad news for me,' interrupted the president.

'Yes, and you're not going to like it.'

'I haven't liked anything you've said so far, so I'm sure this can't be any worse, or can it?'

'According to Nash, the guard's conscience got the better of him. He returned to the Towers on the morning of 9/11. He was in the South Tower when the first plane struck. He said he'd heard small explosions, so he went to investigate.

'This is the bummer, sir – he managed to find two of the devices that hadn't exploded, and he has the evidence, in a number of pictures he took …' He suddenly stopped talking, waiting for some kind of reaction.

Very calmly, the president asked him where the pictures were now.

'We've no idea, Mr President.'

'You don't know. For Christ's sake, I thought you were my Secretary of Defense. You couldn't defend my coat. Get hold of Nash straight away, tell him to find them, and soon. I'm not bothered what he has to do, but by God, he has to find them.'

'Mr President, I'll get on to it right away. But in the meantime, what do you want me to do about this so-called group?'

'Listen, 9/11 was six years ago, and each year at this time, these irritating shits appear, trying to stir up trouble. And what happens? Nothing, apart from Nash's problem, which can be dealt with if we act immediately. If the press had had a sniff about Nash's discovery, it would have been splashed all over the front pages of every newspaper around the globe, also my telephone would have been red hot with calls throughout the night from the leaders from all over the world. Look, these guys get the publicity they want, small as it is, and they hide away for another twelve months, then they come out of their holes, and once again they start spouting about the same facts,' shouted the president. He carried on ranting. 'Don't worry; our secret is safe, for now, as long as we keep it to ourselves. But first, we must find those pictures, that's if there are any to start off with. It could be a red herring; anyway, we could always say the pictures are false, they could have been taken anywhere. I can't imagine there being anything else incriminating in the pictures which would verify this guard's story. It's not in our interest to start panicking now. Relax, we've been through worse moments than this over the past six years, and we've always come out of it; unscathed.'

Until now, the SoD thought, despairingly, sweat beading on his face.

'Just to be on the safe side,' said the president. 'When you do get hold of Nash, inform him from me that he has to tread very carefully. We don't want to arouse their suspicions, we can't be having these annoying assholes thinking they are on to us.'

The SoD nodded nervously, desperately wanting to get out of the president's presence.

'Do you have any more bombshells to throw at me or can I carry on running the country?' asked the president, annoyingly.

The SoD scarcely dared mention the British national's involvement.

'There is one other small matter, Mr President; there was a British citizen involved in the fracas last night, which leads Nash to believe that he may be a visiting member of an outside alliance. He also reckons this Brit may have the pictures.'

'Christ, that could become embarrassing if Nash is correct. We can't afford to upset the British government, especially after all the support they've given us over the past few years. Just keep me informed of any developments will you. I don't want too many complications to sort out, especially as regards to the Brit. Anything else?'

'I think I've said and done enough this morning, don't you? As soon as I have any news, I'll report back to you at once.'

Putting on a false grin, the SoD left the Oval Office feeling frightened, and somewhat relieved to be out of the presence of the President.

'THE PLANE FACTS'

September 10 2001: Former President Bush is with a brother of Osama bin Laden at a Carlyle business conference. The conference is interrupted the next day by the attacks. (Washington Post, 16/3/01)

September 10 2001: A number of top Pentagon brass suddenly cancel travel plans for the next morning, apparently because of security concerns. Why isn't this news spread widely? (Newsweek, 13/9/01 Newsweek, 24/9/01; more)

September 10 2001: Defense Secretary Rumsfeld announces that by some estimates the Department of Defense 'cannot track down $2.3 trillion in transactions'. CBS later calculates that 25 per cent of the yearly defence budget is unaccounted for. A defense analyst says, 'The books are cooked routinely year after year.' (DoD, 10/9/01; CBS, 29/1/02) This announcement was buried by the next day's news of 9/11.

September 11 2001: Recovery experts extract data from thirty-two WTC computer drives revealing a surge in financial transactions just before the attacks. Illegal transfers of over $100 million may have been made through some WTC computer systems immediately before and during the disaster. (Reuters, 18/12/01; CNN, 20/12/01; more)

Chapter Nine

'When the character of a man is not clear to you, look at his friends.'

Japanese proverb

SEPTEMBER 12 2007, 1 a.m. – Chelsea Hotel

It was the incessant ringing of the hotel's telephone that eventually woke Alex up from a deep sleep.

'Who the hell can this be?' he moaned, rubbing his eyes. 'No one knows me in New York, and a call at this hour could only mean one thing, bad news.'

Glancing at his watch, which read 1 a.m., he picked up the phone, expecting to hear one of his sons on the other end. It wasn't, it was Harry Pinchpeck's voice he heard, and he sounded excited, and frightened.

'Alex, it's Harry, the detective you met tonight … listen, you need to get some clothes together, and get the hell out of the hotel, fast …'

Alex was still floating around in a dreamlike state, trying to work out what Harry was ranting on about.

'Harry, what the hell's up with you, it's only …?' He tried to talk over Harry's frantic babbling, but Harry didn't let him finish.

'Alex, shut up and listen to me will you … a few minutes ago Nash showed up back here at the station, and somehow he's come to the conclusion that either you or Larry have the pictures. He must have checked Tony's pockets over at the hospital, so he's now on his way over there, so for Christ's sake, move your butt.'

Alex assumed Harry must have divulged the name of his hotel to Nash; if he hadn't, he would have been implicated. One thing's for sure, Alex thought, I'm not letting on that Larry was asleep just a couple of floors from his. That was his refuge, but only if he managed to get out of his room before Nash appeared.

'Alex, are you still there?' Came the voice down the phone.

'Yes,' acknowledged Alex. 'Where the hell do I go? I don't know anyone, apart from you, ' he lied.

'Do as I suggested last night, and head across town to the terminal, then hopefully I'll meet up with you there in the afternoon, and no offence Alex, but there's always an assortment of down-and-outs wandering around the area, so if you have any creased or dirty clothes, I would suggest you wear them.'

'I haven't got much choice in the matter, have I?' responded Alex, yawning.

'No, and you haven't got much time either, so move it,' shouted Harry.

'See you tomorrow some time, Harry, and thanks for the warning.' Alex cut the connection.

Alex quickly dressed, and began to rush around the room like a madman, collecting as many items of clothing he could lay his hands on, along with his books and shoulder bag, forcing them into any available space in his case.

Knowing that he couldn't squeeze anything else in his case, he pushed the top down so he could fasten it, hopefully without bursting the zips. Picking up the discarded clothes he couldn't force in, he flung them under the bed, trusting they would be still there, once this nightmare was over. Yet Alex wasn't feeling too confident at this moment in time.

'Shit, the pictures,' cried Alex, dashing over to the bed to collect the envelope from under his pillow. Ensuring none had fallen out, including Tony's handwritten note, he carefully secreted the envelope in his inside pocket of his jacket.

Slowly easing the door open, he started to listen for any movement, or the sound of the creaking lift being used. There was nothing; thankfully all was quiet.

Easing the door shut, making sure it didn't slam from the draught coming down the corridor, he made his way to Larry's room.

'What number did Larry say? Oh yes, forty, here goes,' he muttered, once again listening out for any movement of running feet, or the slamming of doors.

It was a long way to Larry's room, especially dragging a bulging case up two flights of stairs – he daren't risk using the lifts. After a great deal of puffing and panting, sweat dripping down into his eyes, which he wiped away with the back of his hand, he eventually reached the landing of Larry's floor. Gingerly opening the door, satisfied that it appeared to be deserted, he made his way along the corridor. He'd only moved a short distance, when to his alarm, he noticed a young lady struggling to insert her key into the door of her apartment.

'Work, will you,' she shouted.

'This I don't need,' muttered Alex under his breath.

Trying to look as inconspicuous as possible, Alex breezed past her without offering to help, which he normally would have done under different circumstances.

'Excuse me, young man, can you help me? I'm having difficulties with my key,' asked the young lady.

Shit, thought Alex. I suppose I can't ignore her now, especially after she called me young man. She must be drunk.

Propping his case up by the wall, he came across to assist her.

'Here, let me try,' he said, taking the key from her trembling hand.

After a few seconds of fiddling around, Alex was relieved to hear the click of the lock, and the door yawned open.

'Thank you very much,' the woman said to Alex as she disappeared into her room.

'No problem,' responded Alex to a closed door.

Collecting his case, he made his way down the corridor, searching for Larry's apartment, which he soon found.

Trying to muffle the sound of his tapping with his sweater, and kneeling down, he began trying to attract Larry's attention by whispering between the gap at the foot of the door.

'Larry, Larry, are you awake, can you hear me? It's Alex.'

Alex just hoped and prayed that no one came out of their apartment to investigate the disturbance. After what seemed like hours, he eventually heard the sound of the door being unlocked from the inside, and the voice of a tired, irritable man.

'Who is it?'

'It's me Larry, Alex, open up will you, quickly,' whispered Alex, panicking.

Cautiously, Larry opened the door, peeking around the edge to confirm it was him. Wiping his eyes with a tissue, he eventually invited Alex inside.

'What's all the fuss about? I was just having an exquisite dream with a long-legged brunette who was just about to slip into bed with me ...' He stopped mid-sentence, noticing Alex dragging his case in the room. 'What's the problem? Not paid your bill?' he quipped.

'I wish it was that simple. Harry rang me about half an hour ago to warn me that Nash was on his way over here.' Alex repeated what Harry had said to him over the phone. 'I hope you don't mind me coming here, but I couldn't think of anywhere else to go,' he apologized.

'It's fine, don't worry, and don't concern yourself about Nash finding us. The apartment's registered in my sister's married name, so Nash is going to be one disappointed asshole when he doesn't find you.'

Alex slumped down on the nearest chair, letting out an almighty sigh.

'I'm worried for Harry, Nash is bound to find out he tipped me off,' he commented.

'From what I've heard from you, Harry can look after himself. Anyway, how will Nash know – you won't tell him, and I certainly won't,' said Larry, moving to the window, slyly pushing the blinds to one side, checking outside for any sign of Nash or his associates.

'I can't see anything unusual out there,' he said, 'only the normal late-night revellers making their way home.'

Larry wandered into the bedroom, only to return with blankets, which he threw over to Alex, suggesting he use the couch, which he could vouch was comfortable. As Alex was preparing his makeshift bed he started to survey the room and was surprised by the lack of furniture.

'The room is a bit minimalistic. Does your sister prefer that look?' he asked.

'If you look carefully Alex, you will also notice that there are no sharp edges on any of the furniture. That's because Summer – that's my sister's name, by the way – is partially sighted – in fact she's registered blind. She can't afford to have sharp edges anywhere in any of the rooms, or she would have bruises all over her body.'

Alex's face suddenly went red; realizing he'd just put his foot in it.

'I'm so sorry, Larry, I didn't know. I hope I haven't offended you?'

'Don't be so daft; you weren't to know. Come on, relax, and settle down in your comfy little nest – we both need to be alert in the morning, or we'll be no good to anyone.'

They decided that they would take turns standing guard, listening out for any unusual movement in the corridor or out in the street.

'When Nash arrives,' said Larry, laughing, 'be ready to crawl out of the window, and clamber across the railings of the balconies. Unfortunately the only way down from the outside is by a fire-escape ladder over on the other side of the building, so if we do have to take off, we will need to go across the front of the hotel. Thankfully the iron railings are black, so it should give us some degree of concealment.'

Alex wasn't too happy with Larry's description of the potential escape.

'Get some sleep, Alex, you're going to need it, and don't worry too much about Nash. When he gets round to checking my address he's going to be disappointed. I haven't had one since just after 9/11. I decided to sell my apartment, so apart from living here on and off over the last six years, I've been freeloading with my mates. So I can't imagine Nash coming across my name on any of their databases for a while. No doubt in time he will probe into my family's background, check to see if I have any brothers and sisters. At that stage he may get lucky, but that's going to take him some time.' Alex began to relax a little, wrapping the blankets around him, trying to make himself as comfortable as possible. 'Goodnight, Larry, and thanks again,' he remarked. Sliding one of the chairs up to the door,

Larry prepared himself for an uncomfortable few hours. 'Don't forget to give me a nudge when it's my turn, will you?' muttered Alex. 'Don't worry, I will,' answered Larry. Once again, Alex noticed him wiping his eyes.

During the time Harry was on the phone to Alex, Nash was organizing his troops to drive across to the hotel, hopefully to apprehend Alex.

'What the hell's keeping you?' he barked to the four agents who were slipping on their shoulder holsters, and buttoning up their coats.

'By the time we get there, he'll probably have got up, dressed, had breakfast, and be on his way for a jolly good walk,' he added, in a pathetic British accent.

'Now listen,' he snapped, 'don't go rushing in like Rambo on speed. This hotel is a fine establishment with a long history. When we arrive, we'll split into two groups, one to check if there is a rear exit, and I'll go in the front with you two.' Pointing at two bored-looking agents. Climbing into the two waiting unmarked police cars they drove away, no one uttering a word en route.

Pulling up opposite the hotel; with Nash once again repeating his instructions; the two groups split up. Nash stormed through the front entrance towards reception. Showing the desk clerk his badge, he asked for Alex's room number. The clerk wasn't used to having government agents on his shift, and he started to get flustered.

'I'm not here all night, son,' shouted Nash, 'so I would suggest you do as you're told – go on your computer, and give me the goddamned information I've asked for.'

Trying hard to compose himself, the clerk eventually stammered out the information.

Nash made his way to the stairs, checking to make sure his companions weren't trailing behind. As he wasn't one to stand on ceremony; when they arrived at Alex's room Nash instructed the two agents to break down the door with their shoulders. Both men lined themselves up, and from the way they were positioned they were clearly aiming to hit the door at either end, hopefully resulting in the door coming off its hinges. One of the agents started to count down under his breath; when he got to one, both of them hit the door.

The noise was deafening, prompting the residents to come out into the corridor to investigate the disturbance. The force of the impact caused the door to come clean off its hinges, leaving it and the two agents sprawled out on the floor. Nash didn't bother to ask if they were all right, he just barged his way in, expecting to see Alex sat up in bed. But to Nash's disappointment, the bed was empty, and from the way the bed covers had been tossed about, it appeared to him that the occupant had left in a mighty hurry. After a few seconds, searching the bathroom, Nash came out shaking his head, tut-tutting to himself under his breath; empty handed.

'Looks like Mr Monroe has flown the coop. It also seems he may have friends in high places.' Nash moved around the room, checking through the bedside drawers and closets, ending up kneeling down by the side of the bed, peering underneath. Nash pulled out the assortment of clothes which Alex had put there.

'It seems he left in a hurry,' remarked Nash, clambering over the horizontal damaged door. He made his way down the corridor, whilst shouting out orders to the two red faced agents, who were still adjusting their clothes. 'Start questioning the residents on this floor, and don't worry, they won't be asleep; the racket you've just made will have woken up most of Lower Manhattan. If you have no luck, start on the rest of the floors. I want this Alex Monroe caught, and quickly.'

He stopped walking just before he reached the door to the stairs, and proceeded to punch numbers on his cell phone.

'Holmes, sorry to wake you up so early, I didn't disturb you, did I? I'm over at the Chelsea Hotel. I was hoping to have a chat with Mr Alex Monroe, and guess what? He's not here. I wonder why? It seems you may have a sympathizer at the station, and I have a damn good idea who it is. Sort it out, or I'll come down on you and your little band of misfits and sort them out myself. Holmes? I need half a dozen of your men down here right away. I require them to conduct a thorough search for this fugitive. He must be here somewhere. I wouldn't have thought he would have had time to get out. Oh, and one more request. Check out this Larry Underwood's family. Does he have any brothers or sisters? As far as I can tell, the guy doesn't even exist. One final request, Holmes; have a good night.' Closing his cell phone, chuckling to himself, Nash carried on making his way downstairs to reception.

'There is only one reason why Mr. Alex Monroe isn't tucked up in bed and fast asleep, as they say in England? He must have the pictures,' whispered Nash, feeling relaxed, now knowing who to apprehend.

Whilst shuffling around in his chair, trying to find a comfortable position, Larry heard an unusual number of car doors slamming outside in the street.

Easing himself up, he made his way cautiously over to the sleeping form of Alex. After a couple of shakes of his shoulder, Alex turned over to see Larry indicating for him to be silent. Jumping off the couch, Alex followed Larry over to the window. Sliding the shuttered blind to one side, they guardedly peered out of the window.

'Shit,' cried Alex, 'that's Nash down there. Who else is with him?'

'It looks like he's brought a few of his mates along. You must be important,' whispered Larry.

Alex sighed. 'I don't want to be important, I just want to go home, and they'll soon know which room I'm staying in. Nash won't be too happy when he finds out I'm not there. Anyway, you've no need to worry Larry, it's me they're looking for, not you. So if they decide to start searching the hotel, we may get away with it.'

'I don't think it's going to be as simple as that Alex. If Nash has any sense he would have already arranged to have our mug-shots printed, and handed out to the agents.'

'How could he have managed to get hold of mine so quickly? I've only been in the country a short while,' raged Alex.

'Alex, you're in America now, not some backward tin-pot country. Since 9/11, our government have enacted what we call the Patriot Act. This means they can do what they want, without asking, and your great British government have agreed to assist them all they can. So as far as we're concerned, mister, I have no reason to doubt that your picture, along with mine, is in Nash's slimy little hands right now.'

'I'm coming to the conclusion that my trip to New York was a bad idea,' stated Alex.

'Don't panic, we haven't been caught – yet,' replied Larry, dabbing his eyes with a tissue.

Larry peered once again through the blinds, checking to see if any of the agents had been ordered to patrol the outside. Observing it was clear, he moved back over to Alex.

'Oh Christ, I've just remembered!' cried Alex. 'As I was making my way along the corridor to your apartment, I helped a young lady with her key; she was having difficulties getting into her apartment. So if and when she's questioned, she may remember me.'

'Luckily,' replied Larry, 'we do have a slight advantage over them. We're on the fourth floor, so it will be a while before they arrive, so the best thing you can do is sort out what you need from your case – you seem to have too much in there, judging by the bulges on the sides. I have a couple of backpacks we can use – they'll be easier to carry around.'

Alex had accepted the fact that they may have to crawl over the balconies in order to escape, although he'd hoped it wouldn't have to come to that.

Quickly opening up his case, Alex started emptying its contents on the floor, sorting through what he needed.

'Bloody hell,' he moaned, 'I'm going to have to leave all my books. Never mind, they'll be secure here, and if I do get out of this safely, I can always come back for them. But if I do get caught, I can always get someone to come for them, at least I'll have something to read whilst I'm locked up in prison,' he said, with a trace of fear in his voice.

Larry came back in from the bedroom with two medium-sized backpacks, dropping one beside Alex.

'You can use this one, but don't fill it, you don't want to be hauling too much weight around, especially if we are on the run for a while.'

Alex looked up into Larry's watery eyes, trying to work out if he was as scared as he was.

'You'd be wise to check out the side pockets.' Larry advised him, smiling. 'You never know, Summer may have left some of her panties in one of them.'

Alex thought Larry was only joking until he embarrassingly pulled out a pair of swimming briefs, along with a white fold-out cane.

'Won't your sister be wanting this?' he asked, holding the cane out to Larry.

'No – she hasn't much use for it now, not since the laser treatment she had last year. Keep it – you never know, it may come in handy . . .' Larry suddenly stopped talking, having heard the sounds of someone hammering impatiently on one of the apartment doors down the corridor, also the voice of an irritable man, demanding that the door be opened, immediately.

'Come on Alex, it seems as though Nash as organised his men to do a thorough search of the hotel. We need to get out of here – now.'

'Christ Larry, they haven't wasted much time getting up here, have they?' whispered Alex.

'No they haven't, so unless you want Nash and his friends to find you, move yourself,' ordered Larry.

Once they were sure they both had enough clothes packed, they once again checked outside to see if the street was clear.

'I can't see anyone at the moment,' commented Larry. 'I would have thought they'd all be inside, in the warmth, rather than freezing their butts off outside.'

Larry began to unlock the window, slowly easing it open, the sudden rush of incoming cold air causing them both to take a step back into the warmth of the room.

'Bloody hell!' shrieked Alex. 'It's cold out there.'

'Don't worry,' replied Larry, 'once you start swinging from balcony to balcony like a monkey, you'll soon warm up.'

Alex knew Larry was only trying to ease the situation with some light banter, but it wasn't working. He was scared.

After they had both carefully climbed out onto the balcony, Larry eased the window shut, also ensuring that there were no unseen agents creeping up from the sides or wandering around below in the street. Glancing over the balcony, Alex was shocked to see a drop of about fifty feet. Luckily he wasn't afraid of heights, so it didn't bother him too much. Larry reminded him that they would have to make their way across the front of the hotel towards the fire escape, which was positioned above a tattoo parlor. There were four balconies to navigate; unfortunately they overhung the building, meaning they would have to stretch across to reach them. Alex wasn't too concerned, but he did notice that the railings were coated in rainwater, mindful that this may hinder their escape. After they had adjusted the backpacks on their shoulders, specifically checking that the buckles on the straps at the front were securely fastened, Larry cautiously mounted the iron railings, all the while swiping away the rainwater from the top, hoping it would give him a firmer grip. After a nervous five minutes he finally found himself seated on his backside on the second balcony, sweat trickling down his face.

Once Larry had made it safely across, Alex painstakingly made his escape, tracing the same route, hoping the railings would be dry. He was taking slightly longer, as he was being more cautious; there was also the fact that he wasn't in as good a physical shape as Larry.

Alex was just in the process of reaching out to grab hold of the top of the slippery railing when he suddenly lost his footing, resulting in him falling backwards towards the sidewalk, and certain injury, or even death. Alex didn't have time to see his life flash before his eyes, as within milliseconds of him falling to the ground, he abruptly stopped mid-flight, leaving him dangling fifty feet in the air, the straps around his shoulders and back beginning to bite into his skin.

'F-u-u-c-k.' Alex cried out, in wide-eyed terror.

Alex raised his head up, only to see to his relief, Larry struggling to hold onto the straps, also attempting to hook his left arm around the top of the railings for support.

Suddenly becoming aware of the predicament he was in, Alex quickly clamped his right hand around the base of the railing to steady himself, before reaching out with his left foot, hoping to wedge it between the brick work in the wall. The sweat that was beginning to stream into his eyes was making it difficult for him to see what he was doing.

'Sshh!' whispered Larry, his voice breaking up with the strain of holding onto the straps of Alex's backpack. 'I think I heard someone moving about below us.'

Gripping hold of the railing for dear life, with his legs precariously suspended in mid-air, Alex twisted his head around to peer down towards the sidewalk over to his right, only to see to his horror, one of the agents having a sly smoke by the entrance. 'Fuck, what do we do now?' murmured Alex panicking, his grip on the slippery railing becoming weaker by the second.

'Just hold on, I can't imagine him hanging around for too long,' wheezed Larry.

'I don't think I will be able to,' sighed Alex, the muscles in his arm beginning to seize up. Because it was becoming difficult by the second to keep hold of the straps, Larry decided to slip his left hand between the railings, aiming to reach out as far as possible towards

Alex's right hand. With an exerted effort, stretching his arm as far as the railing would allow him; his face pressed up hard against the cold wet metal, Larry managed to grip hold of Alex's right wrist, hoping to give him some additional support, and breathing space; which luckily it had. 'Thanks Larry, I don't think I could have held on much longer,' stammered Alex, his strength slowly ebbing away.

After a few tense minutes, the agent tossed his cigarette butt far out into the middle of the street, and went back inside. Much to Alex and Larry's relief.

Still clinging dangerously fifty feet in the air, it was the awful thought of not seeing his sons again which gave Alex the incentive he needed to climb to safety.

By this time, sweat was also starting to pour down Larry's face with the exertion, and to make matters worse, the straps were beginning to dig into the palm of his sweaty hand, causing them to painfully, and slowly slip from his grip, delaying the inevitable. Recognizing the discomfort Larry was in, Alex slipped his hand from Larry's grasp, and quickly reached up, seizing one of the flowered motifs on the railings; hoping he could pull himself up sufficiently for Larry to grab hold of him. After a great deal of effort from both of them, Larry eventually managed to seize hold of Alex by the scruff of the neck with his free hand, before pulling him with all the strength he had left, dragging Alex unceremoniously over the railings, leaving him in a heap on the floor.

'Christ Almighty, Alex, I thought you were a goner there,' remarked Larry in a breathless voice. Slowly lifting himself off the wet floor, Alex began to shake with fear at the realization of what could have happened.

'You thought I was a goner, you should have been in my shoes. Thanks Larry for saving my life. I don't think I would have survived the fall.'

When they had eventually composed themselves; controlling their breathing, they scanned the area below them once more, aware that the noise they had made may have alerted the agent if he happened to be positioned near the entrance. Certain it was all clear, they began to crawl across the remaining balconies, and where possible keeping out of sight of any prying eyes below. The climbing and the thought of falling once more made Alex feel apprehensive, and exhausted. Sweat was trickling down his back, his whole body was beginning to shake.

'Can we have a rest for a minute, Larry? I'm totally burned out.'

Larry admitted that he was also tired, and a rest would do them both good. Once they felt they were ready to carry on, Larry began climbing over the last balcony, hoping he would reach the ladder without anyone unexpectedly appearing below them. Alex wasn't sure if his fifty-eight-year-old body could cope with any more of this climbing and crawling, yet quickly coming to the conclusion that he had no choice.

'If Marie could see me now, she'd wet her pants ... Jason Bourne, move over, here comes Alex Monroe,' he mumbled to himself, chuckling, trying to relieve the tension.

'Just follow me, Alex, and don't look down. By the time you reach the ladder, the rungs should be reasonably dry to grip.'

Once again checking to make sure his backpack was secure, Larry started to release the ladder from its holding position, without any success.

'That's all we need, it won't move. Just keep back in the shadows. I'll have to stand on it – hopefully my weight will release it.'

Cautiously climbing up to the top rung of the ladder, Larry started to jump up and down, hoping to disengage it.

'Geronimo,' he whispered, as the ladder slowly started to descend. Taking one step at a time, Larry managed to land on the pavement, unscathed. After quickly surveying the area, he indicated to Alex for him to start his descent. Alex began to compose himself, checking one last time that it was all clear, before advancing towards the ladder. All his life he had always taken his time when doing anything, and this was no exception, especially after his last scare. In no time he was on the ground, and once he had managed to push the ladder back to its original position, he moved over to Larry, who was by now standing well back in the shadow of the tattoo parlor's door.

'Well, that was easy enough, wasn't it?' chuckled Alex. The tension and adrenalin rush caused them both to suddenly burst into fits of laughter.

'Sshh, be quiet,' whispered Larry, 'someone may hear us.'

'I can't help it,' Alex whispered back, covering his mouth with his hand.

Alex was just about to make his way out of the shadow of the doorway when Larry pulled him back with an unexpected jolt.

'Just hold on, I can hear a car coming, and it sounds as though it's in a hurry. We may have some additional unexpected company.' Larry was correct in his assumption, as within a few seconds, two police cruisers had pulled up in the street, opposite the hotel. Seconds later, six pissed-off-looking NYPD policemen wandered across the road and entered the hotel. After controlling their nerves, Alex and Larry cautiously slipped out of the doorway, always checking behind them, making sure no one had wandered unexpectedly out of the hotel's entrance.

'Where are we going?' asked Alex.

'The Grand Central terminal, where your friend Harry suggested. It's going to take us a while to get there, and on the way we'll need to find somewhere safe to hide. Central Park will probably be the best place, and it's not too far from the station, also the Park is large enough for us to disappear in. Come on, Alex, cheer up. I've a feeling the next few days are going to be interesting.'

As they were making their way, Alex turned to Larry and asked him why he was so determined to find out the truth.

'I don't like to talk about it, but since we are both in this together, I'll confide in you my experience of 9/11.'

'I can remember it as if it was yesterday,' said Larry, with a touch of sadness in his voice. 'Our unit was the first to arrive as the second plane struck the South Tower. I was taking firefighters up in the elevator to the twenty-fourth floor to get in position to evacuate the workers. On our last trip up a bomb went off. We all thought at the time that bombs were being systematically set off in the building. It felt as though someone was sitting at a control panel, pushing detonator buttons. You could hear the explosions coming from what seemed to be various floors, one after another, from top to bottom. Also another thing that struck me whilst I was in there ... the sprinkler systems weren't fully working ...' Larry hesitated for a moment, trying to control his emotions, wiping his eyes once more.

Feeling the hurt and pain Larry must be going through, replaying the horrors he had witnessed, Alex decided it was best not to say anything while Larry struggled to find the words.

'I had asked a colleague to come with me, which was a good thing because we got trapped inside the elevator, and he had the right gear to open the doors to get out. When we managed to open them we noticed at least five hundred people trapped in the stairwell. Suddenly the power went off. It was dark, everyone started to scream, and panic. We had a few oxygen masks with us, which we shared out whilst we were ushering the workers down the stairs. We were the lucky ones, we managed to get out safely. At that stage I knew at least thirty firefighters were missing. I lost a great number of colleagues that day.' Larry stopped talking, as the events of that horrific day suddenly came flooding back to him, causing him to fight back the lump in his throat. After a few seconds he carried on.

'Once we were outside, I went back in to try and assist with the rescue, but I was so messed up and tired. It was then that something struck me on the side of my head, which caused me to collapse unconscious onto the floor. I don't know how long I was out, but the next thing I remembered, I was wandering the dust-filled streets, disorientated, in a dream. I started to look around for a landmark through all the dust and charred paper which was falling all over the place like a heavy snowfall. I eventually saw a glimpse of the sun up ahead, so I headed in that direction. As I was slowly making my way, I noticed scorched shoes hanging from branches in the trees by the side of the road. I assumed that they had been left there by some of the lucky people who had escaped from the burning buildings. I stopped to look back at the Towers. Flames were pouring out from some of the top floors, and debris was falling everywhere – it reminded me of the ticker-tape celebrations on New Year's Eve in Times Square. By now I was covered in ash, not unlike the rest of the people who were wandering about, all looking like their hair had turned prematurely grey. When I think back to that day, I still find it hard trying to come to terms with the carnage, along with the vast amount of debris floating about in the air. Sometimes at night, while

I'm drifting off to sleep, I can still sense the soot and dirt covering my face, plus the horrible sensation of my throat becoming clogged up with the thickening dust.' Larry hesitated again. No doubt reliving that horrible and frightening experience, Alex assumed.

Controlling his thoughts, wiping the moisture from his eyes with the back of his hand, Larry proceeded with his tale.

'I can vaguely remember staggering into a shop doorway, throwing up as I was attempting to clear the air passages in my throat. All of a sudden, emerging through all the swirling dust and ash, a shimmering image of a man appeared clutching a large bottle of water against his chest. That's when I bumped into Moon. No words were spoken, he just smiled, and turned the bottle upside down and poured the contents over my head, and I can tell you this, Alex, that was the best sensation I've ever experienced in my whole life. I must have fallen unconscious again, because the next thing I remembered, I was in hospital, with bandages covering the top of my head. I found out later from one of the paramedics that Moon had carried me to one of the hospital shelter's that had been set up a few blocks from the collapsed Towers. When I thank Moon for what he did, he just shrugs it off with a wave of his hand as though it was an everyday occurrence to him.' Larry paused long enough to control his feelings.

'You've no doubt noticed that I have to continuously wipe my eyes. That's because, when I was inside the Towers, some of the dust particles and soot floating about in the air ended up in my eyes. My first reaction was to wipe them, which unfortunately I did with the back of my hand, consequently it damaged the tear ducts in both eyes. It's something I'm going to have to live with for the rest of my life. I suppose it's a small price to pay after all that's happened, don't you think?'

'Yes, I suppose so,' responded Alex.

Larry carried on. 'I kept on trying to tell the doctors about the explosions, but they said I was suffering from concussion and shock, and it was just my mind playing tricks. I even mentioned it to the investigators who came to debrief me, and I have to say, the look on their faces told me that I might have hit a nerve. They said it would be in my best interests to keep the theories to myself. So now you see, Alex, I knew all along about the explosives, I just wanted someone to confirm my suspicions, and Tony has done that, thank you very much.' By the time Larry had finished, they were only a short distance away from the entrance to the park.

'Why didn't you mention it to me before, about the explosions?' asked Alex.

'Because at first I didn't know whether to trust you or not, but after tonight's escapade I think I can, and I'm sorry for being suspicious of you, Alex.'

'After what you've been through, I'm not surprised you were wary of me, I would have been wary of me,' replied Alex with a chuckle, hoping to ease the tension. They carried on silently for a while, both trying to come to terms with their situation.

'Who's the guy on top of the column?' asked Alex, pointing up in the air.

'Columbus. We are at the entrance to the west side of the park. This is Columbus Circle,' replied Larry.

'Very impressive Larry, like most things I've seen whilst I've been here. It's a pity I can't enjoy it more,' moaned Alex.

'Once this is all over, I will give you a Larry Underwood guided tour of New York, including all the seedy parts,' smiled Larry, draping his arm around Alex.

151

'I'll look forward to that. In the meantime we need to find some-where to hide, and hopefully get some sleep,' remarked Alex.

Larry noticed a building to one side which was in the process of being renovated. 'Come on Alex, we may find something over there we can use to keep dry if it decides to start raining through the night.' He gestured with his head.

Sneaking around to the side of the building, Alex came to a hole in the fence. 'Larry,' he whispered, 'I think I can see a sheet of tar-paulin over there in the mud. If I can manage to wipe it down we may be able to use it to cover us. Here, help me widen this, so I can squeeze through.'

Pulling the wire apart, Larry eventually managed to make the gap wide enough for Alex to climb through, and in no time Alex had wiped down the tarpaulin as best he could, before clambering back out.

'This will do,' he remarked, 'at least it will give us some protec-tion if it starts to rain.'

Rolling the tarpaulin into a manageable size, they trudged across to the relative safety of the park, mindful of the fact that they were getting some threatening and puzzled looks from the resident down-and-outs. It didn't take them long to find a concealed spot under one of the many bridges dotted around the park, which, by the looks of it, had been used recently. There was evidence of a few pieces of wet cardboard, plus a stained blanket lying on the damp floor. There was also the distinguishable odour of stale urine. Whilst Larry was orga-nizing the shelter – by carefully hanging the tarpaulin on two rusty broken nails that were jutting out of the crumbling plaster on the wall, Alex began searching the area for any dry cardboard that might have been left around by the park's other residents. It didn't take him long to come up with enough waste for them both to lie down on. Ensuring the shelter was as waterproof as possible, also there weren't any shady characters wandering around, they both settled down on their makeshift beds. Protecting their backpacks by using them as pillows, and satisfied they were reasonably safe – especially under the extraordinary circumstances they'd found themselves in; they tried to get some sleep.

'Right, listen up,' shouted Nash to the police officers who had just arrived in the lobby. 'This is the guy we're looking for,' he said, handing out pictures of Alex which he'd had sent over to the fax in the hotel's reception. 'Don't go knocking on every door in the hotel, that's already in hand, just start searching the corridors for anything unusual. Also a couple of you can go and check out the fire escapes, plus any rear exits. It's important we find this guy, and soon, and if you find anything, get word back to me immediately. Got it?'

After a laborious and unsuccessful fours hours, Nash decided to call off the search, sending his agents and the NYPD policemen home.

Nash wasn't beaten. He would move heaven and earth to find Alex.

He had to, his and the government's future were in his hands.

'THE PLANE FACTS'

Crash in Pennsylvania

Why was the debris from this plane spread out over eight miles? The official story is that the plane crashed after the passengers stormed the cockpit. But normally when planes crash into the ground the debris ends up in a relatively small area. Often the fuselage and wings remain near each other. The debris scattering over eight miles is very odd. Is the official story believable?

Numerous eyewitness accounts suggest the plane was shot down by another, marked plane. (9/11 timeline)

Attack on the Pentagon

Why won't the Pentagon release their video footage of this event? It was perhaps the most bizarre of all. The Pentagon oddly chose to release five still frames from their security cameras' footage. One of these five frames shows something that might be a plane or a missile or a grey smear. The other four show an exploding fireball on the side of the Pentagon.

There was barely any debris from whatever caused the explosion, and yet supposedly the remains of the passengers were all physically identified by the FBI. So the explosion completely vaporized tons of steel, yet didn't destroy human remains. Also, the hole in the side of the Pentagon was too small for a 757 to fit into.

Why won't the Pentagon release the rest of the footage? (9/11 cover-up)

Chapter Ten

'War is too serious a matter to entrust to military men.'

Georges Clemenceau (1841–1929)

BIGGS AIR FORCE BASE (El Paso, Texas)

Up to 1966, the base was part of the Strategic Air Command, which operated heavy bombers.

In 1966, the air force departed from the base and it became an army airfield. The base would probably have been abandoned, except for the fact that Fort Bliss surrounded Biggs.

Since 9/11, the passengers and crew from American Airlines Flight 77 have been secretly hidden away in a heavily guarded facility, some thirty miles from Biggs Air Force Base.

One of the passengers was Nathan (Nat) Ford, Harry Pinchpeck's former partner.

The facility was surrounded by four barbed-wire fences, each fifty metres apart, the outer two being electrified. The two inner fences had stainless-steel boxes welded to every third fencepost. These were self-powered security relays monitoring the hundreds of pressure points set in the ground at regular intervals around the perimeter of the complex. Also integrated intermittently within the high outer fencing were manned watchtowers. In addition, there was a double security-gate system, with two checkpoints, each guarded by armed, military-looking personnel. An array of security cameras and infrared imagers monitored the facility 24/7.

Any visiting dignitaries were put through a rigorous security check before being admitted, involving retinal scans, fingerprint checks and, for final confirmation, a brainwave scanner, which reads an individual's synaptic trace.

For added internal security, the American servicemen stationed at the site, along with the workforce (in most cases they were non-English-speaking), had bar codes tattooed on the inside of their left wrist.

The security within the complex was monitored by the most up to date cutting-edge technology available from a security center located at the far northern side of the base. Besides all these impressive safeguards, there was also a twenty mile no-fly zone in force.

The facility was the most secure and well-kept secret in the whole of America; indeed, in the world.

It had its own state-of-the-art hospital and school. The living quarters were positioned in the centre, close to the main facilities, which contained the canteen, plus all the leisure amenities, including a swimming pool; a small cinema; a ten-pin bowling alley and a library.

There was also a cemetery, located well out of the way.

Over the last six years people had married and died, and not surprisingly, a small number of children had been born, some in wedlock, some not.

During the first few months of their incarceration, the passengers and crew constantly rebelled, demanding to be told the truth; some even threatened to go on hunger strike unless they were released. They soon gave that up as a bad idea once they knew they were to be there for a long time.

The authorities said they had to be patient, owing to the mounting problems in America which had to be resolved before they could be notified of their future.

After a while the passengers and crew decided they would elect a committee, to oversee the day-to-day running of the facility, ensuring discipline was controlled correctly. The authorities weren't seen too often. The only contact they had was on a weekly basis, with the committee, helping to sort out any infighting and grievances that needed to be handled at a much higher level. When they did ask further questions about why they were being held prisoner, they were once again told it was for their own good.

The authorities finally informed the 'detainees' that on Tuesday, 11 September 2001, terrorists, in hijacked commercial aircraft, dropped a number of 'dirty bombs' throughout the United States, resulting in lethal radiation covering the greater part of the country, and it would be years before it was safe enough for them to return home.

They also said they were truly sorry, but all their loved ones would have perished at the time, but if it was any consolation, their deaths would have been sudden, they wouldn't have suffered.

Accepting their predicament, the committee decided to organize various social events, such as baseball games between the men and women and chess tournaments, and with the help of the facility's authorities, they built themselves an indoor and outdoor playground for the children with a small farm attached. This was to encourage them to grow their own food, and to be as self-sufficient as possible.

Nat had never believed in any of the explanations that had been put to them. He knew there was cause for alarm, well before 9/11, as he was already investigating sightings of known terrorists in the United States, reportedly preparing for an attack on American soil; yet he didn't want the authorities to be aware of this, as he knew it may jeopardize his future whilst he was being held at the facility.

Propped up at the top of his bed, both hands clasped behind his head for support, Nat began to reflect back to when his nightmare had begun.

He could still remember the day he left Washington Dulles airport ...

The flight had only been in the air for forty minutes when he sensed the aircraft turning full circle. He'd been on this flight a number of times, and he couldn't ever remember this manoeuvre occurring before. He kept on asking the flight crew questions, and to his surprise they weren't aware of anything untoward. Glancing through his window he observed to his alarm, an F-16, flying dangerously close to their aircraft. Also, further over towards Washington, he could see the sun reflecting from the wings of another plane, which he thought was unusual, as he knew that most of Washington, especially around the White House and the Pentagon, had been designated a no-fly zone.

What the hell is happening out there? he thought. He began to wonder if there was a problem with the aircraft. But nothing's been said over the intercom, he reflected, starting to feel anxious, worried that terrorists might be on board. Unbuckling his seat belt, he moved across to the other side of the cabin, checking to see if he could locate the F-16. Scanning the area over to his left, he unexpectedly noticed the Pentagon, which was by now only a few miles away. Now he was worried. If the aircraft had been hijacked, what more prominent building was there to crash into than the American military command centre?

All of a sudden, the plane banked sharply to the left, causing Nat to lose his balance, making him crash heavily onto the cabin floor. The plane proceeded to climb.

It was at this stage a voice came over the intercom.

'Good morning ladies and gentlemen, this is the captain speaking, your pilot on this outward-bound flight from Dulles Airport to Los Angeles. No doubt you have noticed that we have returned to Washington. The reason for this is that we have been requested by the FAA to take part in a government exercise, which, I may add, is still in progress, and we will shortly be returning to our original flight path. I will inform you of any more additional changes during the course of the flight, where necessary, and I thank you for your patience.'

After lifting himself off the floor, by holding the top of the seat in front of him for support, Nat noticed the F-16 heading straight towards the west wall of the Pentagon, and what looked like a plume of smoke coming from the fighter's right wing. A missile, he realized, in horror.

Nat shouted out, 'Christ almighty …'

That was the last thing he remembered, until he woke up with a sore head. Finally coming round, aware he was not on the plane any more, but lying on a hospital stretcher, with a king-size headache, he tried to cast his mind back to what had happened.

Then he remembered the F-16 heading towards the Pentagon … and the missile.

'Oh my God,' screamed Nat, lifting himself up, only to find that his arms and legs had been restrained. 'For fuck's sake, get me out of here, can anybody hear me?' he shouted, frantically. He kept on shouting for ten minutes, but to no avail. After a while, he decided he would save his energy. He might need it to escape, if the opportunity arose, he thought.

They eventually released him fours later, incarcerating him with the rest of the passengers and crew from Flight 77.

It all came flooding back to him. All those lonely years and months, not knowing what was going on in the outside world.

'Get out of here! It must be nearly six years, and in all that time no one has ever believed me,' he groaned. They had said he'd had a panic attack on the plane, which ended up with him having to be sedated. He was becoming a danger to the rest of the passengers.

'Bullshit,' he said to no one in particular. But did they drop 'dirty bombs?' Have I been wrong all these years? he wondered.

SEPTEMBER 9 2007

The janitor pushed the rickety old trolley containing his cleaning utensils along the corridor towards Nat's apartment. He was wearing the standard grey overalls with his security badge hanging from a cheap, tarnished silver chain around his neck. The name on the badge read Jack Goodman. He had an iron-hard muscular frame, complemented by a thick neck and black hair shot through with a small amount of grey.

Over the past six years Jack had been responsible for the cleaning and upkeep of Nat's single story apartment complex. He was also a government agent. Jack was always respectful to Nat, or 'the detainees', as the passengers and crew from Flight 77 were known.

Jack never bothered to knock before entering Nat's room – that was one of the many rules of the facility. Nat was already up, dressed and in the bathroom as Jack walked in.

'Good morning, Jack,' Nat shouted from the bathroom. He knew that there wouldn't be anyone else but Jack in his room at this time in the morning.

'Morning,' replied Jack. 'Ready to be escorted to the breakfast hall?'

'Ready as I'll ever be.' Came the usual reply from Nat.

Satisfied that everything was in order, Jack escorted Nat to the canteen for his breakfast, along with the other passengers and crew from the flight.

On a number of occasions Nat had tried questioning Jack about the facility, only to be answered as usual with a blank stare. Only a few months earlier he had actually started to have a conversation with Jack. But once again, nothing came of it.

Everyone on the facility ate breakfast in the canteen. The rest of the time, the meals were prepared by the detainees in their rooms. They were each given a small amount of money to buy basic essentials. The other spending money came from jobs some of them had volunteered to take on. This gave them some self-respect; it also made the days less boring. Nat had volunteered for the upkeep of the gardens. He had always been a keen gardener, and there was always something to do around the facility. Early on during his incarceration, he wondered whether he could escape by hiding in the garbage truck when it did its weekly collections. When he saw the guards prodding the waste with long pitchforks, and the pneumatic crushers being constantly turned over, he quickly gave up on that idea, and when he noticed the weird bar-code tattoo on Jack's left wrist, he suddenly realized escaping was definitely out of the question.

After the ritual group breakfast, Nat made his way back to his room to change into his work clothes. Entering the house through the kitchen door, he found to his surprise, Jack sitting by the kitchen table, looking anxious.

'This is an unexpected pleasure Jack; do you need me for anything?'

Jack didn't answer him at first, but lifted himself off the chair and moved across towards the kitchen window, checking to see if there was anyone in the back garden. Satisfied it was clear; he walked back to his chair.

'Nat, you'd better sit down, what I'm going to divulge to you may cost me and my family our lives, so you need to listen carefully, also you must promise not to repeat anything of what I'm about to say to anyone, under any circumstances, understand?'

Nat was beginning to get excited.

'I promise. Am I going to be told the truth, at last?' Nat enquired.

'Do you know what day it is, Nat?'

'What day it is? Come on, Jack, I sometimes don't know what fucking year it is,' responded Nat.

'It's September the ninth 2007. Nat, you, along with your fellow passengers and crew from Flight 77, have been locked up in this facility for nearly six years, and during all that time I have been constantly trying to come to terms with the guilt and shame of holding you all here against your will.'

Nat was now starting to become eager to find out exactly what Jack had on his mind.

'Jack, as you're aware, I've always known that there was something not right about this place, and the real reasons why we are all kept here. I don't know if you heard about my outburst when we were in the air? I know it's, what, six years ago now, you say. When we first arrived, I kept on trying to tell the authorities about the F-16 I spotted flying towards the Pentagon, and the missile I saw heading towards the west wall. They just didn't listen to what I had to say. They said I had become hysterical during the flight and I had to be sedated. The drugs must have affected my brain. What a load of bullshit. As a police officer you have to be alert at all times, which in this case I definitely was.'

'I did hear something to that effect,' replied Jack, 'but I didn't take much notice. Over the years, there have been many lies and distortions of the facts, but I can tell you for certain, Nat, you were correct, you did see an F-16, and from what I've heard, it fired a new-generation missile: an AGM-type missile, which was armed with a hollow charge with a depleted-uranium BLU tip. When it struck the Pentagon, there would have been an instantaneous fire, which would have given off heat in excess of 3,600 degrees Fahrenheit ... Nat? One hundred and twenty-five innocent civilians died in the Pentagon on that day.'

Nat was shocked. He'd always had an idea that something terrible had happened, but when the truth is put in front of you, it's very difficult to comprehend, he thought.

'Shit! I know it's not the right thing to say, but it seems I was correct all along. But it doesn't alter the fact that the American government must have been involved somehow ...' Nat decided to stop talking, hoping Jack would divulge more. He didn't have long to wait.

'Nat, I never wanted to carry on being part of this operation, it's just that all my family were threatened, and I've another confession – I'm sorry, Nat, I'm not just a janitor, I'm also an undercover government agent assigned to watch over you.'

Nat kept quiet for a while.

'Nothing surprises me, Jack, and don't worry. Over the past years you've treated me well, with respect, I have no grudges against you. Please carry on.'

Jack felt relieved that Nat had taken the news so well.

'I know a great deal about your life Nat. Your family, your job as a detective working on suspected terrorists in the Washington district. I even know about your partner, Harry Pinchpeck. And don't worry, he's alive and well. You might be interested to know he's been transferred to New York.'

'That will please him, he always said he'd like to work there,' commented Nat, smiling.

'I need to explain what actually happened on September eleventh 2001. Or, as the rest of the world has come to know it as, 9/11. Then you will be able to work out for yourself why I am confiding in you,' said Jack. 'But first of all let me begin by telling you a little bit about myself. My name is Jack Goodman. I was born and brought up in the Bronx, and I live with my wife and two small children two miles from here ...' Jack then paused to compose himself. 'I'm sorry to be the bearer of bad news, Nat ... your father passed away two years ago, after a long illness.'

Nat's eyes suddenly shot open, then after a few seconds he dropped his head into his hands.

'The murdering fuckers . . . just wait until I get my hands on the ones responsible for all this,' cried Nat.

Jack waited to give Nat time to regain his composure, before carrying on.

'I'm fine now Jack, thanks for letting me know, I appreciate it.' Nat's voice was wavering with emotion.

Leaning over to rest his arms on the table, Jack carried on.

'I was deployed overseas for three years, then posted back to the States for special services. After 9/11, I, along with dozens of other servicemen, volunteered for this assignment. We were originally told that we would be guarding well-known American sympathizers of Osama bin Laden, plus terrorists who were arrested after 9/11. So you can imagine there was no shortage of volunteers. Yet after the atrocities that happened on 9/11 were documented, we all realized that something wasn't stacking up. But we had to carry on with the deceit. I think it's about time you were told of what actually happened on the day you were all brought to this facility. Let me start on the morning of September eleventh 2001, the day that changed the mood of the nation; which ultimately resulted in the citizens of America being made aware that the United States of America could be intimidated and terrorized by unknown factions. I can only tell you what I know, but that will be sufficient for the moment. Also, I can't be hanging around here for too long, as one of my colleagues may become suspicious.'

Over the next fifteen minutes Jack gave Nat as many facts as he could about the events surrounding 9/11. When he had finally finished, Nat noticed that they'd both been crying off and on.

'I knew there was something not right during the flight, especially the part about a government exercise, also the F-16 I spotted heading for the Pentagon. What I can't understand is how did they manage to force the pilot and crew to fly here?'

'That's a good question,' replied Jack. 'The announcement from the captain about the flight being part of an exercise was correct. Unfortunately, he was not involved in the rest of the set-up. When he radioed back to air traffic control that they had arrived back at the Pentagon, he was immediately given a new flight path, then escorted by the F-16 to a secret airfield where he was to land, for his own safety and that of his passengers. So you see Nat, this is how you all ended up here.'

Nat was getting more angry and distressed the more he heard.

'You know what Jack? I can't believe the American government could have been involved with something so corrupt and evil. Thousands of innocent lives lost, and for what?' he asked.

'Oil! We all knew at some point in the near future we would run out. And where else in the world is there a surplus of oil? Iraq. The American government just needed a sound reason to invade the country. At first they blamed Osama bin Laden for 9/11, suddenly changing their minds, accusing Saddam for the attacks on America, also claiming he was manufacturing weapons-grade uranium for producing weapons of mass destruction, or WMDs as they were commonly known to the gullible public. Yet there was no evidence to back it up.'

Nat sat there, not knowing what to say. 'So I have been stuck in this hellhole for six years because our greedy government wanted more oil?' screamed Nat.

'Apart from the oil, you also have to consider the arms industry. There hasn't been a full-scale war for a number of years, not since Vietnam, so consequently there is now a large stockpile of new-generation military aircraft, tanks, guns and millions of rounds of ammunition out there. They have to be used somehow. Also the directors and shareholders of these arms corporations need to make a return on the investments they have put in over the years; and we are talking in trillions of dollars here, Nat.'

Nat was trying to take it all in. 'I can remember reading years ago,' he commented, 'President Roosevelt allegedly knew that the Japanese Air Force were going to attack the American fleet at Pearl Harbor. This was the only way he could involve America in the war.

At the time there was also a stockpile of army vehicles and guns. It was said that he ensured none of his brand-new aircraft carriers were docked at Pearl Harbor – only the old rusting warships were moored there.'

'Nat, you may be right, but it doesn't alter the fact that I have put my life on the line, and we need to think clearly about our next move.'

'Let's both sleep on it. I'll go and do some work in the gardens, it's nice and fresh out there. It may clear my head for some serious thinking. You go back to what you have to do, and let's get together again this time tomorrow,' suggested Nat.

Jack agreed that was the best thing to do, and left the room.

Nat left by the front door, Jack by the kitchen door.

Nat couldn't concentrate; he knew he had to be careful. Not look agitated or concerned. Yet he kept thinking back to his father, dying without telling him how much he missed, and loved him. Also his mother, now all alone, not realizing her son was alive and well.

It was starting to get dark, so Nat decided he'd had enough for the day. He washed his hands in the sink in the shed he had been given to store his garden implements. Slowly walking back to his apartment, he kept looking round to make sure no one was following him.

I'm now becoming paranoid, he thought.

A few minutes later he entered his apartment, where he went straight to the fridge, looking for something he could cook quickly. On reflection, he decided he didn't feel like eating. He had lost his appetite, especially when he kept thinking about his father – also the thousands of innocent victims who perished six years ago. After sitting, thinking things through for a while, he finally decided he would have his favorite meal of scrambled eggs on toast; he needed to keep his strength up. He always had this when he was a young boy, when he was worried about anything, or depressed, which, at the moment, he was.

'One microwave meal and toast coming up,' he proclaimed to the room.

He went across to the table he and Jack had sat at a few hours ago, and began to reflect back to what Jack had said. There was so much to take in, he thought. The good news, though, was that his partner Harry was still alive, and well, which made him smile.

'I need to find a way of sending a message to Harry. I wonder if I could persuade Jack to send it. Hell, why not, he's virtually put his life on the line already, and let's hope he can track down Harry's address in New York.' Nat was now feeling excited

He started searching through his kitchen drawers and cupboards, looking for something to write on, but, as expected, there was nothing. He knew the authorities at the facility were nervous that a stray piece of paper may end up in someone's backyard, miles away. He decided he would use some toilet paper, which luckily for him wasn't the quilted type. He came up with the idea of asking Jack to type the message down on a standard piece of paper – it was going to need an envelope anyway. I'll see what he says, he thought.

'But what do I write?' he asked himself. 'There's so much to tell him.' After mulling it over for a while, he came up with a answer.

'I'll just let Harry know that I'm alive and well somewhere in the desert.' He'd need Jack's help with the location, also the coordinates, if he knew them, he thought.

When he had finished, he folded the paper up into a small package, making sure it was small enough for him to swallow, if by any chance he was caught with it on him. The excitement of the day had worn him out. He just wanted to get out of this prison, and find out the truth. He also needed his sleep, as he couldn't afford to get complacent, and get caught. He was too close to a result.

He knew he had to be careful. If the government could allegedly murder thousands of its own citizens, they certainly wouldn't lose any sleep over two more.

It was a warm night so he decided to sleep in his shorts. Lying on top of the sheets, he was soon fast asleep.

September 10 2007

If he dreamt, Nat couldn't remember his dreams when he woke up, but he did try to remember the events of the day before. It all came rushing back to him, which made him sit up and search his room, just in case there was anyone unexpectedly watching over him.

'You're getting paranoid again,' he said, shaking his head.

At 8 a.m., Jack walked into Nat's room, unannounced.

'Morning Nat. Did you manage to come up with any ideas?' whispered Jack.

'Yes, but I'm going to need your help. Let's get breakfast over with first, and I'll explain my proposal,' suggested Nat.

Sixty minutes later, Nat and the rest of the group made their way back to their apartments. Jack was already seated at the kitchen table when Nat entered through the front door.

'Nat, we need to be extra careful. The chief noticed me missing for longer than usual yesterday. I told him that I had a bad stomach, and I had to use your bathroom. I can't be having a bad stomach two days in a row, so we need to be quick. Let me hear your plan.'

Nat outlined his idea of sending a message to Harry in New York, which he said he'd already written down on a piece of toilet paper, asking Jack to add the location, and, if he had them, the coordinates, also suggesting Jack type the message down on some more suitable material. But more importantly, would he be able to locate Harry's New York address? Jack acknowledged that he did know the coordinates, and also it wouldn't be too much of a problem tracing Harry's address.

'An excellent idea and I have the answer to our prayers as to a way of sending the message,' Jack said excitedly. 'My wife's flying over to New York tomorrow, and I'll suggest that I take her to the airport. She always visits her sister each year on the anniversary of 9/11. The sad thing is, her sister's been seriously ill for the last few years.' Jack stopped to compose himself before he carried on. 'Unfortunately, her sister was only fifty yards away when the Towers came down, consequently she swallowed a great deal of lead, glass fibers and asbestos. Since then her sister has had trouble breathing. The doctors have said her lungs are severely damaged, and she hasn't long to live. I know it could be dangerous involving my wife, but it's the only thing I can come up with at the moment. I can ask her to post the message to your partner when she's in New York. Hopefully, no one will be any the wiser.'

'Do you think you can persuade your wife to post it, and more importantly, will she think it's odd posting a letter from New York, instead of you sending it through the normal channels, here at the facility, which I know is out of the question, especially with the strict security procedures you must have to go through.'

'Maybe, but I think she may have too much on her mind to realize what I have asked her to do. Just think, Nat, if and when your partner receives your message, the shit will hit the fans all over the world.'

'That's sorted,' Nat said. 'Let's hope your wife doesn't say anything to anyone about the letter on her return from New York.'

'I will let you know what my wife says this afternoon when I come back to do my rounds. I can't be hanging around here too long. As I have said before, someone may start to get suspicious. And don't forget, act normal.'

'As a matter of interest, which airport are you referring to Jack? I've never, ever seen or heard a plane in all the time I've been stuck here,' commented Nat.

'EL Paso International Airport,' answered Jack. 'This whole area has been designated a no-fly zone, similar to the arrangements that are in place around The White House, The Pentagon, also Area 51 which is located somewhere in the Nevada desert. All flights have been ordered not to fly within twenty miles of the facility, for fear you would all come to realize that we had been lying to you all the time.'

'Well, fuck me, Jack,' exclaimed Nat. 'Thanks once again for your honesty, you don't know how grateful I am to you for helping me. I don't think I could have lasted much longer in this hellhole.'

'I'm not just doing it for you; it's also for the victims' families and friends, and myself. I can't carry on living a lie like this, knowing what I know. It's about time the truth was made known to the American public,' replied Jack, somberly.

Sliding the piece of toilet paper out from his trousers' pocket, handing it over to Jack, Nat reminded him to make sure he added the location plus the coordinates, also instructing Jack to flush the note away, once he had copied the text, which Jack acknowledged he would.

The next few hours were going to be the longest Nat had known. He was used to staking out houses for days on end, but this was total-ly different. If everything went to plan, he could be home, soon. Nat carried on as usual throughout the rest of the day. He changed into his work clothes, and leisurely strolled down the street. He began to prune the bushes, followed by weeding the communal gardens.

It was a warm day for September and Nat kept thinking about freedom, standing in Central Park, a bottle of ice cold beer in one hand and a large hot dog smothered with mustard in the other, watching all the young ladies walking by.

Once Jack had left Nat's room, he went straight home. Jack had been married to Angie for seven years. They had two children, a girl of five, and a boy of two. Their marriage was sound, yet Angie was always worried when Jack was posted overseas. Being on this base made her feel safer, she kept on reminding herself.

As usual, Angie was sitting in front of the television watching her favorite talk show as Jack walked in. He asked her if everything was organized for her trip in the morning, suggesting he take her to the airport, just in case she became upset, knowing her sister was seriously ill. She thanked him for his concern, saying she would like that.

Because their quarters were situated two miles from the facility, there was no way the passengers could get access to any of the families, or, more importantly, a television. The only news the detainees received was from a newsletter which was read out each week during breakfast, reporting stories from other countries, which was only bad news about civil wars, tsunamis and starvation, adding that this had come about because of the atrocities of 9/11; yet another good reason for the passengers and crew to stay here. Nothing important or revealing was divulged about what was going on around the world.

During the afternoon, when Jack was making his way back to the office before his rounds, he noticed Nat digging out a stubborn tree root. He wandered over, asking him if he needed some help, suggesting he could send for some men from the engineering department if the tree was causing him any trouble.

Nat looked up, squinting into the afternoon sun. 'No thanks, I can handle it, shouldn't take too long, it's starting to come loose now.'

At that point Jack bent down to whisper in his ear. 'Everything's fine, for the moment. I won't be giving her the letter until the last minute; it will be safer that way. You never know, Nat, the cavalry might come charging through the gates with your friend Harry leading them.'

After Jack had left, Nat carried on with his gardening, praying that Jack's wife would post the message.

September 11 2007

After driving his wife to the airport as promised, Jack helped her to carry her bags over to the check-in desk.

Angie waited in line with the rest of the passengers. There weren't too many in front of her, so she soon found herself at the front of the queue, and handing over her tickets and identification to the counter clerk. After collecting her boarding pass, she made her way over to where Jack was nervously waiting.

Right, he thought, this is it, as they cuddled each other, with Angie planting a kiss on Jack's cheek.

Jack said in a pleading voice, 'Angie, I was wondering if you could do me a big favor? I was given this letter from the chief this morning to send in the first post. I completely forgot all about it in my haste to get you here on time. I just remembered it while I was waiting back there. If you post it when you arrive in New York, it will get there sooner than if I have to take it back to the base. Do you mind?' Well, that's it, I've done it. Will she or won't she? he thought.

'Jack, you forgetful man. Only if you pay for the stamp. Only joking, here, let me have it. Who's it addressed too? Mr H. Pinch-peck, that's an unusual name.' Angie gave a piercing laugh.

'Angie, please be quiet, will you, the correspondence coming out of the base is highly confidential, you can't go shouting out names for everyone to hear,' said Jack, hastily scanning the faces around them, panicking.

'Well, if that's all the thanks I get for helping you out, you can send it yourself,' she responded, turning her back on him.

Shit, thought Jack, I've done it now. Keeping as calm and composed as possible under the circumstances, he gently turned her around to face him, and once again hugged her. After planting a kiss on both cheeks, he apologized to her in a pathetic voice.

'I'm sorry, I shouldn't have shouted at you like that. It's not easy you know, having to watch over the detainees twenty-four hours a day without getting hacked-off.' He hoped that had pacified her.

'Apology accepted, but promise me, when you get back, you'll have a word with the chief. Tell him I said you need some time off, and if he doesn't grant it, he will have me to answer too.'

'Yes, all right, I will, as soon as I get back. Come on, let's move across to the departure gate. You can go through to the lounge, and relax a little before the flight.' He gently guided her with his hand on her back.

Jack had noticed whilst he'd been groveling, that he had been sweating profusely, which surprised him that Angie hadn't remarked on his condition. Some spy I would have turned out to be, he thought.

Angie eventually made her way through to airside. Walking through the doors, she looked over her shoulder and waved. Jack returned the wave; he also let out a big sigh of relief. 'Well, that's it. Let's see what happens now.'

Slowly making his way back to his car, always checking to see if there was anything out of the ordinary, he felt as if a great weight had been lifted off his shoulders.

He was now looking forward to the morning, and informing Nat of the good news.

September 12th 2007

Nat was already up, and pacing around the apartment, waiting anxiously for Jack to appear. He kept looking at the time. 'Come on, you should be here by now,' he groaned.

Nat suddenly had an awful thought. What if the plan hadn't worked, what if the authorities had found the note? The possibilities were endless, and frightening. He was just about to walk over to check the corridor once more when he heard the squeaking of Jack's trolley.

'Phew! I can relax, I hope,' he sighed.

'Morning Nat, and don't worry, she's taken the letter,' said Jack, with a smile.

'Thanks. Now it's just a matter of time before we know whether the note's managed to find Harry,' remarked Nat.

'Be patient Nat, you've waited six years, what's a few more days?' said Jack, feeling elated for Nat.

'THE PLANE FACTS'

Insider Trading

Who were the big investors who knew 9/11 was about to happen? Although the stock trading on American and United Airlines was up by 1,200 per cent the day before 9/11, no public investigation into who profited was undertaken. Hundreds of Arab-looking Americans were rounded up and interrogated for little apparent reason, but neither the SEC nor the FBI arrested any of those who made millions from uncanny 9/11 stock trading. The FBI's reason? They say they know who made those trades, and the traders had no conceivable connection to al-Qaeda.

(Internet)

Was Flight 93 shot down?

A small furore was created in late 2004 by an off-the-cuff remark from Donald Rumsfeld during a surprise Christmas Eve visit to troops in Iraq. Recalling past terrorist events, Rumsfeld said, '… The people who did the bombing in Spain or the people who attacked the United States in New York, shot down the plane over Pennsylvania and attacked the Pentagon…'

The Pentagon later said this was simply a misstatement, not some sort of Freudian slip of the tongue. (Jim Marrs, The Terror Conspiracy)

Chapter Eleven

'Nil desperandum.'
Never despair

Horace (65–8 BC)

SEPTEMBER 12 2007, Central Park, New York, 8 a.m.

Alex began to wake up from a disturbed and often broken sleep. Ever since that tragic day in July 2005 he hadn't slept soundly, and the previous night had been no exception, especially after the unpleasant conditions he'd just endured.

Alex found it difficult at first to open his eyes, as they felt heavy. Crawling on his hands and knees, he cautiously made his way out into the open, blowing into his hands, stretching his legs, rubbing the cramps from them.

The sun was just beginning to break through the wispy clouds, giving him some additional warmth, helping to take away the chill from his elderly bones. His whole body felt damp.

Suddenly the reality of his predicament once again came home to him.

Appraising the scene around him, he noticed dozens of people jogging around the park, and he had to smile at the sight of a young man taking four well-dressed dogs for a walk.

Moving back towards their makeshift shelter, making sure he wasn't overheard, he called out to his friend. 'Larry, are you awake?' He bent over, listening out for some kind of reply or movement from the inside. It was the rustle of paper which indicated to him that Larry was beginning to stir.

'Jeez! It's c-c-cold in h-here, what's it like out there?' stammered Larry.

'Slightly warmer – the sun's just breaking through the clouds. Are you coming out? We can't be hanging around here too long.' Alex pointed out.

It was the aroma of ground coffee along with the bouquet of freshly-baked bagels and pretzels which interrupted his thoughts. Looking to see where the aroma was coming from, he spotted a street vendor by the entrance to the park.

'There is no point in starving. We must eat or we won't have the energy to move very far,' he remarked. 'Come on, Larry, there's a large hot cup of coffee, and bagel with my name on, waiting for me over there.' He glanced back towards the entrance.

Larry emerged from the tent, yawning, shivering and once again, wiping the moisture from his eyes.

'Larry, I've only a small amount of loose change on me, do you have any money?' enquired Alex.

'Just hold your horses will you, the one thing I didn't forget to bring with me in our haste was my wallet. Here, take this, twenty dollars should be enough.'

'Cheers Larry, I won't be long.'

With his collar turned up, hands thrust deep in his pockets, he trudged through the park towards the aroma of food. I must look like a bum, thought Alex, bleary eyed, unwashed and unshaven. As he was making his way across, he glanced down, only to see discarded newspapers flapping in the wind at his feet, the headlines highlighting the previous day's ceremonies.

'It seems a lifetime ago now,' he muttered.

The aroma of food, mixed with the warmth drifting in the morning air, was intoxicating. I wish I could stay here all day, he thought. He ordered two large coffees to go, and noted that the $20 was enough for a bagel and a pretzel each.

'Absolute heaven, I can't wait to sink my teeth into these,' he drooled.

Gratefully taking the order, he wished the owner a good day, and carefully carried the food and coffee, by balancing the two cups on top of the box.

Larry had already cleared away the garbage and wet litter from the area, giving them somewhere dry to sit.

'That sure looks fine,' remarked Larry, salivating.

'Sure does,' replied Alex, in a pathetic attempt to sound like an American.

Larry sneaked a look towards him, indicating his reaction, and again they burst out laughing.

After their moment of madness, finally finishing off the food and coffee, they collected their backpacks from under the tarpaulin and headed towards the park's exit, discarding the litter in the nearest waste basket on the way.

'We need to get hold of Sally and Guido, we won't bother with Moon, I've no idea where he hangs out, he just appears like magic,' commented Larry.

'Are you going to risk using your cell phone?' questioned Alex.

'No, I'll use a landline; It'll be safer, just in case Nash has managed to find out that my sister lives at the hotel, and if he has, and checks through the bills I always seem to hang on to, he'll know which cell-phone company I use.'

They'd only walked a few blocks before they came upon a vacant phone booth.

Larry started to sift through his wallet, searching for Sally's business card with all her numbers listed.

'Got it,' he declared. 'I'll try her at home first, just in case she went back for some sleep after visiting the hospital.' Larry dialed the number, and waited patiently for Sally to answer. After a minute he hung up.

'There's no one in, it's just gone over to the answering machine. I'll try her cell phone.' Larry dialed, hoping Sally was awake, or at least she had it switched on.

Sally answered after the third ring.

'Sally, it's Larry, is it alright to talk?'

'Larry, thank God you called, and yes, we can talk, I'm back at the hospital … Larry, you're not going to believe this. The bald-headed agent at the park last night, it was Nash, the one who bribed Tony for the keys … Tony managed to inform me it was him before he slipped into a coma. Also Nash followed me to the hospital, the creep … I'm sorry, but Tony's pictures have gone missing, they must have fallen out of his coat pocket during the scuffle last night.'

'Sally, please listen to me, it's important. Yes, we know about Nash, and the pictures are safe, they're with us …'

'With us? Larry, who the hell is us? Are the others with you?' interrupted Sally.

'I'm going to have to be quick as we don't want to be loitering around here too long. Do you remember the tall guy who jumped in to help you and Tony last night? The guy I was just about to introduce to you all; the Brit?'

'Yes I do, what happened to him? Larry, is he the us?'

'Yes, and it seems that before Tony fell unconscious, he somehow managed to slip the envelope with pictures into Alex's coat pocket. Also, after you left us to go with Tony to the hospital, Nash had us both taken down to the local police station for questioning, insisting we be kept there all night. Luckily for us we were released late on in the evening, and that's not all, whilst Alex – he's the guy by the way, who's standing next to me – was being questioned, the detective doing the questioning admitted that he was sympathetic to our cause, and get this, he also has a theory about Flight 77, the one that allegedly crashed into the Pentagon.' Larry paused to get his breath, bringing his thoughts back into some semblance of order.

'Sally, are you still there?'

'Yes . . . I wondered what had become of you both after I left the park. Larry, what a story this could turn out to be.'

'Oh! Sorry Sally, I forgot to ask, how is Tony? It's just with all I had on my mind, it made me completely forget to ask.'

'Don't apologize, I know what you must be going through, and thanks for asking. Tony's still in a coma, but at least he's being looked after ...'

'Sally, sorry to interrupt, but we need to meet. The detective who was with Alex last night, Harry Pinchpeck ... and don't laugh, I know it's an unusual name, God only knows how he got on in First Grade. He wants us to meet up with him tonight at four p.m. at the Grand Central Station. Will you be able to make it?'

'No one's going to stop me Larry, not with what this Harry guy has to say, plus Tony's pictures ... If I can come up with a decent story to go with them I will try to persuade my editor to print them.'

'Sally, I hope your phone's not monitored, or we will all be in the shit.'

'Larry, you know my philosophy – what will be, will be. Must run. See you this afternoon at four?' She then cut the connection.

After ending the call, Larry quickly briefed Alex on his conversation.

'Come on, it's ten thirty, so I suggest we take our time, act as though we're tourists, enjoying the sights, and we can gradually make our way over to the station.'

'Good idea,' replied Alex. 'At least I will be able to tell everybody, when I eventually return home, that I've seen something of New York.'

As they made their way cautiously across the bustling city, with Alex pausing now and again to stop and admire the brightly colored neon lights as they passed through Times Square, which gave the effect that it was night-time, Larry eventually managed to get hold of Guido, informing him of the situation, and the meeting arranged for 4 p.m. Guido said he couldn't wait, confirming he would definitely be there.

It had just turned 3.30 p.m. by the time Alex and Larry finally arrived at the station's main entrance. As they stealthily made their way inside, Alex was overawed by the sheer size of the building, also the vast number of people milling around. At the building's heart was a giant station hall, with an elaborate marble floor, which he was standing on. There were domes above him, painted with an artificial sky, with what seemed to him to be thousands of stars nesting inside the structure.

Larry mentioned to Alex that the twinkling constellations on the main concourse ceiling were drawn in reverse, as if seen from outer space, allowing New Yorkers to see something they never saw: 'a night-time sky above the Big Apple'.

Alex also noticed a giant brass clock, with chandeliers, just above the information windows.

'Magnificent,' he proclaimed, in awe.

'Come on, Alex, we can't afford to stand here all day, we need to find the others. Keep close to me; I don't want you wandering off.' Larry grabbed hold of his arm. 'By the way Alex, I'm not surprised you reacted as you did to the sight of the inside of the building. I did the same when I first came to visit the terminal – you just get used to it.'

Creeping around the marble floor, keeping as close to the walls as possible, they eventually came across Harry, who was standing next to the west wall steps, sipping a cup of coffee, closely monitoring the crowd around him.

Alex and Larry slowly moved towards him, all the while expecting to see armed agents appearing at any time. Nothing happened, to their relief.

'Am I relieved to see you both, especially you Alex. I didn't know if you'd managed to get out of the hotel in time,' remarked Harry. Alex then surprised Harry with his account of the night's escapade.

'Christ, guys, you were damn lucky to get out, but well done, it's nice to know you got one over on Nash. Now you can relax for a while, so what can I get you?' asked Harry, shaking his empty coffee cup at them. They both ordered tall black coffees, and cheekily a cheese-and-ham sandwich each, which Harry bought without any comment.

While they were waiting for Sally and Guido to appear, they gave Harry more details of their escape from the hotel, including Alex's frightening near-death experience. It wasn't too long before both Sally and Guido walked in, hand in hand, giving the impression that they were lovers. Larry stood up on his tip-toes, waving, trying to attract Sally's attention, which he did after a nervous few seconds.

187

It was Alex, Sally noticed first. She immediately made her way over to him, and in a show of gratitude embraced him.

'Thank you Alex, for your help last night, it was very brave of you.'

Alex wasn't one for hugging strange ladies, but in this case he thought he'd make an exception, and he started to enjoy it.

'No problem. How's Tony? Has there been any change since this morning?'

'No, but thanks for asking. I hope to visit him again tonight.'

'Come on guys and gals,' said Larry, anxiously, 'we need to decide what to do next, also you need to meet Harry.'

Alex performed the introductions, leaving Sally until last. It was Harry who took the initiative to talk first.

'Sally, I'm sorry about your brother being injured last night, but the pictures and his confession don't alter the fact that he was partly responsible for the collapse of the Towers and the loss of hundreds of innocent lives. But once you've heard and digested what I have to say, I will leave it up to you and your friends to decide whether to print the information or not. My theory is just that, a theory, nothing more, but I do think Tony's revelations should be brought to the attention of the American public.'

'Let me listen to what you have to say first, also I need to check out these so called pictures Tony managed to take, then we can all decide what to do next,' replied Sally. 'I don't know about you guys, but I haven't eaten for hours,' she added, 'so why don't we find a seat at Michael Jordan's Steakhouse – the last time I ate there it was fabulous. It's my treat for your help last night, and for just being here, supporting me.' There was a slight quiver in her voice.

Noticing her emotion, Larry came across, placing his arm around her, giving her some comfort and support, which Sally accepted with a grateful smile.

They managed to get seated quickly, and after they had each ordered the 'house steak', Alex secretly handed over the envelope containing the pictures and Tony's confession to Sally for her and Guido to examine.

Certain he had all their undivided attention, Harry began to re-lay his beliefs to them, knowing full well that Alex and Larry had heard it all before.

After Harry had finished, Sally and Guido sat back in their seats, stunned. It was Sally who broke the silence.

'If only we could prove your theory is correct. What a story that would make, also we're not one-hundred percent certain these pictures of Tony's are of explosives planted in the Towers. '

'Now listen up all of you,' ordered Harry, 'I am still a law enforcer, and I still have to follow the correct procedures, and uphold the law. If this ever gets back to my superiors, I will be suspended without pay, or worse, arrested and sent to jail, so you now realize how serious it could be for me.'

'You've no need to worry, Harry,' responded Alex, looking around the group, 'we're all in this together, aren't we?'

They all nodded in agreement, echoed with a 'Yes'.

'Right, it's getting late, and I need to get back to the station,' Harry informed them, 'I can't be seen with you any longer than necessary. If we bump into Nash, well, that will be it. Have you two anywhere to sleep tonight?' He looked at Alex and Larry for a response.

Both Alex and Larry shook their heads.

'You can stay with me tonight if you like,' said Harry, 'and Sally, you're also welcome to stay, you may need some TLC tonight, especially after your next visit with Tony.'

'Are you sure that's wise, Harry? Nash may come round to visit you,' queried Larry.

'Nash will be so engrossed in his search for you two, he won't even be thinking about me, so the offer still stands. My apartment?'

'Thanks Harry, we'll take you up your offer,' all three answered.

'All agreed, good. Here's my card with my address on, and my spare set of keys. Make yourselves at home until I get back some time later tonight. Sally, you may also want to think about what we need to do about the stories,' Harry concluded.

'I have a good idea already what I'm going to write, but I will think about it some more until we meet up again tonight,' replied Sally.

After saying their farewells, with Sally seeing to the bill, as promised, they went their separate ways, all looking forward to meeting again that evening.

It was at this point, Guido came across to have a private chat with Larry. 'Larry, I'm sorry, but I think it may be best for me not to get mixed up with the group any longer. My wife is becoming concerned about all the publicity we're getting, and she's worried that if my boss finds out that I'm involved with the group, and he doesn't totally agree with what we are trying to achieve, I may end up losing my job, and with four hungry mouths to feed, that's the last thing I need.'

'I can well understand your dilemma, so if you feel that way, that's fine by me, and not to worry, if anyone asks, I'll tell them that you need to spend more time with your family, which I know they will fully understand. But thanks for all your help and support over the past few years.' Larry gave Guido a friendly hug, shook his hand, and wished him all the best for the future.

'Thanks Larry, and take care of yourself.' Guido headed over towards the exit, a worried, mixed up man.

It didn't take long for Alex and Larry to find Harry's apartment. It was situated near the City Hall Park, and it was like most normal Victorian terraces, with trees lining the street, kids cycling up and down the path, being a nuisance, like most kids of today.

Once inside, and having adjusted their eyes to the darkness of the room, they both commented on the neatness, and the homely feeling to the sitting room.

'I wish my house was as clean as this,' remarked Alex.

'It looks as though he's a bit of a tidy freak,' replied Larry, 'we'll have to make sure we don't mess it up for him – he is helping us out.'

Leaving their mud-stained backpacks and shoes by the front door, they both slumped down and relaxed on the two welcoming chairs close to the open fire, which luckily for them still had some life in it.

The noise of the front door being closed woke both Alex and Larry up with a start.

'Hi guys, I hope you've both made yourselves at home?' shouted Harry.

Looking round, making sure everything was where it should be, Alex and Larry replied with a 'Yes thanks'.

'By the state of the kitchen it looks as though you haven't eaten yet?' commented Harry.

'No, we thought we would wait for you. What time is it anyway?' asked Alex.

'Nine thirty. Have you heard from Sally?' asked Harry.

'No, do you want me to phone her?' replied Larry.

'No, we can wait a while, it will take me an hour to prepare the meal, she may have arrived by then. Chilli and rice OK for you both?'

'Yes please,' came the reply.

Harry was just about to start serving the meal when there was a knock on the front door. Cautiously, he walked across to open it, first checking through the spy-hole to see who was there. 'It's Sally.' Letting her in, and taking her coat, Harry escorted her to the two waiting, hungry men.

'Hi Sally,' called Alex, 'how's Tony?'

After easing herself down into one of the chairs, she dropped her head in her hands. Tears began to stream down her cheeks, tears that had been building up over the past few hours. Quickly jumping out of his chair, Larry sat down on the arm of the chair, wrapping his arm around her shoulder, her head resting on his arm.

Harry silently went back to serving the meal, placing the plates on the table, waiting for Sally's tears to subside. Wiping her eyes with a tissue Larry had pushed into her hand, she glanced up to see three friendly faces. 'Sorry about that, guys, I've been holding it back all day, and seeing you all there, with concerned looks in your eyes, it made me start.'

'Sometimes it's best to let it all out, you'll feel much better now,' commented Larry.

'Supper's ready, so tuck in, as they say in the UK,' stated Harry, hoping to ease some of the tension in the room.

Sally excused herself, popping into the bathroom to freshen up. Returning to the table, apologizing once again, she ate her meal without further comment.

When they had finished eating, they cleared up the plates, and sat down to discuss their next move. When Sally informed them that she would like to report the findings in her newspaper, the conversation became excited.

'If it's all right with you all, I'd like to write an article about the "alleged" pictures, and if Harry's agreeable, sketch out in a separate article a "what if" scenario about Flight 77.'

'On one condition,' Harry said, staring at them all. 'You mustn't mention Nat's name. If you do, and if I'm right about him being held prisoner, they may cause him some harm, and that's the last thing I want.'

'Agreed,' said Sally.

After chatting for a while longer, Sally announced that she needed to go home to grab some sleep, before she visited Tony again in the morning. Once again Harry offered her a bed, if she wanted it.

'Thank you for your kindness, Harry, but I will be better off at home.'

They all agreed that was probably the best thing. They fixed another meeting for noon the next day at the west entrance to Central Park, where Sally said she would update them, all four deciding it would be best if they changed their meeting places each day, just in case anyone became suspicious.

'I haven't said anything to Mum yet about Tony. I'm afraid if I do, and Tony doesn't make it, it would kill her. I'm going to wait until I'm certain Tony is out of danger. Don't worry, I won't be naming him in the article about the photos, I'll just say they've come from a reliable source, as usual.'

She collected her coat and made her way home, whilst the rest of them made up their beds before going to sleep.

They were all feeling exhausted, especially Alex and Larry after spending the night before huddled together outside in the rain, and cold.

'THE PLANE FACTS'

THE COLLAPSE OF THE TWIN TOWERS

Why did the Towers collapse? No steel skyscraper had ever collapsed because of fire. Repeat: In the 100-year history of steel skyscrapers, none had ever collapsed because of fire. The steel used in skyscrapers doesn't melt at temperatures that fire can attain when burning in open air. Jet fuel is essentially refined kerosene, which burns at around 700ºC in optimal, perfectly aerated conditions. Even if the fires did get this hot, it's not nearly hot enough to melt (even significantly weaken) structural steel, which melts at around 1,535ºC. Also, given the shocking speed and neatness with which both Towers fell, the seismic evidence of small earthquakes moments before they fell, and the fact that the buildings were pulverized instead of falling in chunks, it appears that the Towers actually fell owing to a controlled demolition rather than fire. It is imperative that an investigation into what happened on 9/11 examine the readily available evidence and this unsettling possibility. **(Internet)**

THE COLLAPSE OF WTC 7

Don't forget about this building. Yet another steel skyscraper collapsed from fire that day. None ever, and then three, in one day. WTC 7 was another building in the World Trade Center complex, but it was the farthest of the buildings from the Twin Towers. It was located on the next block. Little debris struck it, and there were no large fires burning inside. Yet, as that horrendous day was ending, at 5.20 p.m., WTC 7 collapsed in a remarkable seven seconds. Nearly freefall. It fell in what appeared to be a perfect demolition. Yet the official story is that it collapsed, the whole building 'pancaking' neatly, floor by floor, to the ground. This seems impossible, both because an explosion in the basement wouldn't cause a neat implosion but rather a toppling, and because the fifty-seven floors of the building couldn't have 'pancaked' individually and still reached the ground level at freefall speed. **(www.wtcnet/videos.html)**

Though the media claims fires brought the building down, the building's owner, Larry Silverstein, later recounted the story of the collapse of this fifty-seven-story skyscraper in a PBS documentary, America Rebuilds. 'I remember getting a call from the fire department commander … I said … maybe the smartest thing to do is to pull it. And they made that decision to "pull", and then we watched the building collapse.' **(PBS Documentary)**

The term 'pull' is industry slang for the controlled demolition of a structure.

Chapter Twelve

'A single arrow is easily broken, but not ten in a bundle.'

Japanese proverb

SEPTEMBER 13 2007, Harry's apartment, New York

Alex woke up to the sounds of someone noisily moving around in the kitchen, combined with the radio playing in the background. Easing himself up off the bed, stretching his arms and back, with some difficulty, he gradually ambled off towards the commotion.

'Morning Alex, did you manage to get some sleep … scrambled eggs and toast all right?'

'Good morning to you and a big yes to the other two questions, thanks. Is Larry up yet?' asked Alex wearily, heading in the direction of the bathroom.

'No, he's still fast asleep. I'll give him a shout when the food's ready,' replied Harry.

Returning to the kitchen, Alex found Larry seated at the table with a mug of steaming coffee in his hands.

'Morning, Alex.'

'Morning, Larry.'

Helping himself to a mug of coffee, Alex examined the food on the table. Harry had set it with a large pot of steaming coffee; scrambled eggs and a stack of toast coated with lashings of butter.

'This sure looks good,' remarked Alex in his phony American accent, 'and once again, thanks, Harry.'

Smiling, Harry glanced up at him. 'You won't be getting any more help from me in future if you try that pathetic accent again.'

They all looked at each other for a second before bursting out in fits of laughter. It feels good to be able to have some fun, thought Alex. Especially after all we've been through. I need to keep my sense of humor.

It was almost 10.00 a.m. when they had finished breakfast. Harry started clearing away the dishes, stacking them in the sink.

'What time did you say we were meeting?' Harry asked.

'Noon, at the west entrance to Central Park,' replied Alex.

'Good, that gives us two hours. That's more than enough time to get there,' Harry said. It was the sound of falling envelopes on the hall floor which made them all suddenly stop what they were doing.

'Don't panic, guys, it's only one of my neighbors dropping off the mail,' said Harry.

'We're all getting a bit jumpy, let's all just calm down,' stated Alex.

After collecting the envelopes from the floor, Harry made his way to the window for some additional light in which to read them, noticing that one of the envelopes had a New York postmark, yet not recognizing the hand writing. After tearing open the envelope, he lifted out a folded piece of paper. Alex and Larry noticed that Harry had gone a deathly shade of white, his hands were trembling.

'I can't believe it. This can't be right. Oh! Christ, guys,' exclaimed Harry.

'What's the problem Harry? You look as though you've seen a ghost,' said Larry.

Harry handed over the letter for them both to read. 'I can't believe it,' he repeated, staring out of the window, shaking his head.

Alex came over to read the contents of the letter with Larry.

Harry

It's me, Nat, your partner from six years ago. No, it's not a hoax. This is serious. I have been held prisoner at a secret air base since the morning of September 11 2001. As you know I was on my way to Los Angeles from Washington on American Airlines Flight 77. The one that supposedly crashed into the Pentagon.

When we arrived at the base we were told that terrorists had flown a large number of aircraft into buildings throughout America, each containing 'dirty bombs' and for our own safety we had to stay at the base until the air was harmless. We were also informed that vast areas of America were uninhabitable, and it would remain so for a considerable number of years.

Harry, it was a missile that was fired into the side of the Pentagon, and I also know about the other terrible events that happened on 9/11.

I have a friend on the base who hopefully has managed to get this letter to you. Harry, he will be in as much danger as myself if this letter becomes public knowledge. I would please ask you not to divulge my name. If they find out it was me who has sent this letter, the authorities here will probably take me out into the far reaches of the desert, and put a bullet in my head.

Another piece of important information you need to be aware of – the pilot and crew of the flight are also being held captive.

This is where we are being held:

Biggs Air Force Base – El Paso, Texas

The coordinates:

Latitude: 31° 50′ 58″N

Longitude: 106° 24′ 47″W

Decimal degrees:

Latitude: 31.84944

Longitude: 106.37972

Always your buddy,

Nat

PS: Harry, just in case you may think this note is a wind-up, one night when we were both on a two-day stake-out, we divulged to each other our middle names. Yours happens to be Milhouse (with an 'e', unlike Nixon's). And mine is Lennon, after John Lennon.

I hope that convinces you.

HARRY – PLEASE BE CAREFUL

Alex and Larry had to read the letter more than once, as they were both astonished by its contents. Larry passed the note back to Harry, wondering if this was just a big joke.

'Harry, what do you think, is it from Nat, or is it a wind-up from some of your mates down at the station?' he enquired.

'I haven't discussed my theory with anyone in the department, only my family and closest friends, plus you four yesterday after-noon. Yet it's the mention of our middle names that gives me reason to think it may be Nat whose sent this letter. I have always hated Milhouse as a middle name; Nat and my family are the only one's who know it, apart from you two now.'

'What do you think we should do now Harry?' asked Alex.

'The first thing we have to do is try and get hold of Sally. Her "what if" scenario has suddenly taken on a new meaning,' answered Harry.

'He says he's at the Biggs Air Force Base in El Paso, let's look it up on the Internet, to see if it really exists,' suggested Alex.

Harry went straight to his computer, logging on to Google. Within seconds he had Biggs Air Force Base on the screen.

'Christ Almighty, Harry, it looks like the note could be kosher, and your buddy may be alive,' cried Alex.

'That still doesn't mean Harry's note's not a hoax. Let's phone Sally, see what she suggests we do next, also we can't afford to put her in danger by printing something we are not completely sure about,' suggested Larry.

Larry picked up his cell phone and rang Sally's number, hoping she would be awake.

'Hi Larry, what's the matter?' answered a tired-sounding Sally.

'How do you know something's wrong? I may be just ringing to check that you got home safely last night.'

'Come on, Larry, what's the problem? I can sense there's something not right in the tone of your voice.'

'Sally, remember Harry's theory? I think he may have been correct. I don't want to divulge too much information over the phone, but it's imperative that you get back over to Harry's as soon as you can?'

'Sounds interesting, I'm on my way.'

Larry closed his cell phone, informing them both that Sally was coming straight over. 'Can you imagine what would happen if this information was printed in the papers?' Larry asked.

'Look guys,' said Harry, 'we are in enough trouble as it is, so we have to be extra careful, and I'm still not sure if the note is from Nat.'

'If Sally can put together a good argument in the article, always qualifying the findings with "allegedly", we may get away with it,' advised Alex, who was now becoming excited.

During the course of the next thirty minutes, the atmosphere in the room became subdued, as each of them tried to contemplate what the repercussions would be if the stories were found to be true.

It was the rapid knocking on the door which brought them out of their musing.

'That will be Sally,' said Larry as he made his way to the door.

Dashing through the door, Sally demanded to know what all the fuss was about. Harry passed the envelope over to her, advising her it would be best if she sat down to read the note.

After digesting it, Sally looked towards Harry.

'Do you think it's from Nat, Harry?' she asked.

'Yes, I'm certain, especially with him mentioning my middle name.'

'What do you want me to do about the article now that this has arrived?'

It was Larry who answered, before Harry could reply.

'Sally, we have to be certain that you are not put in any danger when you disclose all that we know. The reaction from the American government will be explosive. No doubt they will deny everything, but if we are all agreed, I think we should go all the way, print everything.' It didn't take long for them all to agree.

'Can I take the note with me?' Sally asked Harry. 'Don't worry, I'll make sure it's safe, and I'll make certain no one sees it. I just want to pick out some of the details. I think it would be best not to divulge the location, just yet. We need to see what reaction we receive first.' The other three agreed to her suggestion.

'Look, I'm going over to visit Tony, see if his condition's improved overnight. That's where I was going before you rang. Then I'm going to sit down and type up the articles, and show them to my editor. That's when we could come up against a brick wall. If he thinks it's too risky, we're fucked ... sorry ...'

'You don't have to apologize. I'm surprised we haven't all gone mad after all we've been through during the last thirty-six hours,' replied Alex.

Sally said she would let them know the outcome of her meeting with her editor as soon as possible, hopefully some time in the afternoon. After she'd left, Alex and Larry began to sort through their backpacks for a clean change of clothes.

Harry had to report back to work, so he left them in the apartment, suggesting they relax, and to be ready for Sally's call. Larry started to watch an old black-and-white western on cable TV, which he said he had seen a dozen times. Alex sat back on the couch, reading one of the many dog-eared paperbacks Harry kept in his bedroom; annoyed with himself for not tucking one of his books in his backpack.

It was late afternoon when Larry's cell phone rang, causing them both to jump up from their seats. Larry quickly picked up the phone.

'Hi Larry, it's Sally.'

Sally gave Larry the good news that she had been given the go-ahead to print both articles in the next day's early edition.

'Woweee,' shouted Larry down the phone, 'that's great news, Sally.' Then, in a caring tone, he asked her to be careful.

'I will, Larry, and thanks for your concern,' she replied.

Alex and Larry couldn't wait for Harry to arrive home, to give him the good news.

Opening the front door, Harry shouted over for some help.

'Pizza and fries OK guys?' he called.

Alex rushed over to help Harry carry in the fragrant-smelling boxes, at the same time frantically informing him of Sally's good news.

'That's great; now let's see what response we get from the rest of the media.'

Initially they were all too excited to eat, but they eventually managed to finish off all the food.

They scraped the remnants into the waste bin, along with the pizza boxes, and called it a night, all echoing the same thought – that the next day was going to be exciting and frightening at the same time.

'THE PLANE FACTS'

September 12 2001: 'Inside Help' for Terrorists at Airport?
Billie Vincent, a former FAA security director, suggests the hijackers had inside help at the airports. 'These people had to have the means to take control of the aircraft. And that means they had to have weapons in order for those pilots to relinquish control. Think about it, they planned this thing out to the last detail for months. They are not going to take any risks at the front end. They knew they were going to be successful before they started … It's the only thing that really makes sense to me.' (Miami Herald, 12/9/01)

May 30 2002: FBI Agent Wright formally accuses the FBI of deliberately curtailing investigations that might have prevented 9/11. He is threatened with retribution if he talks to Congress about this. (Fox News, 30/5/02; more)

May 23 2002: President Bush says he is opposed to establishing an independent commission to probe 9/11. (CBS, 23/5/02) Vice-President Cheney earlier opposed any public hearings on 9/11. (Newsweek, 4/2/02; more)

March 26 2003: Though the investigation into the space shuttle Columbia tragedy cost $50 million, and the Ken Starr investigation of Whitewater and Monica Lewinsky ran to $64 million, the White House baulks at increasing funding beyond $3 million for the 9/11 Commission's investigation into the worst terror attack, ever. (Timeline, 26/3/03; MSNBC, 20/9/06)

Chapter Thirteen

'If you can't stand the heat, get out of the kitchen.'

Harry Vaughan, associated with Harry S. Truman

SEPTEMBER 14 2007, 8 a.m. – Harry's apartment, New York

Harry was the first one out of bed, dressed and on his way down to the news-stand for the early morning edition of the *New York Times*. He bought three copies as he knew they'd all be eager to read the articles.

Once through the door to his apartment, he noticed that Alex and Larry were eagerly awaiting his return.

'Here you are guys, hot off the press,' he said, throwing the papers towards them.

The silence in the room was deafening. All three stopped reading at the same time, and all three let out a big sigh.

'I wouldn't want to be in the White House at this moment in time,' commented Alex. 'Turn the TV on, will you please, Harry,' he went on. 'Let's see if there's any reaction to the articles on any of the morning talk shows.'

'Fox News is always the best for reporting,' suggested Larry.

'Fox News it is, then,' replied Harry.

September 14 2007, 7 a.m., the White House

The President was pacing behind his desk in the Oval Office, waiting impatiently. He had been woken up unexpectedly by his Secretary of Defense, who had sounded excited down the phone.

Whilst he was wondering what all the fuss was about, there came a sudden knock at the door.

'Enter, and be quick about it will you,' demanded the president.

The Secretary of Defense tentatively walked across the thick carpet, holding a copy of the first edition of the *New York Times*, which he handed over to the president, before stealthily backing away.

'Mr President, I am sorry I had to disturb you at this early hour, but I think it's crucial that you should read the articles in this mornings *New York Times*.'

Taking the newspaper, the president made his way to his large leather chair, slumping down heavily, making the chair groan under his weight.

Sliding his glasses up his nose, and resting his elbows on the desk, he started to read the articles.

American Airlines Flight 77 – have the passengers and crew come back from the dead?

A World exclusive from Sally Rider

Have they been alive all the time, and where have they been? Facts relating to the incident of Flight 77 in Washington on 9/11 have come to light. A letter has turned up, allegedly from one of the passengers, accusing the United States government of murder and deceit. According to its contents, the passengers and crew of Flight 77 have been held prisoner in a secret government facility for the past six years. The letter goes on to describe how they are being guarded 24/7 in a large complex, believed to be located somewhere in the desert. Other details disclosed state that a missile was fired at the Pentagon, and the flight was diverted to an airfield some hundreds of miles away. The authorities in charge of the facility informed the passengers and crew that terrorists had crashed a number of aircraft into buildings throughout the United States, each of them containing 'dirty bombs.' They then announced that the air around America was poisonous, making vast areas uninhabitable and it would remain so for a considerable number of years, and for their own safety they would be looked after until the air was harmless.

How the letter managed to find its way out of the facility is a mystery at the moment.

Mr President, what do you have to say to these accusations?

ALSO: A reminder of what we know, but still have no answers to after six years:

Did 4,000 Jews skip work on 9/11?

Why was the steel and debris quickly removed before there could be a significant investigation?

Not one steel-framed building in history has collapsed owing solely to fire.

How did the Towers come down so easily

when they were supposedly built to withstand earthquakes, tsunamis and truck bombs in the parking garage?

More than a dozen countries tried to warn US authorities that an attack on American soil was imminent, some days before the events.

There are standard procedures when a plane is suspected of being hijacked. Jet fighters would have been sent up to intercept within ten minutes. Had the plane then not responded, it would have been shot down.

From September 2000 to June 2001, sixty-seven planes steered off course, and the air defense systems worked as they should, and interceptors were launched.

In the first days after the terror attacks on New York and Washington, Saudi Arabia supervised the urgent evacuation of twenty-four members of Osama bin Laden's extended family from the United States. This was in a private jet, which flew around the USA days after 9/11?

... so whilst thousands of US citizens were stranded, the Government allowed this to happen ...

... When a senior United States intelligence officer was asked why no one considered detaining the members of the family, he replied,

'That's taking hostages, we don't do that.'

A growing number of whistleblowers within the federal government have pointed to evidence that various agencies were well aware of the possibility of attack but were prevented from mounting investigation by senior officials.

Within a few hours after the 9/11 events, the FBI had released names and photos of the suspected hijackers, although later many of those named turned up alive in the Middle East.

We need a response, and now!

****

Evidence of controlled explosives in the Towers?

Another World exclusive from Sally Rider

I have another explosive story for you. What is the government hiding? Are they going to come clean? More information that has come to light during the past two days indicates that there has been another cover-up over the past six years by the President and his advisors.

Evidence from a reliable source has been passed on to me. This individual, who at the moment doesn't want to be named, was employed at the Twin Towers. He states that he was approached by a government agent a few days prior to 9/11. My source was ordered to keep away from the Towers for at least two weeks. He didn't trust the agent, so he took it upon himself to go back to work, on the morning of 9/11. He arrived shortly before the plane crashed into the North Tower. His first instinct was to help the walking wounded. Whilst doing so he heard the second Tower being hit. He couldn't remember how long he was inside the Towers, but whilst he was there, he heard a number of explosions going off above him.

My informant tells me that he managed to collect his camera from his office, and with the help of a fleeing colleague managed to find and take a number of pictures of two unexploded devices.

Why did the agent send my informant away days prior to 9/11?

Were all the hundreds of eye-witnesses correct in saying that they heard small explosions prior to the Towers collapsing?

Did agents, along with other accomplices, plant the devices?

ALSO, was there a 'power down' over the weekend before 9/11?

Also, why haven't these questions been answered?

Why did several of the F-16's, which are normally airborne and going at full speed in under three minutes, all take longer to get up on 9/11?

Physical evidence suggesting that what hit the Pentagon could not have been a Boeing 757 coexists with the testimony of several witnesses to the effect that whatever did hit the Pentagon was far smaller than a 757.

Why on the same day on which jet fighters were unable to protect the Pentagon from an attack by a single airplane did the missiles that normally protect the Pentagon also fail to do so?

The only plane that was evidently shot down, Flight 93, was the only one in which it appeared that the passengers were going to gain control.

The evidence that Flight 93 was shot down after passengers were about to gain control coexists with the fact that the flight control transcripts for this flight were not released.

That coincidence coexists with the fact that when the cockpit recording of Flight 93 was released, the last three minutes were missing.

Evidence showing that the US government had far more specific evidence of what was to occur on 9/11 than it has admitted coexists with evidence that it actively blocked investigations that might have prevented the attacks.

****

'How the hell did those damn photographs get into her possession, and what's this about a goddamned letter from the base? And look … just fucking look at all those questions she's asking, again,' shouted the president. 'Who is this bitch reporter, Sally Rider? Never heard of her. This is Goddamned serious. I want this reporter's work phone, fax, email, BlackBerry, if she has one, home phone, tapped right away … better still, put her under surveillance, that way we may be able to find out where she is getting her information from. We need to find out soon if these allegations are genuine, or is it just the paper trying to increase its sales figures.'

'Mr President, the problem is … it's all true, and we know it is. We do have the passengers and crew of Flight 77 held in a secure facility, and it also seems that Nash didn't manage to find the pictures after all. I'm surprised all this hasn't come out in the open before now. How we have managed to keep it a secret for so long beats me …'

'Shut up, will you,' shouted the president, interrupting the SoD. 'I need to think about this very carefully.' Raising his worried body off his chair, the president made his way over to the window overlooking the Rose Garden.

'How in God's name did that letter get out of the complex? I've been told repeatedly that the security in there is the best in the whole damn country. It doesn't look like that to me, does it to you?' he asked, staring at the SoD.

'No, sir, it doesn't. I've got my people looking into it right now,' the SoD replied, sweat slowly trickling down his spine, causing him to shiver.

'Listen, I will find out who is responsible for this, and when I do, they will be severely dealt with,' screamed the president. 'We can't be having a repeat of these same allegations year after year.'

'Sir, there is one other important matter I must raise. I have already checked out this reporter, Sally Rider. She's heavily involved with the group who call themselves the Plane Facts. It's the same group that caused a disturbance the other night on the anniversary of 9/11 at Ground Zero. She is also the sister of Tony Rider, the same Tony Rider who was injured when Nash tried to arrest him, the one who took the photographs in the Towers, sir.'

He knew the president was concentrating, as he had become still and quiet for the moment.

'This is more serious than I thought. Call an urgent meeting, but only with those who know the exact details about our involvement. It's imperative we nip this in the bud right away. I also want the names, addresses, telephone numbers and places of work of all the members of this group available for the meeting. Did you mention to me before that one of the group was British?'

'Yes, sir, Alex Monroe. He's over here on vacation,' replied the SoD.

'Well, one thing's for sure, you have been busy, well done. Now let's get this show on the road. We need to sort this mess out over the next twenty-four hours.' With those parting words, the president left the Oval Office.

The Secretary of Defense made his own exit, heading straight to his office to make an urgent call to the one person who hopefully may be able to shed some light on the situation.

'THE PLANE FACTS'

The clean-up looked like a cover-up:-

Why was the debris from the Pentagon and the World Trade Center destroyed immediately after 9/11? Normally forensic teams examine all evidence from a crime scene. Yet the steel from the collapsed WTC was immediately shipped to Korea and China, where it was melted down within days. That steel would've indicated whether the buildings collapsed owing to fire, something that had never happened and that would mandate drastic redesign of tall buildings. That steel also would've told the tale if the buildings had collapsed owing to another cause – like an explosive demolition. It was the same at the Pentagon: the surprisingly small amount of debris was swiftly whisked away to an undisclosed location.

(9/11 cover-up)

Vice-President Richard Cheney was placed in charge of anti-terrorism training and military preparedness exercises by Bush on 8 May 2001. This gave him command authority during the 9/11 attacks because as many as nine war game exercises involving military and intelligence agencies were occurring simultaneously.

(9/11 cover-up)

Chapter Fourteen

'We report, you decide.'

Fox News slogan

SEPTEMBER 14 2007, Fox Studios, 9 a.m.

'Good morning viewers, my name's Randy Myers and welcome to *Fox News Forum*. Our guest this morning is the Democrat Senator Gerry Helleman from Detroit, who has kindly accepted our invitation, at short notice, may I add, to discuss the astonishing revelations which have appeared in this morning's edition of the *New York Times*.

'Just in case any of our viewers haven't read or heard about these articles, I will quickly go through them for you. The first story states that one of the passengers from the aircraft which supposedly crashed into the Pentagon, American Airlines Flight 77, has somehow managed to send a letter to a friend in New York. It is understood that he, along with the rest of the passengers and crew, are being held captive at a government facility.

'The second story accuses the American government of planting explosives in both Towers, days prior to the attacks, with photographs to prove it.

'Senator, these are very serious allegations. What's your reaction to them?'

'My reaction, Randy, when I first read them, was total shock. I was also worried for our fine, upstanding nation. What would the backlash be if these reports were found to be true? I am sorry to say that I was also surprised. Surprised that evidence has now suddenly come to light after six years surrounding the hijackings, and the cowardly attacks on America on 9/11.

'I am also conscious of the fact that the evidence has yet to be proven, but as everyone is aware, I have been repeatedly claiming that this government was either party to the attacks, or had prior knowledge of them, a claim which they chose to ignore. Randy, for an event of this magnitude to be successful, it would have to involve dozens of high-ranking individuals. If these stories are true, and this was made known, it would be news that would explode around the globe in minutes. Its ramifications would be enormous, economically, politically, and also because of the horror of our government's alleged involvement, eruptions would be heard all over the world …' The senator was now in his element, using the broadcast as a platform, making his feelings known to the vast viewing audience.

'… No one would trust their government any more, if the most powerful country in the world could do such a thing to its own people, the repercussions, which would no doubt reverberate around the globe, would be catastrophic.'

'Senator, that is one hell of an assumption, yet we have always been aware of your stand on these issues. But if these stories are found to be true, will the President come out and admit to it? Will he be impeached; can he be arrested for murder? There are many questions that we need to ask this administration, but more importantly, do we now need an unbiased public inquiry?'

'Randy, we can't all of a sudden start scaremongering, going around accusing people of murder. Firstly, we must find this so-called government facility, and soon, if it does exist, and secondly, we need to talk to this person who claims the government secretly planted explosives in the Towers, verify the pictures. Randy, let's not lose sight of the fact, out there are families who have been suddenly confronted with this amazing news. They have had six years of grieving, six years of not knowing the truth. Let's not forget them.'

'One thing's for sure, Senator, we haven't heard the last of this. Thank you for your comments and once again for accepting our invitation to discuss these revelations.'

The first thing the three men noticed on the screen was Sally's picture in the background of the studio; secondly, the interviewer, discussing Sally's articles with what seemed to them to be a senior government official.

Making sure his eyes never left the television screen, Larry reached out for his cell phone on the table.

'We need to reach Sally, and fast,' he declared, punching numbers, and in his haste having to dial three times to connect.

'Sally, it's Larry. Where are you?'

'I'm heading over to the hospital. Why, what's wrong? I picked up a paper on the way. I can't imagine there being any reaction to the articles yet. Or has there?'

'Sally, they're debating your articles on *Fox News Forum*. Just wait a second, let me see who the guest is. Christ, Sally, it's Senator Helleman, and from what he's saying, it seems he's on our side. Sally, you need to be careful. I can imagine Nash will appear at the hospital at any moment, assuming you will be visiting Tony, and knowing how Nash works, he will probably take you in for questioning. How far are you from the hospital?'

'I'm just driving into the parking lot now. Listen, Larry, if I'm lucky, the agent guarding Tony's door may not be aware of the articles, or the debate on the TV, so I'm going to risk it, then I'll get the hell out of here. OK?'

'Sally, when you leave, I suggest you use either the side or rear exit, and make your way over to Harry's apartment, we are all still here,' suggested Larry, concern in his voice.

'Give me an hour, will you, I need to make sure Tony is on the mend. It looks as though I may not have the opportunity to visit him again for a while. See you soon.' Ending the call, Sally casually made her way through reception to Tony's room, unheeded.

Larry dropped his cell phone on the chair, relaying his conversation back to Alex and Harry.

'Harry, I hope you didn't mind me instructing Sally to come over here. It was the first thing that came to me.'

'It's fine. Anyway, at least we'll be together.'

While they were waiting, Harry decided to make some fresh coffee. Alex showered and shaved, whilst Larry paced the room, worrying about Sally. He decided to check the corridor leading to the front door, hoping Sally would appear. He didn't have long to wait. The emergency exit door to his left started to creep open, with Sally's worried face appearing around the side. Feeling somewhat relieved at seeing Larry, she quickly sprinted down the corridor towards him.

'Thank God you're safe,' cried Larry, ushering her quickly into the room, slamming the door shut.

'That was close. I'm not sure, but I think I noticed Nash's car pulling up in the hospital car park as I was leaving. Don't worry, I don't think he saw me. Anyway, I've borrowed my mum's car, so he wouldn't have known it was me leaving.'

'How's Tony?' asked Harry.

'No change, which the doctors said was a good sign – at least he's no worse.'

After calming down, Larry updated Sally on the debate on the television.

'Well, at least we have someone on our side who has a voice in the Senate,' said Sally.

'Come on, we need to contact Fox studios right away. We need Senator Gerry Helleman's help,' suggested Alex.

'What a good idea Alex, you're a genius,' cried Sally, wrapping her arms around him. Alex was now becoming used to this show of gratitude, which he didn't mind.

Harry quickly searched around for the telephone directory, which he found in one of the kitchen drawers. Flicking through as fast as he could, he eventually found what he was looking for and dialed the number, handing the phone over to Larry.

Larry informed the switchboard that he had vital information relating to the morning's debate about the articles in the *New York Times*, and he needed to speak to the senator, urgently. He was put through to the receptionist, who informed him that they were not allowed to put through calls to guests, especially senators. She did mention though that the senator was to be a guest in an afternoon talk show, and if they wanted to leave a message they would have to go through the senator's personal secretary. Larry insisted that she pass on his message to the senator's secretary as soon as possible, adding that the writer of the articles they had been discussing was the person who wanted to speak to the senator. The receptionist said she would, if she had time, as the reaction from the earlier program had caused a large number of people to congregate outside the building and in the foyer, which she had to oversee.

As Larry was passing on the information to the rest of the group he slowly placed Sally's hands in his. 'Let's just think about this for a moment. If and when we sit down with the senator, and pour out all the facts, we'll all be putting ourselves in danger.'

Sally had already come to that conclusion when he was on the phone.

'Look guys, I am fully aware of the situation, including the dangers, but we've made it this far. Let's see what the senator has to say when we show him the evidence, and then we can decide what action to take.'

'Let's hope he will see us,' replied Larry, shrugging his shoulders.

Both Alex and Harry agreed they wanted nothing more than that the truth be known.

'If you're up for it, I am,' exclaimed Sally. 'Where's the studio?'

Checking the directory, Sally wrote down the address. 'It's in the Rockefeller Center, on Sixth Street.'

'It's not too far. Come on, let's grab a cab before we change our minds. We can work out a strategy on the way,' said Larry.

'You three go,' suggested Harry, 'I've got to go into work, but if I hear of anything, I'll phone you straight away. In the meantime, I suggest we meet up again here tonight. Everybody agree?'

They all said yes to his suggestion.

Pulling up in front of the studios, they were shocked to see the large number of people milling around on the sidewalk. Most of them were gathered near to the main entrance, waving placards and shouting.

'Looks like there could be trouble,' commented the cab driver, 'are you sure you have the correct address?'

'It's the correct address all right, and don't worry, I don't think there will be any trouble. In fact, I think history's in the making here today,' replied Larry.

After paying the fare, they made their way to the main entrance, fighting their way through the crowd of people. On leaving the apartment, Harry had handed Sally a baseball cap to hide her face, as he didn't want anyone to recognize her going into the building. As she was approaching the desk in reception, she turned to face Alex and Larry.

'We need to find the senator's secretary as quickly as possible. If the senator realizes that the crowd out here is for him, he may become nervous, and refuse to speak to me. You two find out which studio the senator is in while I try and locate his secretary, OK?'

They both nodded.

'Hi, good morning,' Sally greeted the girl at the desk. 'My friend rang earlier asking if I could meet with Senator Helleman.' She bent across the desk to be near to the girl, whispering, 'I'm Sally Rider from the *New York Times*.' That was it, if anyone had heard her, no doubt she would be besieged by reporters and their camera crews. Luckily no one heard, and the young receptionist didn't respond to her name.

'I did eventually find the senator's secretary, and as you can imagine, after this morning's program, everyone wants to talk to him. But he did say the senator would see you for fifteen minutes, no more, so if you wouldn't mind sitting down over there by the water fountain I will inform his secretary that you've arrived. I thought I saw you arrive with two gentlemen, is that so?'

'Yes, they have just called into bathroom – weak bladders, it's their age,' she said, smiling.

Just then Larry came round the corner, with a grin on his face. 'I've checked, the senator's still here. Some rookie floor manager let me have a peep into the studio where he is waiting to be groomed.'

'Yes, I know, they are trying to contact his secretary now. Hopefully we will be able to go somewhere a bit more private. If the crowd out there spots him, we may have a riot on our hands.'

'You know what, Sally, reading the placards, listening to their comments, I honestly believe they're on our side. They don't seem to be angry with him; they look to me to be on the senator's side.'

Sally heard the sound of footsteps down the corridor. Turning her head, she looked up to see a grey-haired, well-dressed gentleman coming towards her.

'If you wouldn't mind following me, please, the senator will see you now,' the man said, informing her that he was the senator's personal secretary.

As they both stood up, the secretary stopped and put his hand on Larry's shoulder. 'I'm sorry, but the senator said he would only speak to the young lady, there was no mention of this gentleman attending.'

Larry was about to protest when Sally intervened. 'Larry, you needn't worry about me, I'll be fine. You know who I'm with, and the main reason we came here was to find someone who would listen to us. Hopefully he's the one.'

Larry knew she was right, so he turned around and sullenly sat back down on his chair.

'Fingers crossed,' said Sally over her shoulder as she disappeared into a side room.

Alex sauntered around the corner, balancing three Styrofoam cups in his hands.

'Cup of coffee Larry? Where's Sally?'

'You've just missed her, she's just popped into one of the rooms down the corridor,' answered Larry.

'Fingers crossed, then,' replied Alex.

Larry took a coffee from Alex, and started to wander up and down the corridor, looking worried.

To Larry's relief, the door slowly swung open to reveal Sally walking out with a silver-haired gentleman, who was immaculately dressed in a black pin-striped suit with an open-neck white shirt, revealing a deep red cravat exploding out of the top. Both of them had smiles on their faces, and when they parted he bent down to kiss her on both cheeks, casually whispering in her ear.

Sally confidently walked across to a nervous-looking Alex and Larry.

'Well, how did you get on?' asked Alex.

'Let's get away from here first, please. But let me just say one thing – we have at last found someone who is willing to listen. Come on.'

Larry was eager to find out what had been said and his patience was waning.

'Will you please stop, Sally, I think we are far enough away not to be noticed. What was his reaction?'

Gathering her thoughts, Sally spent the next ten minutes relaying to them the conversation she'd had.

'He is totally convinced that there is a cover-up, and the current American government were behind the events surrounding 9/11. But trying to get the truth out was a different matter altogether. He also said that the president and his advisers may plead the Fifth Amendment – that way we wouldn't find out anything. What we need is a whistleblower, and with the amount of media coverage, along with the outcry from the public, someone may come forward.'

Larry and Alex stood there, taking it all in.

'A whistleblower,' Alex said. 'If you take into account the incidents on the day, I would imagine there would be someone out there with a guilty conscience. Did he say anything about pursuing the letter about the facility or the photographs?'

'At this moment in time, we only have Tony's word about the explosives, and as for the letter; it could be a hoax. So in the meantime the senator is asking his friends in Congress to assist him. You know what? I don't think the people of this country realize how many members of Congress believe there was a cover-up, or an "inside job", as they are saying on Capitol Hill. They have just been too frightened to voice their opinions.'

Alex was now becoming confused and frightened.

'Look, you two, I know how desperate you are in finding out the truth, but I'm just here on vacation, I don't want to be involved in all of this, I just want to go home. I'm sorry.'

'I can well understand your feelings Alex,' said Larry, 'but to be honest with you, I don't think you'll be able to leave the country. No doubt Nash would have alerted all the air and seaports, ordering them to arrest you on sight. As far as he is concerned, you have the incriminating evidence, and whilst he thinks that, you are unfortunately a wanted man. I'm sorry, Alex.'

'Shit. Come on then, let's get back to Harry's, we need to let him know what's been happening,' said Alex, sullenly.

Pulling her cap down to cover her face, they all walked out of the entrance to the studios towards the road, before hailing a cab to take them back to Harry's apartment.

Harry had only been in his office ten minutes before the phone rang on his desk. He glanced down towards the ID screen. It was the chief, Detective Jordan Holmes. He answered after the third ring. 'Good morning Chief, what can I do for you?'

Holmes never wasted time getting to the point. 'Harry, get yourself in my office right away.' He abruptly slammed the phone down.

After putting his jacket on, Harry ambled through the bustling squad room to find out what the chief had to say.

Knocking on the door, and walking straight in, to his surprise there was another person in the room. Harry suddenly recognized him; it was the mayor of New York.

'Let's not stand on ceremony. Mayor, this is Detective Harry Pinchpeck. Harry, this is the mayor of this fine city of New York.' Harry tentatively sauntered across the room to shake the mayor's hand.

'Mayor, Harry here came into contact with these so-called troublemakers the other night, so he can easily identify them all. We are aware we cannot just throw our taxpayers into jail when we feel like it, but now they have gone one step too far – don't you agree, Harry?'

After taking a deep breath Harry began to explain his situation. 'Chief, Mr Mayor, over the past six years I have listened to the group's concerns, and heard all the facts, which, I may add, have also been reported in the press and published in hundreds of books. I honestly feel that these people may be correct in what they are saying. But at the end of the day I have sworn to uphold the law.'

The chief waved his beefy hand in the air, as if trying to brush Harry's comments away.

'Harry, have you read this morning's articles in the *Times* about a so-called government facility? Also some alleged photographs of explosives planted in the Towers?'

'No, but I did overhear a number of people discussing the articles as I was making my way to the office this morning, but to be honest, Chief, it sounds a bit far fetched, don't you think?' Harry knew he had to show his allegiance to them both.

The chief handed Harry the morning's edition of the *New York Times*. 'Just check out the stories on the front page.'

Harry took the paper and collapsed into the chair opposite the chief's desk, knowing full well the contents of the articles.

'Where is this reporter getting her information from, Chief? No one else is printing these allegations,' Harry pointed out.

'Well, I can tell you where she got the one about the explosives. Her brother, Tony,' announced the chief. 'We think he may have made it up so he could help out his big sister with an explosive story.'

Harry couldn't believe what he was hearing. They must be using Tony to get to Sally; that was the only conclusion he could come to.

'That's a serious allegation, Chief, what evidence have you got?' Harry was now becoming worried. He needed to find Sally and the rest of the group to let them know the situation.

'Son,' the mayor interjected, 'we are fighting a war against terrorism in this fine country of ours, so if the President and his advisers has any reason to believe that this guy is lying, well, that's good enough for me and the chief. Got It?'

'Well,' interrupted the chief, 'Tony Rider won't be going too far. He's in hospital, in a coma, I believe. And according to Nash, Tony has been on the wanted list since 9/11. It seems that he's been trying to blackmail the government. The guy was up to his neck in gambling debts, extorting money from Nash by forging those photographs.'

Harry knew about the gambling debts; he also knew the pictures were genuine – or he hoped they were. They were using Tony as a scapegoat.

'I would suggest you go out there and try and find out how this Sally Rider managed to get her hands on this so-called letter, also those dammed pictures,' said the mayor. 'Earn your pay, son.'

Harry hated anyone calling him 'son', especially an overweight politician who wouldn't be able to find the door without his help.

'Thank you for the advice mayor. Now, if you will both excuse me, I will go and earn my dollar. Good day to you both.'

Harry stormed out of the office, slamming the door behind him, causing the glass in the door frame to shake.

He knew he had to get home as quickly as possible to see if the rest of them had returned from the studios.

Harry usually made his way home by the subway, but in this case he needed to get home quickly, so he stopped a cab, and he was home in next to no time.

There was no sign of anyone in the apartment, so he started to make a spaghetti Bolognese for supper. He needed to concentrate, and cooking a meal always helped him.

As he was finishing preparing the meal, all three came in together.

'You had me worried there for a while,' said Harry. 'You'd better all sit down before I tell you what happened to me this morning – you're not going to like it.'

Harry went over the details of the meeting he'd had with the mayor and the chief, waiting for a reaction, especially from Sally.

'I'm not surprised,' responded Sally, 'especially after what's been discussed on the TV, and that was a cheap trick trying to say Tony had been blackmailing Nash.' She hoped he hadn't.

Whilst eating their supper the group updated Harry on Sally's meeting with the senator, Harry getting excited once he'd heard the good news about the senator's offer of help.

Once the realization of their predicament had sunk in, they all sat back and relaxed, wondering what to do next. It was Alex who broke the spell.

'So what do we do now?' he asked. 'Hellfire, I seem to be repeating myself.'

'The first thing we'll do is finish our meal. Then you need to get out of here – if you are caught in my apartment, I will lose my job, and probably be arrested for harboring criminals,' stated Harry.

'We're not criminals, for God's sake,' shouted Alex.

'We are at the moment. You see, Alex, we have something the government desperately want,' responded Sally, concern evident on her face.

'While I'm washing the dishes, I would suggest you both collect your belongings and be ready to leave as soon as you've finished. I'm sorry, but there is no alternative,' apologized Harry.

'We know that, Harry, don't apologize. Come on, let's not overstay our welcome,' ordered Larry.

'Alex, it may be better if you keep hold of this,' said Sally, handing over Harry's letter. 'Following my articles, they'll be out there looking for me as well as you.'

Alex was stunned, but he reluctantly took the note from her, placing it safely inside the envelope with Tony's, along with the photographs; and suddenly wondering where they were going to sleep that night. Hopefully not outside again, he thought.

Once they were all ready; carefully easing open the door that led to a small communal garden at the back, Harry glanced around, looking for any conspicuous characters.

'Before you leave, we'll need to decide where to meet up tomorrow – somewhere well away from here,' he said.

'Ellis Island,' chipped in Sally. 'It's a long way from here – it will also give Alex an opportunity to see some of the sights.'

'That's fine by me, if it's OK with the rest of you? Ellis Island it is, then,' Alex said cheerfully.

Harry, once again checking that the coast was clear, wished them all good luck. Alex responded by thanking Harry for his hospitality, adding, 'See you later'.

Creeping slowly down the steps towards the rear of the garden, listening for anything out of the ordinary, they safely made it to the gate which opened out to an alley that ran the full length of the back of the houses. Larry held up his hand, indicating for Alex and Sally to wait, whilst he checked out the immediate area.

Relieved that they were safely on their way, Harry locked the back door and made his way across to the kitchen sink, hoping that nothing untoward happened to any of them.

'THE PLANE FACTS'

Non-existent Air Defence:-

Why weren't air force planes sent up to intercept the hijacked planes? In the year before 9/11, jet fighters were sent up routinely (at least sixty-seven times) whenever, according to the FAA's own standard operating procedure manuals, an airliner went off course by two miles or by fifteen degrees. On 9/11, the FAA was notified by a frantic stewardess that Flight 77 had been hijacked fully twenty-five minutes before it crashed. The Pentagon has the most advanced radar and air defence in the world, and Andrews Air Force Base, which is charged with defending the Pentagon and has fighter jets on ready alert, lies a mere eleven miles away (one minute's flying time). The plane that supposedly struck the Pentagon was known to be hijacked fully forty-five minutes before it crashed after two other planes had already been hijacked – yet it flew unchallenged over the most protected airspace in the world. (9/11 cover-up)

Chapter Fifteen

'Nearly all men can stand adversity, but if you want to test a man's character, give him power.'

Abraham Lincoln (1809–65)

SEPTEMBER 14 2007, WHITE HOUSE, 9.05 a.m.

For two hundred years, the White House has stood as a symbol of the Presidency, the United States government, and the American people. Its history, and the history of the nation's capital, began when President George Washington signed an Act of Congress in December 1790 declaring that the federal government would reside in a district 'not exceeding ten miles square … on the River Potomac'.

The SoD had only been seated at his desk for a short while after leaving the president, when the Vice-President stormed into his office, his face ashen with worry.

'You'd better come with me to the Oval Office. There's a debate on Fox News which we should all witness – the others are on their way,' said the VP, and turning to leave, not giving the SoD time to react to the intrusion.

The President tilted his head down so he could look over the top of his glasses at the people who had entered his office. Standing in front of him was his Vice-President, the Secretary of Defense and, making up the group, the former National Security Adviser; now the current Secretary of State, all looking as though they'd sucked on a lemon.

'I don't like it when you all suddenly storm in here unannounced,' remarked the president, scanning the faces with a quick jerk of his head.

The Secretary of State took it upon herself to turn on the television, tuning to Fox News. 'Mr President, I think you should listen to this.'

The four of them stood transfixed in front of the screen, concentrating on what the senator was discussing. The program had only been on the air for a few minutes so they hadn't missed much of the debate …

It was the VP who broke the tense silence in the room, once the debate had finished.

'Mr President, you must seriously consider addressing the nation – calm the waters, pacify the citizens of America. You have to convince the American people that what's being printed in the papers and discussed on the news is a total fabrication, adding that the perpetrators will be brought to justice, and dealt with severely …'

'Don't tell me what I need to do. I can see what is required, I will deal with it, and in my own way,' interrupted the president, his face turning red with anger.

The SoD tried to cool the situation. 'Sir, we have known each other for a number of years, and I have always looked up to you for help and guidance, yet I'm afraid in this case you must consider the possibility that the truth may come out. We only need one whistle-blower to verify what's being said is true, then we could all end up being charged with murder,' he stated, trying to keep his voice from trembling.

'Look, we all knew at the time what we were getting ourselves into when we organized the hijackings, and I am certainly not going to let some young upstart of a reporter have me shaking in my boots. Got it?' responded the president.

'Yes sir. So what are you intending to do?' asked his SoS, sweat starting to slowly trickle down between her breasts.

'Firstly, the most important issue at this moment in time is for us not to panic. Secondly, I want you to have a serious talk with the editor of the *Times*, inform him in no uncertain terms that he must divulge Sally Rider's sources, and then you need to put all available resources into finding her. I take it you haven't managed to find her yet?' said the president, staring over the top of his glasses at his SoD.

'No, sir, we are still searching,' answered a very nervous SoD. 'I will get on to that right away,' he went on, 'and in the meantime we also need to put out an A.P.B. on the rest of the group, especially this Alex Monroe character. As we are all aware, he's from England on vacation. I will just remind you, just in case you have forgotten; we tried to apprehend him at his hotel the other night but he somehow managed to escape. We are certain he was warned. That's still being investigated. The others are Larry Underwood, an ex-firefighter who I have found out recently was in one of the Towers when it collapsed. There is a cab driver in the group, known as Guido – he was dropping off a fare when the first plane hit the North Tower. There is one other person, he goes by the name of Moon, he assisted Larry Underwood after he was injured in the Towers, since then they have become friends. I am sure it's possible to obtain pictures of them all. There are a few others, but they are just bit players who are no threat to us. Mr President, I have a great deal to organize. I will instruct the heads of the agencies to meet up for an emergency meeting today to work out a strategy. Once that's in place I will report back to you with any news. If you don't mind, I will take my leave.' The SoD didn't wait for a response, but moved away from the group, quickly closing the door behind him. When he was some way clear of the Oval Office he let out an almighty sigh of relief.

The president started pacing around the room, alternately glancing out of the window and staring back at his colleagues.

'We will meet again in twenty-four hours, in the situation room. Let's hope we will have some good news to report. I've still got sixteen months left as President, and I am not going to go through all this shit again. We have to nip this in the bud, now. Go about your business, but please give the Secretary of Defense as much help as you can in finding a way of ending this debacle.'

Looking at one another, coming to the conclusion that the meeting was over, they slowly made their way to the door, saying their goodbyes, leaving the president standing by the window, staring up at the sky, unaware that he was all alone.

As the Secretary of Defense was heading down the corridor, he spotted Nash leaning against the wall by his office door.

'I hope it's good news,' the SoD said.

'Couldn't be better,' Nash replied, smirking.

The SoD asked his secretary to hold all his calls as they were entering his office, securely locking the door behind them.

'What's the good news you've got to tell me then? By God I need some, especially after what I've just been through,' said the SoD.

'I've been a busy man; you're going to be really proud of me. I have always known Harry Pinchpeck was sympathetic to the so-called Plane Facts group, so I've been delving into his past, and what do you know? His previous partner was one of the passengers on Flight 77, and if I was a betting man, which I'm not, as you know, I wouldn't be surprised if this so-called letter came from him.'

'Nash, for God's sake, keep your voice down. You never know who's listening. There are only a few of us who know the truth about Flight 77, and if that was made common knowledge, they will cut off our balls.'

'Ouch, nasty!' cried Nash with a squeamish look on his face.

'So what are you thinking of doing now, Nash?'

'I'm going to pay a visit to Harry's apartment. I have a feeling he is harboring the rest of the group, and if I'm right, Harry Pinchpeck is going to have a lot of explaining to do, don't you think?'

'Certainly, but be careful Nash, we can't be having any more bad press at the moment. If Sally Rider is there, we may end up in tomorrow's papers.'

'Trust me, will you? Our secret is safe. Oh! By the way, my youngest boy is starting college soon, and I could do with a little help with the fees. I don't think that will be a problem, do you?'

'Nash, don't push your luck. The President isn't too keen on you at the moment. Get me some results, and I will see what I can do.'

'That's very kind of you. We wouldn't want anyone knowing what really happened, now would we?' Nash grinned.

'Nash, get out of my office before I have you thrown out,' cried the SoD.

Nash realized he'd managed to upset him, which had been his intention from the start.

The extra money would come in handy, he thought, as he fancied another condo in Florida, under an alias – he wasn't that stupid to use his own name.

'Next stop, Harry's place,' he said to himself. 'That's when the fun will begin.'

Once Nash had arranged for half a dozen agents to meet him at Harry's apartment in the evening, he made his way out of the White House's main gate, after organizing a cab to take him to the airport; catching the first flight to New York.

By the time he arrived at JFK, it was just after 6 p.m.

He collected his black Chevy suburban from where he had left it in the long-stay car park at the airport, and promptly made his way over to Harry's apartment, with the intention of confronting him, and hopefully the rest of the group that had caused so much grief and anguish, not only to him, but also the President.

Just as Nash was about to hammer on Harry's front door, Larry, Alex and Sally were making their way down the path of the back garden towards the gate.

'THE PLANE FACTS'

May 2001: For the third time, US security chiefs reject Sudan's offer of thick files on bin Laden and al-Qaeda. A senior CIA source called it 'the worst single intelligence failure in the business'. (Guardian, 30/9/01; more)

Mayor Giuliani was warned of the collapses of the Towers.

The core of WTC 1 failed below the third floor.

An explosion was reported on Flight 93.

The Secret Service were not concerned about the safety of the President on 9/11.

Dick Cheney left Washington undefended on 9/11.

The President was in no hurry to get out of Booker Elementary School. (Internet)

Chapter Sixteen

'The truth is rarely pure, and never simple.'

Oscar Wilde (1854–1900)

SEPTEMBER 14 2007, LANGLEY AIR FORCE BASE, WASHINGTON, 9.10 a.m.

It was an exceptionally hot September morning, which was why most of the windows in the games room had been left wide open. However, the sound of Jets taking off and landing close by made it almost impossible for anyone to hear what was being debated on the television; which the majority of the servicemen in the room were trying to do.

'Turn it up, will you,' came a booming voice from the back of the room.

Moving across to the television, Ray turned the volume up to its maximum.

While he was listening to the senator's contribution to the debate, Ray suddenly realized that the terrible secret he had been protecting over the last six years had finally come back to haunt him. He had always wondered what had become of the crew and passengers of Flight 77 after he had watched the plane land safely at the secret airbase in the desert. Now hearing it on the television, he had finally found out … only if the story was true, he thought. Also over the past six years Ray had heard and read about the large number of people who had allegedly heard small explosions in the Twin Towers, seconds before their collapse. He just assumed that was their confused and muddled minds during all the commotion and turmoil that was going on around them at the time.

Or was it? he pondered.

Gary was sitting just a few feet away from Ray, listening to the same debate.

Over the last few years, Gary had had frequent nightmares about his involvement on 9/11. He had always been afraid that one day his role in the shooting down of Flight 93 would come out into the open. Fortunately for him that hadn't been mentioned in either the debate or reported in the early morning edition of the *Times*.

Gary and Ray knew they'd both been involved in some way or another with the events on that fateful day, as they were the only two pilots who were scrambled on that morning.

Were their secrets about to be revealed? They both wondered.

Once the debate was over, Ray pushed himself off his chair, and made his way to the break area where he grabbed a cup of black coffee. Gary decided he would follow suit. As they stood shoulder to shoulder, Ray turned towards Gary, whispering in his ear, 'You want to be very careful Gary. All through that program, I noticed a few signs of panic on your face whilst you were concentrating on what was being discussed.'

Gary carried on with what he was doing, trying not to give anything away.

'Listen, Gary, I know for a fact that we were the only two pilots scrambled on the morning of 9/11. I certainly know what I did, and I've a gut feeling that you may have been involved. Am I correct in my presumption?'

Gary stood motionless, trying to gather his thoughts, considering, is now the right time to talk to someone? Moving his head slowly, he glanced up to face Ray. 'Yes, I do need to talk to you, but someplace more discreet, with no one around to hear what I have to say, and am I right in saying that you may have something you need to get off your chest?' Checking to make sure no one was listening; Ray whispered a 'yes' under his breath. 'It took me some time,' confessed Gary, 'but I also found out that we were the only two pilots who were ordered to scramble. I realize that we were only following orders, but that doesn't mean to say we have to agree with the final outcome.'

'Can we meet in the gym at fifteen hundred hours today, just after it closes, it should be secure enough in there?' said Ray. Gary nodded his agreement, whispering, 'Fifteen hundred hours it is.'

The rest of the day dragged, which made them feel anxious about coming to terms with their involvement and, ultimately, their confessions.

The time of the meeting finally arrived, with Gary and Ray making their way nervously over to the gym. There had only been three airmen inside using the free weights when they entered, and they didn't hang around for too long.

Ray walked back to check on the door before sitting down next to Gary on one of the benches nearest the far wall, and handing over a copy of the early edition of The *New York Times*.

'You'd be best reading the articles they were discussing in the debate before we confide in each other about our involvement,' suggested Ray, leaning his head against the wall, staring up at the ceiling.

With the newspaper splayed open in his hands, Gary leant forward, his arms resting on his knees, totally engrossed in what he was reading.

'Well, it seems some of the events have finally come to light, which doesn't surprise me, especially after six years. Who's going to go start, then?' asked Gary.

Ray volunteered to go through his account of his involvement first. During the course of Ray's narrative, Gary mentioned that he had always been curious about the size of the hole in the side of the Pentagon, which as far as he was concerned was no way as big and wide as a Boeing 757. Accepting Ray's detailed explanation of the whole events, Gary's curiosity had suddenly been answered.

When Ray had finally finished, he sat there passively, feeling relieved that at last he had told someone. Gary, on the other hand, was worried that confessing to his role might be a mistake, but he knew had no choice, he had already committed himself. Composing himself, expecting at some stage some kind of reaction from Ray, he proceeded.

After fifteen harrowing and tense minutes, Gary finally stopped talking, wiping away the moisture from his eyes with the back of his hand.

'No doubt you are thinking that I am as bad as the rest of them?' asked Gary.

Ray had thought his secret was controversial. Gary's was downright dangerous.

'No, you're not as guilty as them, Gary, and as you've just stated, it was only after you'd heard about the other incidents, you realized you had been used, like me. You were only following orders from the Vice-President. Christ Almighty Gary, you must have been experiencing a lot of emotions over these past six years, knowing that the passengers and crew must have somehow found a way of overpowering the terrorists. Can you imagine what would have happened if the plane had landed safely, with the terrorists being taken away and interrogated by the authorities. It doesn't even bear thinking about?'

Gary had always known that this day would eventually arrive. Yet now he felt more at ease, knowing that someone else knew what hell he had been going through over the last six years. But it didn't stop him feeling guilty.

'Now that some of the facts have come out in the open,' stated Gary, 'we should try and contact the senator who was in the debate this morning, see if he'll sit down and listen to us. How we do that is a different matter. I would suspect that all of his post being securely vetted and searched by his staff. Also, I can well imagine in the light of the recent interview we witnessed, he may require some additional security. There is bound to be some morons out there who watched the program who didn't totally agree with all of his views.'

Easing himself up from the bench, Ray paced around the floor, trying to come up with a solution.

'Gary, look, we can't afford to panic, not now, especially with all the controversy the debate would have caused. If we do happen to get in touch with the senator and disclose our involvement, the authorities will know immediately that it's us two whose passed the information on. We will just have to keep quiet and sit tight for a while. Let's just hope the truth is made available through other channels. Also we need to bear in mind that there hasn't been any reference at all about Flight 93. So if by any chance a window of opportunity does arise, we may be able to confirm all the facts that have been printed and discussed are true, along with your involvement in the shooting down of Flight 93. At that stage, we will have to decide what to do.'

'You're right Ray. What do you think will become of us, once the truth is made known?' asked Gary.

'I have no idea, and to be honest, I don't think the American public will ever find out. I can't see the government admitting they were involved in any of the atrocities, can you?' replied Ray.

'Not when you put it like that, no. Ray, the guilt, and shame, we've both had to live through over the last six years has been enough, we don't want it all brought up again. I agree, we will just have to monitor the progress over the next few days and weeks, and let's see what transpires. Come on, let's get out of here before someone becomes suspicious, especially the base commander – I believe he is the only other person on the base who knows we're both involved.'

'THE PLANE FACTS'

July 16 2001: A New York taxi driver tells of emails warning of an
imminent al-Qaeda attack on New York and Washington:
A Village Voice reporter is told by a New York taxi driver, 'You know, I am
leaving the country and going home to Egypt sometime in late August or
September. I have gotten e-mails from people I know saying that Osama
bin Laden has planned big terrorist attacks for New York and Washington
for that time. It will not be safe here then.'
He does in fact return to Egypt for that time. The FBI, which is not told
about this lead until after 9/11, interrogates and then releases him. He
claims that many others knew what he knew prior to 9/11.
(Village Voice, 25/9/02) Paul Thompson, The Terror Timeline

A veteran detective involved with post-9/11 investigations claims that
rumors in New York City's Arab-American community about the 9/11
attacks were common in the days beforehand. The story 'had been out on
the street', and the number of leads turning up later is so 'overwhelming'
that it is difficult to tell who knows about the attacks from second-hand
sources and who knows about it from someone who may have been a
participant. After 9/11, tracking leads on Middle Eastern employees who
did not show up for work on 9/11 are 'a serious and major priority' (Journal
News, 11/10/01) Paul Thompson, The Terror Timeline

Chapter Seventeen

'Keep violence in the mind. Where it belongs.'

Brian Aldiss (1925–)

SEPTEMBER 14 2007, New York – Harry's apartment, p.m.

Harry was just stepping away from the back door, when there was an almighty hammering coming from his front door, along with a booming voice bellowing through the letterbox, which Harry recognized straight away as Nash's.

'Oh fuck!' cried out Harry in alarm.

Suddenly becoming aware of the crisis he'd found himself in, Harry slowly inched his way across to the front door, hoping that his friends had either heard the commotion coming from the inside of his apartment, realizing the danger they were in, or they were a safe distance from the garden. As soon as Harry had released the lock, Nash barged his way through the door towards the sitting room, with the rest of the agents fanning out around the other rooms.

'Where the hell are they, Harry? I know they've been here, I can even smell a woman's perfume, so they can't be far away. Search everywhere.' Nash ordered the agents with a sweep of his hand.

Making his way over to the window that overlooked the back garden, Nash caught sight of Alex as he was nearing the gate.

'Get around the back now! There, out there, hurry, for God's sake, hurry, hurry,' screamed Nash.

Harry just hoped and prayed that his friends had heard Nash's ranting and raving, and were making their escape.

No sooner had the three of them left the garden when they heard the sound of heavy footfalls and shouting coming from the open door to Harry's kitchen. Then all hell was let loose behind them.

'Stop where you are, and don't move, we have you surrounded.' Came the screaming voice of Nash. They knew full well he was lying about them being surrounded – he just wanted them to think they had no chance of escaping.

Sally was the first to react. 'Run,' she called out, 'and meet up as arranged, and don't worry about me, I'll find you.'

Alex and Larry didn't need to be told twice. They quickly disappeared down a side road to their left, sprinting away as fast as possible, threading their way through the foot traffic, hoping they had enough distance between them and their pursuers.

'Just keep running Alex, and don't stop to look back, I can't imagine them shooting at us, as there are too many innocent bystanders hanging around,' wheezed Larry, as they were skirting their way through the crowd of inquisitive onlookers.

This was like some outlandish nightmare scene, thought Alex, where you were continually thinking. This can't possibly be happening, I'll wake up soon when it's all over. Alex knew it was for real when he realized he was slowly running out of breath, the sound of his heart pounding in his ears. 'I wish I'd spent a bit more time on the treadmill at the gym,' he said, gasping for breath.

Dashing into the oncoming traffic, they tried desperately to dodge in between the fast moving cars, also ignoring the horns and the squeal of brakes, echoing in the evening air. Moments later they managed to rest awhile, after sneakily slipping inside a grocery store.

Holding his right hand over a painful stitch in his side, once again trying to catch his breath, Alex glanced back towards the entrance, checking to see if any of the agents were wandering around outside. Relieved that there was no sign of them, he bent over at the waist, with his hands braced on his knees, taking a few deep breaths.

'I think … we lost … them,' said Alex, breathless. 'Where to … now?'

'Just act normal Alex . . . here, catch,' called out Larry, as he was tossing a big red apple towards him; which Alex caught in mid-air. 'When we make our way out of here, just start eating the apple as though you haven't a care in the world. Hopefully we may not be as conspicuous, also don't run, as that only attracts attention. I picked up that little piece of advice from the TV,' chuckled Larry, as he was standing in line to pay for the fruit. Alex just glanced across at Larry, shook his head and smiled.

Once they'd both got their breath back; certain the coast was clear, they sneakily exited the store with their heads down; both chomping happily on their apples; heading across town towards the Union Square subway station. Following a nervous and tense fifteen minutes they arrived safely at the station's entrance, with Larry pacing around, trying to work out the best place for them to go.

'Alex, we need to split up, and meet up again tomorrow at Ellis Island, with the rest of them. It will be easy for you to find, also there's bound to be a large number of tourists around, so it will be easy for you to lose yourself. But don't get there too early; we need to keep a low profile. Try and arrive about three p.m., that will give me time to search around for Sally and Harry.' Larry stopped talking, trying to get his breath back before carrying on. 'You mentioned to me the other night that you enjoyed reading books. Well, two blocks from here is the Strand bookshop; it's open until ten thirty, so you will have time to browse and lose yourself in the store. Here, you will need some money, take this, it's only a hundred dollars, it's all I have left, it should be enough for something to eat and drink, and don't even consider using your credit card; as soon as the transaction's been authorized, Nash will know immediately where you are, so be careful, find somewhere safe for the night, you must be used to this by now.' Once again he paused to control his breathing; he also began to examine the area, quickly glancing around for anyone who seemed out of place. Certain they hadn't been spotted, he continued. 'You will also need to keep warm. There's a few charity shops in this area, so I would suggest buying yourself a big coat, and a baseball cap. By now your face will be plastered all over the TV screens, no doubt they'll be describing you as a suspected terrorist,' stated Larry, drying the moisture from his eyes with a tissue. 'Let's not hang around any longer than necessary. You've been saying that you haven't seen much of the Big Apple, so here's your chance, and don't worry about me, I'll scrounge a bed for the night from one of my mates. Keep your head down Alex, and I'll see you tomorrow, and take care.' After that advice, Larry headed towards the stairs leading to the subway.

'See you later,' shouted Alex, as Larry disappeared from view, leaving Alex wondering once again. How the hell did I get myself into this shit?

Alex checked the time: 8 p.m. Making sure there were no 'boys in blue' around, or anyone who looked remotely suspicious, he ensured his backpack was securely strapped, before wearily making his way to the bookstore.

The sweat, caused by all the running was now cooling down on his skin, causing Alex to shiver. He needed to find some additional clothing, soon, as he knew it would become much colder during the night, especially if he had to sleep outside again. Hoping it wouldn't come to that. It didn't take him long before he came across a charity shop which to his relief was still open. He spent ten dollars on a well-worn, thick herringbone overcoat, which smelled of mothballs, and a dollar on an old, battered New York Yankees baseball cap. In addition, he also paid two dollars for a pair of Ray-Bans. You never know when you might have to improvise, he thought, with a smile. Storing the glasses away in his coat pocket, and carrying the coat over his arm, he left the shop, feeling pleased with himself. He knew he should only wear the coat when it got too cold; at the moment he was fine. Pulling the cap down over his eyes, hoping it would hide most of his face, he made his way through the bustling crowds making their way home.

Arriving by the entrance to the store, he noted that the Strand bookshop had opened in 1927. It was located on Broadway at 12th Street, occupying 55,000 square feet of space, and reputedly stocked two million books.

Alex was in book heaven. Floors and floors of them. He would have loved to have been able to spend more time wandering around all the shelves. But he knew for the time being it was for only a couple of hours. 'Once this nightmare is over,' he mused, 'I am going to spend some quality time in here. When that will be is anyone's guess.' He couldn't believe the number of science fiction books that were available in America. 'Why can't we have all these to choose from in the UK? We must have only a quarter of this amount,' he said to himself.

He had been so engrossed, flicking through a graphic novel by one of his favorite illustrators, when he was startled by the speaker system informing customers that the store would be closing in twenty minutes.

Ten past ten – how time flies when you're having fun, he thought, with a contented smile on his face.

Knowing full well that he had no intention of buying it, he placed the book neatly back in its rightful place, and made his way to the exit. It had become noticeably colder outside. Where do I go now? he thought. He knew he had to keep moving to keep warm. Checking through his pockets, he counted out what was left from the money Larry had given him: $87 plus some loose change. 'I won't get very far with that,' he remarked to himself glumly. 'I could travel on the subway for a while, that way I will be able to keep warm.' The only worry there, he thought, it won't be safe, and there is always the chance I may be mugged. With just over eighty-seven dollars, I should be able to find a room somewhere around here, he tried to convince himself. I need to find a hotel where they list the room rates outside, that way I won't embarrass myself if I haven't enough money. Carefully, he slid the notes and loose change back into his coat pocket.

After wandering the streets for over an hour he found a Budget Hotel on 38th Street advertising rooms for $70 a night

'Great,' he said to himself. 'Lady Luck is looking down on me for once.'

After secretly peeking through the hotel's glass doors, ensuring there wasn't any unsavory characters asking embarrassing questions of the desk clerk, he made his way cautiously inside. Thankfully the foyer and the corridors were deserted, apart from the desk clerk, who seemed to be engrossed in a glossy magazine.

'Here goes,' he said to himself, confidently walking up to reception.

Alex could see that the clerk was only young, with long, dyed-blonde hair, tied up in a ponytail, which seemed to be the fashion these days, he thought. He also noticed that he was wearing a suit and tie, which surprised Alex – normally kids that young tended to rebel against uniforms. The young man seemed totally lost in his magazine.

'Good,' he said to himself. 'This way he may not remember my face clearly if it appears in the morning papers, or on the late-night news bulletins.'

Alex coughed to attract his attention, which caused the clerk to quickly look up.

'Good evening sir, sorry to have kept you waiting, how can I help?' asked the clerk.

Well, that's another surprise, thought Alex, I didn't expect good manners.

'Do you have a room for the night please?' Alex asked.

'Let me check … yes, we have one on the ground floor, but I must warn you, because it is on the ground floor, there is an emergency exit in the bathroom. But not to worry; we haven't had to use it in the two years I've been here.'

'That's fine,' replied Alex.

'Do you have any means of identification? You know what it's like these days sir, especially with all these terrorists around,' said the clerk, studying Alex's face.

'As you can probably guess by my accent, I'm British,' Alex remarked, as he handed over his passport. Alex was now becoming nervous, and his hands were shaking. He knew he would have to show some identification; he could only hope his name hadn't been splashed all over the newspapers. Alex became nervous, suddenly realizing his name and details would soon be on the hotel's computer, which he hadn't allowed for. He was now having second thoughts about staying at the hotel, wondering whether he should collect his passport and get the hell out of there as quickly as possible. Sweat was beading on his face and his hands were once again beginning to shake.

'Unfortunately the computers have been out of action most of the day, so would you please fill out this card?' asked the desk clerk, handing back the passport.

Alex wasn't expecting this, but after hearing that bit of unexpected good news, he let out a big sigh of relief, which fortunately for him, the young man hadn't noticed. That was a close shave, he thought. Never mind, unless this young man was well up on the day's events, he should be safe. Now feeling relaxed.

'I am expecting someone in during the night to fix the computer, and then I'll be able to transfer over your details,' commented the young man.

'Let's hope they arrive soon. I expect you have a few to file away, especially if it's been down most of the day,' Alex commented, hoping there would be enough of them to keep his till last.

'We've had about fifty guests booking in throughout the course of the day, so once it's up and running it's likely to take me the best part of what's left of my shift to get it all done, that's if it gets fixed soon.'

Alex was now feeling more relaxed; now knowing he had at the most seven hours before he needed to move out of the hotel.

He picked up his key, wished the clerk a good night, suggesting he not work too hard, and casually made his way to his room. The hotel was like most he had stopped in over the years when on business trips. Wallpaper from the seventies, carpets that were threadbare with stains whose origin he didn't wish to think about.

'Could do with a bit of TLC,' he mumbled.

He finally found his room, which was as far away from reception as possible; also there wasn't another room within thirty feet.

'Great,' he said to himself, 'so if there are any unusual noises coming from the corridor, it can mean only one thing – they must have traced me.'

On entering the room, the first thing he noticed was how small it was. Never mind, he thought, at least it smells clean, and the bed seems large enough. Yet to his dismay there was a neon light right outside his bedroom window, sending piercing light and shadows all over the room through the thinly made curtains.

'No wonder it was vacant, the light will keep me up all night,' he grumbled.

Wandering into the bathroom, he saw to his delight that the bath was enormous, also noticing the emergency door in the corner. He walked over to check it out, to see if it would be easy to open if he needed a quick getaway. 'No problem.'

He climbed on top of the bath to open the window, to let in some fresh air. Whilst up there he saw that the emergency door opened up into a narrow alleyway, which was surprisingly clear of rubbish. He was now feeling hopeful, and with some kind of escape plan worked out, he went back into the room to organize his sleeping arrangements. Lifting the blankets off the bed, he carefully placed them in the bath. Some of the pillows he wedged around the taps, so that he wouldn't hurt himself during the night; the rest he carefully positioned at the other end so he had somewhere to rest his head.

He decided he would take only his two large coats off, aware that he wouldn't have time to get dressed if he had to get out of the room in a hurry.

He propped open the bathroom door a crack with his shoes, hoping that he would be able to hear any unusual noises coming from outside in the corridor.

Climbing into his makeshift bed, resting his head on the side of the bath, with his feet carefully positioned by the sides of the taps at the bottom, he tried to make himself as comfortable as possible under the circumstances, knowing full well he would wake up in the morning with a stiff neck and aching back. He didn't care; he just wanted somewhere to sleep, preferably in the dark, without any flashing lights keeping him awake most of the night.

'THE PLANE FACTS'

2006–2007: Over fifty former senior government officials and more than a hundred highly respected professors publicly criticize The 9/11 Commission Report as highly flawed, and call for a new independent investigation. (Professors, officials)

May 17 2002: Fear of Being Unpatriotic Affects Media Coverage after 9/11

CBS anchorman Dan Rather tells the BBC that he and other journalists haven't been properly investigating since 9/11. He says, 'There was a time in South Africa that people would put flaming tyres around people's necks if they dissented. And in some ways the fear is that you will be necklaced here, you will have a flaming tyre of lack of patriotism put around your neck. Now it is that fear that keeps journalists from asking the toughest of the tough questions.' (Guardian, 17/5/02) Paul Thompson, The Terror Timeline

Chapter Eighteen

'Great is Truth, and almighty above all things.'

Bible (Apocrypha)

SEPTEMBER 15 2007 – Budget Hotel, 38th Street, 8 a.m.

Once again Alex woke up to unfamiliar surroundings, with the early morning sun streaming through the small bathroom window, bathing his face in the warmth. Aware he needed to go to the toilet, he carefully maneuvered himself out of the bath, and began to stretch his arms and back attempting to relieve the stiffness from his elderly bones.

After drying his hands, he climbed on top of the bath, checking outside in the alley through the bathroom window, making sure there was no one around. Satisfied it was clear, he started to carry the blankets from the bath back to the bed, suddenly stopping what he was doing, as he could hear movement coming from outside in the corridor. Oh-oh, trouble, he thought. The clerk must have had his computer fixed, and my details have been picked up.

'Well, at least I've had a good night's sleep,' he whispered to himself.

Slowly lowering himself to the floor, he stealthily crept towards the foot of the door, peering underneath for any signs of life. He observed to his alarm a number of large black combat boots milling around outside, and whispered orders, no doubt coming from the owners of them. Also he couldn't be certain, but he thought he could hear Nash's voice in the background.

Carefully, and as quietly as possible, he dragged the bed across to block the door, hoping it would give him some additional time to get out of the hotel. Then as silently as possible he moved away from the bed towards the bathroom.

How long before they charged into his room was anyone's guess. But he wasn't about to hang around to find out. But just to be on the safe side, he also wedged an old wicker chair that he'd found in the bedroom, under the bathroom door handle from the inside, hoping the added barrier would give him a better chance of escaping.

Checking once again that the alley was clear, he slowly eased the emergency exit door open. Ensuring the door was securely closed behind him, he made his escape.

He had no sooner exited the bathroom, when he heard shouting and cursing coming from his room. Fortunately for him, the bed had done its job.

Alex could hear the noise of the police all the way down the alley. No doubt they would be trying to enter the bathroom by now. His quick thinking had given him a head start.

Armed police were shouting out orders for whoever was in the bathroom to come out, with their hands up.

Luckily the alley wasn't too long, and within seconds Alex was on the main road, walking as fast as possible without drawing too much attention. He could hear shouting, plus the noise of dozens of pounding feet behind him. He wasn't about to stop and look, he just pulled down his cap and, as casually as possible, walked towards the nearest underground station. He adopted a steady gait, not too fast, not too slow; he just wanted to look like someone with a reason for being there, and not look out of place. He also needed to find the quickest way to Ellis Island.

In all the confusion and haste he'd lost track of time. He checked his watch: 9 a.m. That's the longest sleep I've had in years, he thought. Also most of the stores will be opening soon, so I will have somewhere to disappear, if I have to.

He had only walked a couple of blocks, when suddenly, he found himself outside a travel agent's. 'There must be leaflets available with directions to anywhere in the city – how I managed to forget to put a guide in my backpack is beyond me,' he chastised himself.

Entering the shop, he wandered over to one of the young lady assistants, asking her if they had any leaflets on Ellis Island, and more importantly details of which subway station or bus to head for.

After asking him politely to sit down, she handed Alex at least a dozen leaflets about the Statue of Liberty, along with its history; she then began to explain some of the trips that were available. He was getting annoyed with her.

'I am sorry, I don't want to sound rude, but can you just tell me the best way for me to reach Ellis Island?'

Startled, and slightly embarrassed, the assistant picked out a leaflet which she said would be suitable for him, then wished him a good day. Alex didn't want to upset her; he just wanted to get the hell out of there as quickly as possible. He thanked her, and wished her a good day in return.

Wandering down the street, he stopped inside one of the many doorways to read through the leaflet. The instructions were clear and easy to follow. He checked the map on the back of the leaflet, trying to find an easy route, noting he would have to pass through Chinatown, City Hall Park, which he was familiar with, and then on to Battery Park.

'Well, that's going to take me a few hours,' he mused.

Walking, taking in all the sights, he suddenly realized he hadn't had any breakfast, so he stopped to count out how much money he had left over, which to his joy seemed to be enough for a drink and a bite to eat. He checked around his immediate surroundings, looking for somewhere to eat, like a deli or sandwich bar.

It was once again the aroma of freshly baked bagels which he noticed before he spied the store a few yards away. It was one of those stores you could eat inside, in the warmth; so within minutes Alex was sitting down with one cheese bagel, and a large black coffee. He'd found himself a table in the corner, facing the door. He couldn't remember being in a place like this before. The walls were covered with framed faded sepia pictures showing New York in the early 1900s. The wooden floor was so clean you could probably eat on it.

This is one proud owner, he thought.

When entering, he hadn't noticed the television over by the counter, and to his alarm, and astonishment, looking back at him from the TV screen was his passport photo. He felt sick to the stomach; he had been enjoying his meal, but now he'd lost his appetite. Carefully picking up his napkin, placing what was left of his bagel inside; he slipped it into his pocket for safe keeping. 'You never know where your next meal's going to come from Alex,' he murmured.

Making sure that no one was paying him any attention, he carefully eased away from the table, pulling his cap down, hopefully hiding most of his face. As he passed the TV, Alex could hear snippets of conversation coming from it, and what he could make out what the newscaster was reporting, he didn't like one bit. They were accusing Alex of being a terrorist, and extremely dangerous, advising the public not to approach him, and if anyone happened to spot him, they had to contact the police immediately.

Alex couldn't believe his ears. 'A terrorist? What the hell are they on about? This must be Nash's doing. He must be desperate to get his hands on the evidence, the slimy fucker,' he mumbled to himself as he was leaving the store.

He now knew it was imperative he got to the subway station as quickly as possible.

'What a way to see the sights,' he said to himself, angrily. 'I should be strolling down these streets, taking my time, and not having to be looking over my shoulder.'

It was the swarm of people pushing and colliding into him that first gave Alex the indication that something wasn't quite right. Most people in New York were used to hearing the screeching of car tires and police sirens, but the droning of a helicopter caused everyone around to stop and look up. Alex just carried on with what he was doing, glancing up now and again to where all the noise was coming from.

I wonder if anyone in the bagel store recognized me. I suppose I do look a bit shifty, which would make me more noticeable, he thought. 'No, it's more likely the agents from the hotel, searching the area,' he mumbled to himself, now feeling totally downhearted.

Fiddling around in his coat pocket for a few seconds, he eventually brought out the sunglasses, and he quickly retrieved the collapsible walking stick from his backpack.

'Larry was right, Summer's white stick has come in handy,' he whispered.

Making sure he wasn't attracting any undue attention, he casually slipped on the glasses, opened the white fold-out cane, and started to act as though he was blind.

He slowly began to blend in with the rest of the curious pedestrians, bumping into them now and again, trying to make it look realistic, and the number of apologies coming from them made him feel guilty about using a disability as a way of remaining undetected.

'Needs must, as they say,' he said, carrying on regardless.

The people around him were now being jostled, with protests coming from some of them. There could only be one reason for that, he thought, there must be police around, searching and checking the hundreds of people in the area. Tapping his stick against the wall, trying very hard to look the part, he decided to bend forward slightly, hoping to help reduce his height. Anything to make him look inconspicuous was all he wanted.

All of a sudden the two women walking towards him were pushed aside by a burly man wearing the obligatory black windbreaker, with NYPD scrawled across the front.

'Keep looking back there,' he ordered, 'he can't have gone too far, we have the whole area surrounded. There is no way he can getaway from here … Sorry, sir, I didn't see you there, do you need any help? It's getting rather crowded around here at the moment, and I wouldn't want you to get injured.'

Alex couldn't believe it; the cop was unknowingly helping him. He replied, trying very hard to disguise his British accent by whispering, at the same time stammering.

'I'm f-f-fine, officer, thank you. I have been blind s-s-since birth so I am used to the p-pushing and shoving, especially in th-th-this area.'

With that explanation the cop started to move away down the street, pushing people aside, shouting out further orders to his men on the way.

Alex couldn't believe his luck; yet he had to be careful as it wasn't easy acting blind, also aware that he was trying to avoid the litter on the floor, which, if he had really been blind, he wouldn't have seen. Trying to make it more convincing, he partially closed his eyes, which helped to make his movements more authentic.

He knew he had to take off the disguise soon, as he might have need of it another time, also, he wanted to be himself again. This way, he had two identities. He also noted it was nearly noon, and he wasn't even close to the subway station.

With that thought in mind, he decided to call in at the next department store, to visit the bathroom so he could put away his glasses and stick, and hopefully walk out of the shop unobserved. It didn't take him long to come across a twenty-four-hour drugstore, with him entering the bathroom, as a blind, stooping old man, and coming out as an upright, sighted old man.

He also needed to find a way of getting rid of some of the incriminating pictures along with Harry and Tony's notes before he left the store, also mindful that he had to keep some of the pictures, as he'd want Nash to think they were all there, if and when they caught him. So he called at the stationery stand on his way out. He bought a padded envelope along with a stamp, and cheekily, he used one of the pens from the counter, before writing down a name and address on the envelope. Feeling pleased with himself, he made his way outside, searching for a postbox, spotting one next to a street map which was located just a few feet from the store's entrance.

After safely posting the evidence, he spent what seemed to him to be a lifetime looking for the nearest subway station on the map, and finally locating one two blocks away.

'Why can't they just have street names like we have, instead of names and numbers?' he mumbled to himself.

Now somewhat relieved, he turned in the direction of the station.

He had gone only a few yards when out of the corner of his eye he saw the movement of a number of dark shadows converging on him, followed by two large hands roughly grabbing him by both elbows, lifting him off his feet, and pushing him up against the wall, his face pressed to one side, the feel of cold metal being placed around his wrists.

'You had me fooled back there, sir. Have they started selling miracles in drugstores? You seem to have miraculously regained your eyesight.'

Alex was stunned. How did they know I wasn't blind? he wondered.

Once the officer was certain Alex wasn't a threat, also there was no way of him escaping, he instructed his men to ease off.

Moving cautiously back from the wall, yet still facing away from the inquisitive crowd that had formed around him, Alex moved his lips to one side in order to try and blow away the dust from the side of his face.

'You're probably wondering how I came to the conclusion you weren't blind? Shall I put you out of your misery? When I asked you if you needed assistance you replied by saying, "No thank you, officer." If you had been blind, you wouldn't have known I was a police officer, now would you, sir?'

'Shit,' replied Alex, 'some rubbish criminal I would have turned out to be.'

When the officer had turned him around so he could clearly see and hear him, Alex was shocked to see the large number of police surrounding him. Nash has certainly done a good job of making everyone think I'm a threat. But there was one consolation, thought Alex. Nash was nowhere to be seen.

'Alex Monroe, I am arresting you on suspicion of a terrorism act. You have the right to remain silent. Anything you say can, and will, be used against you in a court of law. You have the right to have an attorney present during questioning. If you cannot afford an attorney, one will be appointed for you. Owing to the fact that you are a British citizen I am required to inform you of your additional rights. If you are not a United States citizen, you may contact your country's consulate prior to any questioning. Alex Monroe, do you understand what I have said?'

Alex was speechless. He had never been in trouble with the police, ever, yet now he was being accused of terrorism activities in a foreign country.

'Yes, I understand officer,' he replied despondently.

'I honestly believe there has been some kind of misunderstanding, which will hopefully be resolved soon, but in the meantime I need to keep the cuffs on.'

The slack-jawed onlookers started to slowly disperse, as they were used to seeing the bad guy being arrested and taken away. Alex was ushered over to a squad car, which had pulled up outside the store, the officer opening the rear door for him to enter, and being careful that he did not bang his head when getting in. Slumping back in the frayed, worn rear seat, Alex began to reflect over the past few hectic and fraught days.

'I might write a book about my exploits,' he murmured to himself.

'Pardon, what was that you said?' asked the officer.

'Nothing,' replied Alex, 'just talking to myself.'

The traffic was light, so it took less than ten minutes to reach the station, which Alex recognized immediately as being the one from the other night. He hoped Harry would be around to give him some help and advice, if it was at all possible, unless he was inside being reprimanded for sheltering the group, he thought, immediately feeling downhearted.

Alex was escorted through into the main entrance, only to be handed over to the familiar face of the desk sergeant, with the arresting officer turning Alex around so he could slip the cuffs off, which gave Alex the opportunity to rub the cramps from his wrists.

'Can't keep away, can we sir?' was the sergeant's opening remark. The sergeant asked if the prisoner had been Mirandized. 'Yes,' was the reply; the officer also informing the sergeant that Alex was a British citizen, which had to be taken into account.

'Empty your pockets,' demanded the sergeant, 'and take off your shoelaces – we wouldn't want you to hurt yourself, now would we?'

Doing as instructed, Alex placed the contents of his pockets on the counter – a few dollars in loose change, the napkin with the remnants of his uneaten bagel, plus his pair of Ray-Bans, along with the envelope containing the incriminating pictures. The backpack was searched and emptied, leaving odd items of clothing strewn on the counter, along with the white stick, which the sergeant picked up to examine.

'I suppose you will want my passport?' asked Alex.

'Yes, and don't worry, you will be given everything back when we deport you,' replied the sergeant with a smirk on his face. 'You may also be surprised to know that the rest of your so-called friends are being questioned at the moment, just down the hall.' The desk sergeant indicated with his eyes towards the main office.

Alex felt a shade happier knowing that Larry and Sally were somewhere in the building.

Alex balanced himself on one foot by holding on to the top of the counter with one hand, and with his other hand, he laboriously slid his laces out from his shoes. It was whilst he was doing this, he was roughly pushed to one side, with a hand reaching across him, grabbing hold of the envelope with the pictures, which caused Alex to quickly grab hold on to the counter with both hands to avoid falling over.

'I'll take these, Sergeant, thank you very much,' said the owner of the hand.

'What the hell's going on? You can't just walk in here and take what you want. Who the hell are you anyway?' screamed the sergeant.

'Nash, Special Agent Nash, if you want my full title, and yes, I can take what I want, especially when it involves a terrorist, which Mr Alex Monroe is.' Nash flashed his badge under the nose of the desk sergeant, and quickly examined the contents of the envelope. 'Everything in order, Sergeant?' Nash went on, smirking, now knowing he had the incriminating photo's safely in his possession.

'Yes, I suppose so, but in future, ask – and it doesn't cost anything for good manners you know,' replied the sergeant, grimacing.

'Sergeant, please take Mr Monroe to the Penthouse suite. Let him spend some quality time, reflecting over the regrettable situation he's got himself into, also the grief he's caused me over the past few days. We need to be seen to be looking after our friends from the UK, now don't we, Sergeant?' said Nash, laughing as he was making his way down the corridor, with the envelope safely in his grasp.

Alex was escorted down a winding passage, and put in a small six-by-six holding cell, fronted by rusted ancient ironwork that had seen better days, noticing there was also a rusted iron bed in the corner, and what looked like a unstuffed mattress lying on the floor. What it was covering, Alex didn't want to know. Opposite the bed was the customary steel toilet, which he wasn't even going to check out.

'I hope I'm not in the Penthouse suite too long,' he whispered to himself, giggling once he realized the dilemma he found himself in.

Alex did have the satisfaction of knowing that Nash thought he had all the pictures. The only concern was if the envelope he had posted would make it to its ultimate destination.

During the time Alex was being arrested and driven across to the station, Sally had been left by herself in the interview room. She knew the routine. Leave them alone long enough to appreciate their fate, and they always confessed to everything.

The turning of the lock, plus the sudden movement of the door being opened, brought Sally out of her reverie. 'Nash!'

'Yes, and don't look so surprised. Did you think I'd leave you here all on your own?'

He started to pace around the room, stalking her, trying to make her nervous.

'You seem to have upset a few people in high places, Ms Rider.' He waited for a reaction from her.

'I see no reason for you to hold me, and if you are going to charge me, I want to ring my attorney, and I'm certainly not answering any of your damn stupid questions.' Came her reply.

'Not so fast, Miss Smarty Pants Reporter. I'd just like to know how you managed to come across a letter from someone purporting to be a passenger on Flight 77, and also these so-called pictures of explosives. Can't you come up with anything better than that?' barked Nash, in a condescending manner.

'Firstly, I will not divulge my sources, that's confidential and you damn well know it, and secondly I want to phone my attorney, now!' shouted Sally.

'Have it your own way, one call only. Who's your attorney?'

'Senator Gerry Helleman, if you must know, he is one of the top defence lawyers in the country. Also I don't know if you are aware, but he is also one of the leading opponents of the 9/11 Commission. He, along with millions of others in this country, are coming to the conclusion that the President and his close advisers were behind the atrocities surrounding 9/11. So, Agent Smarty Pants Nash, your work will be cut out for the rest of the night. Please hurry up with the phone, will you, I don't want to stay in this dump any longer than necessary. Also I will need my pocket book, there's a card inside with the senator's phone number on.'

The phone was plugged into the wall and her pocket book handed over to her, with Nash leaving Sally to make her call.

She nervously hunted around for the senator's business card.

'Got it,' she said, relieved.

The senator had mentioned to Sally at their meeting that he was still practicing law, and if she was ever in trouble she was to ring him on his private line at any time, day or night.

The phone was answered after the third ring.

'Senator, it's Sally Rider, I desperately need your help. I have been arrested for what's been termed as terrorism acts against America ...'

'Just stay calm, Sally, and under no circumstances say anything. I should be with you within the hour. Don't worry, your arrest will only further our cause. Once it's known you have been arrested, there are going to be a great number of questions thrown at the President. As they say, "there's no smoke without fire".'

After noting down the address, the senator ended the call, leaving Sally hoping and praying that everything would work out for the best.

Nash barged back into the room, bringing Sally out of her daydream.

'Guess what, we have the rest of your tribe under arrest. Yes, that's surprised you, hasn't it – also I have these.' Nash waved the envelope about in front of Sally, marching around the room with a smile that could turn anyone to stone.

She wasn't really surprised; they had been extremely fortunate so far, she thought, now feeling somewhat dejected.

'If my friends are here, I would also like the senator to represent them, and I will expect you to inform him when he arrives. I will also entrust you to inform my friends of the situation. I'm not bothered about you having the pictures – as long as Tony gets better, that's all that counts.'

'How sweet, but without the pictures your stories are worthless. You will find it hard trying to find another job once it comes to light that you have no evidence and also you've been lying all the time,' Nash laughed.

'Just leave me alone, Nash, will you, and don't forget to inform my friends about the senator coming over to help them,' shouted Sally.

Nash had to admit to himself that he had no alternative but to inform all parties of the situation. Walking past the desk sergeant, he ordered Alex to be taken out of the holding cell and moved to an interview room, where he could wait until his attorney arrived, also asking the sergeant to inform the other member of the group about the senator representing him.

'THE PLANE FACTS'

NORAD has told three different and conflicting stories explaining why no jet fighters intercepted any of the four hijacked airliners.

Four days before 9/11, Jeb Bush activated the Florida National Guard: 'Based on the potential massive damage to life and property that may result from an act of terrorism at a Florida port.'
(Internet)

On 9/11 Jeb Bush declared a 'State of Emergency' in Florida (E.O, 01-262). 'I hereby delegate to the Department of Law Enforcement the operational authority to coordinate and direct the law enforcement resources and other resources ... of any and all state, regional and local government agencies ...' And by 2 a.m. on 12/9/01, Jeb Bush was reported to have confiscated the police records in Venice, FL, related to the Huffman Aviation flight school. Two rental trucks full of these records drove onto C-130 military aircraft at Sarasosta Airport and flew out with Jeb Bush on board. (9/11 cover-up)

Chapter Nineteen

'After all, tomorrow is another day.'

Margaret Mitchell 1900-40

SEPTEMBER 15 2007, LANGLEY AIR FORCE BASE, WASHINGTON

Following the articles in the *New York Time's*, a considerable number of other major newspapers had suddenly jumped on the bandwagon, coming up with their own theories of what may have happened on 9/11. Most of their headlines were about the previous day's articles from the *Times* and the ensuing debate, along with the subsequent fracas with the Plane Facts group at Ground Zero. Also mentioning Senator Helleman's keen interest in the group's well-being.

The majority of the articles were accusing the 'group' of being extremists, stirring up unnecessary trouble, causing distress to the relatives of the victims.

There were a few of them who were wholeheartedly behind what the group were claiming, with other groups scattered around America using this as fuel to kick-start the propaganda machine. It was a welcome lifeline.

Once again the call for an independent public inquiry was raised in Congress, with television companies vying for the main protest groups to appear on their talk shows.

'We want the TRUTH and NOW!' shouted one of the paper's headlines.

'Come clean, Mr President,' was another.

'First we had Pearl Harbor, then the assassination of President Kennedy, now 9/11 – what will the government do next?' ran another.

Gary and Ray couldn't believe what they were reading. They had all the various morning newspapers spread out over the mess hall tables, trying to read as much of what had been printed before drawing any undue attention from the rest of the servicemen in the room. If anyone did ask, thought Gary, he would just say he was only taking an interest in what was happening in America, as any normal American citizen would do.

They both felt as though they had somehow been vindicated; as if a great weight had been lifted off their shoulders.

'We need to act now, and fast,' said Gary in a hushed tone. 'We can't wait any longer. Look, it says that the attorney who's linked with the group is the senator who was on that talk show the other day. We need to get in contact with him, let him know that what's been printed is true. He must have a website. Ray, I think the best thing for me to do is to take the rest of the day off – I have some leave due, so I can't see it being much of a problem; and I need to find a quiet, out-of-the-way Internet café in town, and don't worry, I won't divulge our names. The senator's got to take us seriously once he reads the contents of my email. The facts will speak for themselves. Especially when I admit to my involvement with the shooting down of Flight 93.' Gary stopped for awhile, trying to control his thoughts. After a few emotional seconds he continued. 'No one, apart from those who were present at the time, would know the true facts; he must surely accept we are not making it up.' Ray agreed to Gary's suggestion. Wishing him luck, Ray pressed an envelope into Gary's hand.

'What's this?' asked Gary.

'The coordinates of the facility the passengers and crew are being held. I made a note of them. I knew one day they would come in useful.'

'Good call mate, this will surely make the senator sit up and realize we're not lying.' Responded Gary, patting Ray's arm in a show of friendship.

Gary made his way to the main gate of the base, where he caught the first Greyhound bus, which would take him to the centre of Washington. He felt both nervous and apprehensive. He also felt elated. After six long, depressing years, knowing he had shot down an innocent airplane, he may now be able to come to terms with it, once it finally came out into the open.

It took Gary two hot, sweaty hours to reach his destination. Arriving at the bus station; quickly climbing down the steps, Gary paused to take in the fresh air, before stretching and flexing his back. He made his way towards the centre of town, hoping to find a secluded Internet café. During his previous visits he had noticed that there were a large number of cafés springing up. Must be good business, he thought at the time; I might even open one myself when I come out of the air force.

It didn't take him long to find one. It was ideal. He had noticed a young man standing in the cold holding up a board advertising an Internet café.

'Mrs Dot Com's café.' He had to smile. The placard had a map showing exactly where the café was located, and he was opening the door within minutes of following the directions. Gary sat awkwardly at the keyboard as his large legs wouldn't fit under the table. He eventually made himself comfortable and searched for the senator's web page. He tried Google first, and as expected he immediately found the senator's home page, which detailed the history of his rise to the Senate, plus a list of all the committees he was serving on.

To his dismay, there were two addresses, one for his Washington office, the other for his office in Detroit.

He decided to send the email to both addresses; that way he could be sure the senator would read at least one of them. How would he phrase it? he pondered. He had to be certain that whatever he divulged could only have come from someone who was there at the time. He wanted the context of the email to be as convincing as possible, without making it too long, yet he knew that with the addition of Ray's coordinates plus his added confession to the shooting down of Flight 93 would sound more convincing.

When he was certain there was enough information to whet the senator's appetite, he pressed the 'send' key.

I wonder when he'll get round to reading his mail? he thought.

'THE PLANE FACTS'

MAY 16 2002: Nobody Predicted 9/11-Style Attacks, Says RICE. National Security Adviser Rice states, 'I don't think anybody could have predicted that these people would take an airplane and slam it into the World Trade Center, take another one and slam it into the Pentagon, that they would try to use an airplane as a missile,' adding that, 'even in retrospect' there was 'nothing' to suggest that. (White House, 16/5/02) Contradicting Rice's claims, former CIA Deputy Director John Gannon acknowledges that such a scenario has long been taken seriously by US intelligence: 'If you ask anybody could terrorists convert it into a missile? Nobody would have ruled that out.'

Rice also states, 'The overwhelming bulk of the evidence was that this was an attack that was likely to take place overseas.' (MSNBC, 17/5/02)

SLATE awards the 'Whopper of the Week' when the title of Bush's August 6 briefing is revealed: 'Bin Laden Determined to Strike in US' (SLATE, 23/5/02) Rice later concedes that 'somebody did imagine it' but says she did not know about such intelligence until well after this conference. (Associated Press, 21/9/02) Paul Thompson, The Terror Timeline

Chapter Twenty

'The enemies of my enemies are my friends.'

Proverb

SEPTEMBER 15 2007, GROUND ZERO POLICE STATION, 1800 HOURS

The Senator, along with his delegation of aides and bodyguards, strode towards the front desk, with an air of authority.

'Where's my client?' the senator demanded to know impatiently. 'Is there anyone in charge around here?'

Suddenly the sergeant popped up from behind the desk. 'Yes sir, how can I help?' he asked.

Taken aback by the sergeant suddenly appearing before him, the senator composed himself before he launched into his customary attorney preamble.

'My name is Senator Gerry Helleman, and I am here to represent Ms Sally Rider.'

'Ah, yes, we've been expecting you. Do you have any means of identification?' He held out his hand to the senator.

'Impertinent man,' Helleman replied, pulling out his wallet.

Having calmed himself down, the senator offered the desk sergeant his business card, which detailed all his credentials.

'Everything seems to be in order, Senator, thank you. Would you like to see the young lady now?' asked the sergeant, pocketing the card.

'Yes please, and would you be so kind as to bring me a cup of strong milky tea, no sugar, for myself, and one for Ms Rider? It may be a long evening, don't you think, sergeant?'

After instructing the senator's attendants to wait patiently in reception, the sergeant escorted the senator through the busy squad room, before stopping at the first room they came too, where the senator was shown in.

'Thank God you're here!' cried Sally, immediately recognizing him. 'I was worried you wouldn't come.'

'Sally, wild horses wouldn't have prevented me from coming to your aid, not after the revelations that have come to light over the past few days …' The beep of a message being received on his BlackBerry interrupted their conversation.

'Excuse me a minute, will you Sally? I have a message, which must be very important, or my secretary wouldn't have sent it.' The senator moved a small distance away to read the text.

'Good heavens,' he exclaimed.

'What's the problem?' asked Sally.

Safely locking the device, the senator pulled up one of the chairs from the corner of the room, sat down, and began to disclose the contents of the text.

'It seems that I have received an email at both of my offices, from someone professing to be a US pilot. It emerges that he has listed the identical coordinates of the facility detailed in Harry's note. I know my secretary, God bless him, wouldn't have sent the full text over, just in case the FBI have my BlackBerry tapped. No doubt he will print it off, and hand it to me when I see him next. Which will now be tomorrow, unfortunately. Never mind, at least I'll have something to look forward to.'

'Do you think it could be genuine?' asked Sally.

'Put it this way, young lady, the only way the information can be that accurate, is if the person sending the message was present at the time, and it also seems very unlikely that the coordinates from two different sources could be false. The only problem we have is that he hasn't left his name, which, when you think about it, doesn't surprise me. From what I can gather from the small amount of information my secretary's sent me, whoever has sent the email is in the air force, and he will be bound by the oath he took, to defend the United States of America. Ironic, isn't it? Also, if we do divulge the information, the authorities would know immediately who had sent it. We need to hold on to this new revelation for safe-keeping. We may need it later.

'Right, first things first. While you've been held in here, what have you said to them?'

'Nothing. I told them I needed to talk to you first. I also hoped you wouldn't mind representing the rest of the group, who are also being held in the station – please,' pleaded Sally.

'That won't be a problem, but first we need to find out what you have all been charged with, if anything, and if there's no sound reason to hold you, you should all be out within the hour.'

Making his way over to the door, the senator pounded on it hard, hoping to catch someone's attention.

The door eventually opened, and in walked Detective Holmes.

'And who might you be?' asked the senator.

'Detective Holmes. You must be Senator Helleman.' He offered his hand to him. 'Pleased to meet you Senator. I don't know why you are involved with these scum bags; they are only stirring up trouble. We are fed up with hearing about an alleged conspiracy from the groups all over America. Let's get on with our lives?' exclaimed Holmes.

'Nice speech Detective, but unfortunately for you, plus a small number of misinformed people in this country, we may be nearer to the truth than you think, and I see no reason for you to keep my clients locked up any longer, so unless you are going to charge any of them with any serious misdemeanours, I would expect you to release them all immediately,' ordered the senator.

Holmes knew he had to release them all, and soon, as he had no firm evidence that they were likely to cause any further trouble. He just didn't like the man who was standing in front of him, also he wanted to annoy him for as long as possible; plus the insistence of Nash, trying to make a case against the group made him feel he needed to be seen to be doing his bit. Earlier on in the evening, as Nash was leaving the station, he'd called in to his office, ordering Holmes to drop the terrorist charges against Alex and the rest of the group, as he had what he wanted. Much to Nash's delight, he noticed. The little creep, Holmes thought.

'They're all free to go, but bear this in mind. If they step out of line again, I may not be as lenient next time,' Holmes informed them both.

Running over to the senator, Sally wrapped her arms around his shoulders, hugging him.

After the normal formalities of signing for their possessions, the four of them left the police station knowing full well that the hard work was just beginning.

Once they were safely outside the station, Alex informed them about Nash sneakily taking away the envelope; with the pictures.

'I was going to mention it as well,' commented Sally. 'He came barging into the interview room waving the envelope in front of me, the shit.'

'Not to worry Sally,' the senator said calmly, 'with all the evidence we have in our possession, we needn't concern ourselves too much about the pictures.'

Moving closer to them all so he could be heard clearly, Alex confessed to his scam of posting some of the pictures and the two notes to a friend.

'You sly dude Alex; I would never have expected that of you. Who did you address it too?' asked Larry.

'You,' replied Alex. 'Well, not you exactly. I addressed it to your sister at the Chelsea Hotel. The only problem was, I didn't know her married name, so I addressed the envelope to Ms Summer Underwood. You don't mind, do you, Larry?'

'Fantastic,' they all cried out, Larry adding that it wasn't a problem.

'I can't imagine Nash being that astute to realize what you've done. Well done, Alex,' cooed Sally.

'What do you think happened to Harry, after we all left his apartment in a hurry?' asked Alex. 'I can't imagine Nash being too lenient with him. Did anyone see or hear from him whilst we were in there?'

'No, nothing,' the rest said.

'I wouldn't worry too much about him,' said Larry. 'From what I've seen of Harry, he would have given Nash a run for his money – we'll see him soon, you see if I'm right.'

'Come on, I suggest we have a celebratory meal, I'm paying,' announced the senator. After an overall vote of agreement from the rest of the group, they made their way to the nearest restaurant, the conversation switching to other topics, hoping it would ease the tension.

'This looks quiet enough,' commented the senator as they stood outside a warm, cozy-looking restaurant, 'not too many diners inside. Look, there's a table over in the corner which hasn't been taken. Leave it to me – being a senator does have its advantages,' he said, winking at Sally.

Making his way over to the head waiter, the senator politely asked if they could have the table in the corner.

'OK, friends, make yourselves comfortable, we may be here for a while,' invited the senator, gesturing them over to the empty table with a sweep of his hand.

Whilst they were settling down, Alex noticed Harry coming in through the entrance to the restaurant. He stood up and waved, hoping to attract his attention.

'We're over here, Harry,' called out Alex.

Harry scanned the room, searching for the voice.

Acknowledging that he had seen him, Harry made his way over to the table.

'How did you know we'd be in here?' asked Alex.

'A detective's intuition, Alex. No, it wasn't, I'm only bullshitting you. I followed you from the station,' laughed Harry.

'You silly bugger,' said Alex, laughing along with the rest of them.

'What happened to you after Nash unexpectedly appeared at the apartment?' enquired Sally.

'He was completely hacked off when you managed to escape, but unfortunately he came down on me with a heavy hand. He kept on ranting and raving about me being in cahoots with you all – he even accused me of warning Alex at the hotel the other night, which I emphatically denied,' replied Harry, smiling.

'What will happen to you now?' asked Alex.

'Nothing. I was given a stern reprimand by Holmes, who ordered me to stay well clear of you all, and as you can see, I haven't taken his warning seriously – he and Nash can go to hell. You are nearer to the truth than you have ever been, and I'm not deserting you now.'

'Bravo, Harry,' they all cried, even the senator, who didn't even know him.

'Senator, I think it's about time we introduced you to Detective Harry Pinchpeck,' suggested Sally. Harry shook the senator's hand.

Moving off his chair, Alex sat next to Harry to have a chat with him.

'Harry, am I glad to see you. What a nightmare we've all been through,' Alex stated. 'I was aware you were all being held and questioned at the station,' replied Harry, 'but in the light of my involvement, I thought it appropriate not to let on ...'

'Quiet, please, everyone,' shouted the senator, interrupting their banter. 'Before we start boring Harry with today's events, let's all decide what we are eating. I will do the honors of ordering the wine and you can tell me all you know.'

As they were tucking into their meals, the group took turns in updating the senator as to all the facts they had amassed over the last six years. Now and again it got a bit heated, when one or more of them interrupted the flow of the conversation. When they were satisfied they had told him all they knew, it was the senator's turn to inform them of his text message, saying he would have his secretary print off a copy in the morning, so they could all digest the complete text.

Alex was starting to get worried, again.

'This is now becoming serious,' he said. 'We can't just sit on these facts without reporting them to the press, and the main news channels. Once we make the American public aware of these shocking details, we may be in a safer position. I can't imagine anything horrible happening to us once we are in the public eye,' proclaimed Alex.

'Good point Alex, and I totally agree with your sentiments,' stated the senator. 'What we need to do is find a way of us all appearing on one of tomorrow morning's talk shows, and I think I may have the answer.' Getting up from his chair, moving away from the table, the senator started punching in numbers on his BlackBerry. After a few animated gestures, plus what sounded like groveling, the senator wandered back over to the group. 'It's all set. Tomorrow morning, we are all going to appear on ABC's *Good Morning America*. That's if you are all in agreement?' enquired the senator. It was Alex who responded first to the senator's unexpected announcement.

'I think it would be best if I didn't show my face, especially being a British citizen. You two go on the program, you both deserve to be there after all the hurtful comments you've had to endure over the years. Also you need to put across to the viewers all the facts you've gathered,' suggested Alex, looking towards Sally and Larry for a response. They all agreed that Alex's suggestion was the correct thing to do under the circumstances, with both Sally and Larry adding that they would be thrilled to appear on the show,

'I would now suggest that you all book into the hotel I observed on our way over here, and don't look so shocked Alex, it's my treat,' offered the senator. 'Once this is all over, you can buy me a beer, OK?'

Alex just sat there with his mouth wide open, nodding. A soft bed, with warm blankets – sheer bliss, he thought. The senator instructed one of his aides – who had been discreetly watching over the senator and the group throughout the course of the meal, to accompany them to the hotel when they had finished. The senator turned to face the group. 'I will organize a car to collect you all at seven a.m. to take you to the studio. I will be arriving earlier as I need to discuss with the producer the important points we need to raise in the debate. Ladies and gentlemen,' he said, standing up, and giving a bow, 'have a peaceful night's sleep, and we will see each other in, what, seven and half hours' time. I bid you all a good night.' And with a flourish of his hand, he made his way to the door, waving over his shoulder as he left.

Finishing their coffees, the group left the restaurant and made their way to the hotel, all feeling slightly light headed after all the free alcohol.

Alex was feeling concerned that he hadn't been in touch with his sons for a while. I'll try and find some free time tomorrow, he thought.

Once they had all checked in, wishing each other goodnight, they went straight to their rooms, with Harry saying he hoped they would let him know the outcome of the debate, which they said they would. He then headed for home.

Alex didn't bother with a shower; he would have one in the morning. All he craved for at the moment was sleep. He piled his dirty clothes on the floor by the side of the bed. 'Can't get any more creased,' he said to himself, climbing into bed.

Pulling the covers around his shoulders, he curled up, wishing Marie was lying next to him. He recalled the smell of her hair, and the feel of it against his face. If she were here, next to him, her lips would be just … He slowly drifted asleep, with a contented smile on his face.

'THE PLANE FACTS'

'President Bush personally asked Senate Majority Leader Tom Daschle
Tuesday to limit the congressional investigation into the events of
September 11. Tuesday's discussion followed a rare call to Daschle from
Vice-President Dick Cheney last Friday to make the same request.' (9/11
cover-up)

The National Commission on Terrorist Attacks on the United States ('9/11
Commission') was a blatant and obvious cover-up under the control of
Bush administration member and 'Executive Director' Phillip Zelikow.
This cover-up can be proven easily with one example: the time of Dick
Cheney's arrival at the Presidential Emergency Operations Center ('PEOC
bunker'). Secretary of Transportation Norman Mineta testified under oath
that Cheney was present at 9.20 a.m. and issuing 'orders' related to
the plane that struck the Pentagon. Mineta's testimony was completely
omitted from their final report, and a fraudulent time of 9.58 a.m. for
Cheney's arrival was given instead. (9/11 cover-up)

May 30 2002: FBI agent Robert Wright formally accuses the FBI of
deliberately curtailing investigations that might have prevented 9/11. He
is under threat of retribution if he talks to members of Congress about
what he knows. (Fox News, 11/5/02; more) He also accuses the agency of
closing down his 1998 criminal probe into alleged terrorist-training camps
in Chicago and Kansas City. Wright has written a book, but the agency
won't let him publish it or even give it to anyone. (LA Weekly, 2/8/02)

Chapter Twenty-One

'When the President does it, that means that it is not illegal.'

Richard Nixon (1913–94)

SEPTEMBER 16 2007, THE WHITE HOUSE

The White House Situation Room is a 5,000-square-foot conference room and intelligence management centre in the basement of
the West Wing of the White House. It is run by National Security
Council staff for the use of the President of the United States and his
advisers (including Homeland Security and the White House staff)
to monitor and deal with crises at home and abroad and to conduct
secure communications with outside (often overseas) persons. The
Situation Room is equipped with secure advanced communications
equipment for the President to maintain command of US forces
around the world.

The Presidential seal hangs on the wall over the chair at the head
of the table.

That was where the President was at this moment. Also seated
around the table with him were his close friends, and trusted senior advisers: the Vice-President, Secretary of Defense, Secretary of
State, plus high ranking officials from the FBI, CIA and FAA. Along
with the President, these five men and one woman were responsible
for the planning of the attacks on American soil on 9/11.

The President looked up from his newspaper, cleared his throat, and with some effort lifted himself off his chair, gesturing with his hand for the rest of the group to stay seated.

'Vision without action is a daydream. Action without vision is a nightmare. An old Japanese proverb, ladies and gentlemen, and at this precise moment in time we are in our own nightmare. I have called you all here so we can decide what action to take, if any. Another well-known American saying: We need to circle the wagons, because, my friends, we certainly need to stay together during this crisis,' he said.

It was the Secretary of Defense who spoke first.

'Mr President, the amount of publicity this group is receiving is starting to concern us all. I was informed on my way over here, that Senator Helleman has taken an interest in the so-called 'Plane Facts' group. We all know his views on 9/11, and I'm sure he will stop at nothing to get to the truth. My other main concern is, if any whistleblowers come out of the woodwork, we would then have no choice in the matter but to admit our involvement, and ultimately accept the consequences.' Sweat was beading on his face. He was a frightened man.

'I have to agree with the Secretary of Defense,' interrupted the Vice-President. 'It is more likely than not that someone out there is going to squeal sooner or later. With respect Mr President, I vote we ask our Saudi friends for help. We could fly over for an unscheduled visit, inform the press we are in delicate discussions regarding oil supplies – that way, we will be away from the limelight, and we can return when it's all calmed down.'

'What about our families?' questioned the head of the FBI. 'What do we tell them when they read about our alleged involvement? They are going to end up taking all the rage and retaliation from the American public. There is no way I will leave them to be fed to the wolves.'

The president motioned for calm. 'Ladies and gentlemen, we need to stop and consider what options we have; also our families are innocent of any wrongdoing. They have no idea about our involvement, which means they can't divulge any secrets to the press. Yet I have to agree with the VP on this one. A few weeks in the company of his Royal Highness will be beneficial to us all. It will also mean we will be safely hidden away from the press. You all know how tight the security is over there. Are we all agreed? Good. I will ask my secretary to make all the necessary arrangements with the Saudi government, and in the meantime I suggest we head over to Camp David tomorrow whilst all the arrangements are being finalized. That way we won't be inundated by the press badgering us with embarrassing questions. I'll leave it for you all to make your own way there. Don't arrive too late, or you will be left behind.' The president pointed out.

The atmosphere in the room was electric. They all knew what the consequences would be if the truth were to be made known. How would their families react? Would the people in the room be charged with genocide, then, heaven forbid, sentenced to death? All these thoughts were flying around all of their heads.

Acknowledging the fact the president had nothing more to say, the rest of them eased themselves out of their chairs, and nervously started to move out of the room to their respective homes. Hoping upon hope that no more incriminating information came to light before they left the country.

'THE PLANE FACTS'

September 10 2001: Martin Luther King, Jr. New Jersey student warns
teacher to stay away from Lower Manhattan
A sixth-grade student of Middle Eastern descent in Jersey, New Jersey,
says something that alarms his teacher at Martin Luther King, Jr
Elementary School. 'Essentially, he warns her to stay away from lower
Manhattan because something bad is going to happen,' says Sgt. Edgar
Martinez, deputy director of police services for the Jersey City Police
Department. (Insight, 10/9/02) Paul Thompson, The Terror Timeline

September 9 2001: Dallas Fifth Grader Forecasts World War III
A fifth grader in Dallas, Texas, casually tells his teacher, 'Tomorrow, World
War III will begin. It will begin in the United States, and the United States
will lose.' The teacher reports the comments to the FBI, but does not know
if they act on it at the time. The student skips the next two days of school.
The event may be completely coincidental, but the newspaper that reports
the story also notes that two charities located in an adjacent suburb have
been under investigation based on suspected fund-raising activities for
Islamic terrorist organizations. (Houston Chronicle, 19/9/01)
The FBI investigate and decides 'no further investigation [is] warranted'.
(Houston Chronicle, 1/10/01) Paul Thompson, The Terror Timeline

Chapter Twenty-Two

'Start Here ...'

ABC News slogan, 2007

SEPTEMBER 16 2007, GOOD MORNING AMERICA STUDIOS

As promised, the chauffeur-driven car arrived at 7 a.m. by the front entrance of the hotel.

Alex hadn't had time to make a drink, so he grabbed the complimentary biscuits from the tray by the bedside table. 'I'll grab a coffee at the studios,' he said to himself when leaving the room. The rest of the group was already waiting for him by the car.

'Come on, sleepy head,' shouted Sally.

'Sorry,' replied Alex, 'I could have stayed in bed all day.'

'Don't worry,' Larry added, 'you will, once this is all over, but in the meantime let's get moving, this is going to be an interesting day.'

The atmosphere in the car felt like a dentist's waiting room. They were all deep in thought, wondering what the outcome would be, once they had finished the debate.

It didn't take them long to reach the studios. Pulling up outside the main entrance, they noticed the senator making his way through the revolving doors to greet them as they got out of the car.

'Good morning, and don't look so worried, all of you. What we are about to do today could change the lives of thousands of people around the world. The producer has allocated us a thirty-minute slot to put our case forward. I have listed the main items we need to raise, but if you want to add anything to the list, please feel free. Hopefully, if we receive enough reaction from the viewers phoning in, we may be able to stay on the air for a little while longer.'

The senator handed each of them a copy of the agenda for discussion, whilst guiding them towards the studio door. Once inside, Alex started to gaze around the dimly lit room, and to his surprise he noticed there was to be a 'live' audience.

'This will be fun,' he whispered, nudging Larry's arm, gesturing with his head towards the sullen faces.

'OK, everyone, one minute before we're on air,' called the floor manager.

After being escorted to their designated seats, the group waited nervously with anticipation for the debate to start. Wishing them all good luck, Alex made his way over towards a spare seat in the audience.

'Right, everyone, five seconds, four, three, two, one,' then pointing towards the program's host, the floor manager gave the thumbs-up sign for the interview to commence.

'Good morning, I'm Doug Sanders, and this is *Good Morning America*. Today we have Senator Helleman along with two of the group calling themselves the Plane Facts. We are here to discuss the damning revelations about the alleged passengers from Flight 77 being held prisoner since 9/11, also the alleged photographs of explosives planted in the Towers – Senator, I also understand that you have recently received some additional explosive material?'

'Firstly, Doug, I would like to thank you for giving us the opportunity to discuss the facts that have come to light, and yes, only late last night I received some incriminating news from someone who states that he was involved in the events of 9/11. As you will concur, I cannot divulge any of the contents until they have been verified.'

'That is some statement, Senator – how soon before we know if the information is genuine?'

'Doug, I will make sure you are the first to know, I can't be fairer than that, now can I?'

'Senator, I look forward to hearing from you.'

The discussion then began in earnest; firstly they went over the details relating to the shocking revelations about Flight 77; then they discussed in length more of the facts surrounding the alleged pictures taken in the Towers, followed by the large amount of information the group had amassed over the past six years. The audience was completely silent for a while, shuffling in their seats, taking everything in. After fifteen tense minutes, when most of the details listed on the fact sheet had been discussed, the audience erupted into a frenzy.

Waving his arms up and down as though he were shaking a blanket, the floor manager shouted for everyone in the studio to be quiet.

'Settle down, all of you, and please be quiet. Someone's going to get hurt if you don't stop. We all want to hear what the senator and the group have to say.'

Once security had calmed the audience down, the senator gave Larry and Sally the opportunity to go over more of the damning evidence they had compiled over the last six years. They spent some time highlighting the contradictions and omissions from the 9/11 Commission's report, which came as a complete surprise to everyone in the studio. The discussion had already overrun by twenty minutes, however the studio's planners weren't too worried as they were aware that the audience figures were increasing by the minute.

The debate lasted for another ten frantic minutes, with the television company eventually deciding to pull the plug as they were running late for the rest of the day's schedule. The interview came to a halt with most of the audience seemingly on the side of the senator, and the group.

'Well, that was productive,' commented Alex, as he approached the group. 'Let's hope there aren't a lot of angry people waiting for us outside, ready to string us up.'

'I'm one step ahead of you there, Alex,' said the senator, herding them towards the exit, 'we are going out through the back door. I've organized my driver to have the car ready for a quick getaway, just in case.'

As they made their way to the rear of the building, the senator was handed a sheet of paper by his secretary.

'I have printed out the details of the text from last night, as you requested, Senator.'

Quickly glancing through, realizing its importance, the senator stopped to read the details in full, trying to come to terms with the revelation before his eyes.

Senator Helleman,

I don't want to reveal my name, but I have some important and damning information which you need to be aware of.

American Airlines Flight 77 did NOT fly into the Pentagon as reported. A missile was fired into the side of the West wall, and yes, all the passengers and crew are being held in a secret government facility.

They were escorted there by one of my fellow pilots.

The stories in the newspapers are totally correct.

I have the coordinates of the facility. I hope by my disclosing them, you may believe me.

Degrees, minutes and seconds.

Latitude: 31° 50′ 58′′N

Longitude: 106° 22′ 47′′W

Decimal degrees:

Latitude: 31.84944

Longitude: 106.37972

I also have some somber news about American Airlines Flight 93.

It didn't crash as was reported by the authorities. I was ordered by the American Government to shoot it down!

I am only confessing our involvement as confirmation that what's been said is all TRUE, but please DO NOT publicly disclose the contents of this email , as I, along with my fellow pilot, are still serving in the American Air Force.

Good luck

The senator, couldn't believe what he was reading. Was this the breakthrough they were hoping for? Genuine confirmation about the facility. Plus the additional damning information about Flight 93 was making his hands shake with rage. There had been numerous speculations about the flight supposedly crashing into the ground.

Yet there was also a large number of eyewitnesses claiming that they saw the aircraft being shot down.

The senator knew he had to bide his time for the right opportunity to disclose the details. He just hoped confirmation came from the government first, as he was worried he might endanger the lives of the two pilots.

'Alex, here, read this, it's a printed copy of last night's text message. Please pass it on to the others when you've digested it, but don't say anything when you've read it.'

Alex leant against the wall, absorbing the information. He couldn't believe his eye's. The letter from Harry's friend must be true, he thought. But what was this about Flight 93? Everything seemed to be falling into place, Alex thought. The government's statements and the so-called commission's findings were just a pack of lies and distortions.

'When the truth about Flight 93 becomes common knowledge, there's going to be a hell of a lot of ducking and diving from some tormented officials,' Alex mumbled to himself.

He started to look around, searching for Larry and Sally, noticing that the senator had steered them over to one side, asking them to wait patiently, as they must read the message.

Leaving them to read the text, the senator started to phone one of his friends, hoping to organize a plane to fly them to the location detailed in the email, and Harry's note.

Once the three of them had finished, they searched around, looking for the senator, all wanting to discuss the contents. He was still on the phone when they found him by the back door. After finishing his call he asked them all to be patient, as he would update them as to what he intended to do once they were safely back in the car. They were all starting to feel excited. At last, they had something to prove to the American public that they had been correct all the time.

Glancing over towards the main entrance through the large glass window, Alex noticed that the crowd had grown quickly. The press had now started to congregate in force, no doubt hoping for an interview with the senator, or even a member of the group. Alex could see that some of the crowd was in tears, probably clutching to the thought that their loved ones may still be alive after all these years. Also, he thought he caught a glimpse of Moon leaning over by the wall, glaring back at him, then recollecting that he'd only been in Moon's company for a short while the other night. I must be mistaken, he thought.

Ushering the group to the waiting car, the senator opened the doors for them to enter. Once the senator was satisfied they were safely locked inside, he headed towards the excited crowd assembled by the main door, deciding at the last minute to address them, hoping for calm.

'Ladies and gentlemen,' he started to say, raising his voice above the chatter, 'I realize you have heard a great deal of damning information this morning. Please leave us to investigate all the facts we have been given. As you will be aware, we have to pass on to the authorities all the details that have recently come to light; for legal reasons, and I am currently putting together an agenda so I can address Congress as soon as possible. Once that has been carried out, I will propose that we vote for an unbiased public inquiry to be set up.' He hoped that might appease the crowd for the moment.

The majority of the crowd seemed to be satisfied with the senator's statement. There were some shouts from a few of them, all wishing him luck. Ignoring the barrage of shouted questions from the press, he stealthily walked away. The crowd was now reluctantly dispersing from outside the main entrance, which gave the senator the opportunity to walk over to the waiting car unmolested, and to the group, who were anxiously waiting.

The three of them had sat in the car, staring out of the open windows, listening to what the senator had to say. They felt he had won their respect and hearts. After closing the door and fastening his seat belt, he turned his head to face the others sat at the back. He briefed them on the phone call he'd had with a friend who had an executive Learjet, which would be waiting for them at the airport on their arrival, in the next few hours.

This caused the three of them to look at each other in amazement.

'Do you think that's wise senator? We're not one-hundred percent certain the coordinates are correct, and if they are, I would imagine the security around the base being the most stringent in the whole country, I can't see us getting anywhere near it,' enquired Larry.

'There's only one way to find out my friends. Are you with me or not?' shouted the senator. After a few nervous seconds, all three nodded in agreement, crying out. 'We're with you!'

'Great news,' replied the senator, twisting awkwardly around in his seat to shake their hands.

'What are you going to do about the email, Senator?' asked Sally.

'Nothing for the moment, Sally,' replied the senator. 'As the pilot states, we can't afford to disclose it to the media, as this would only jeopardize their safety. Let's deal with finding the facility first, and hopefully by then more discoveries may have come to light, and we won't need to mention it, will we?'

They all agreed that was the best course of action.

'Right, now, where were we ... oh yes. I would suggest,' the Senator said, 'we get in touch with Harry right away. Let's give him the opportunity to come with us. We need someone on hand who will be able to recognize at least one of the passengers, which in this case will be his partner Nat, and what a reunion that will be.'

Sally didn't waste any time in getting hold of Harry on her cell phone.

Harry said he had hoped they would contact him, especially after what he'd heard being discussed in the debate on the television. Sally brought Harry up to date with the email, also inviting him on the flight. Harry couldn't believe what he was hearing. A possibility he could be seeing Nat after all these years, he thought. Once they had got their emotions in check, they agreed to collect Harry, before heading off to the airport.

It took them twenty minutes to drive to Harry's apartment, with the senator and the rest of the group meeting Harry by the front door, with him eagerly waiting to set off.

After saying their hellos, they proceeded to the waiting car, which would take them to the airport.

The Learjet's tanks had been filled up, with the pilot waiting patiently, pacing around on the edge of the runway.

Leaving the car, the senator and the group made their way over.

'Brad, I appreciate your help, and for responding so quickly.' The senator offered his hand. 'What you are going to be involved with today will give you something to talk about for years to come.'

'Senator, you've always known my feelings about the events surrounding 9/11, so if there is any way I can help in finding the truth, I'm in.'

After the senator had introduced the rest of the group to Brad, they all climbed into the jet and strapped themselves in, ready for take-off. The flight time was estimated at two hours.

'What I can't understand is how the government have managed to keep the facility hidden from the public for all these years,' commented Alex.

'Alex, our government are damn good at keeping secrets when it's in their own interest,' said Larry. 'You've only to cast your mind back to the late 1940s when an alien spacecraft allegedly crashed at Roswell in New Mexico. That was quickly hushed up after an Army Intelligence officer, who went to investigate the crash site, reported collecting unusual debris from the site, claiming it was "not on this earth," then he mysteriously changed his original story the following day, saying it was only a weather balloon. The guy must have either been threatened, or he was on drugs. Also, we are still not certain if and what involvement the CIA had in the assassination of President Kennedy, or whether Lee Harvey Oswald was working alone or not. I've also recently heard rumors that the Apollo Moon landings were faked. Accusing NASA of using a large indoor studio to recreate the surface of the moon. I would have thought that would be enough to convince you, Alex?'

'When you put it like that, no, it doesn't surprise me at all,' answered Alex.

They became silent for a while, relaxing in the lush leather seats. Harry used the time to wonder what Nat would look like, but more importantly how would he react, once he was free. He was brought out of his reverie by Brad announcing that they were only ten minutes from their destination.

Harry's hands were beginning to sweat; his heart was thumping in his chest – he was nervous and exhilarated at the same time.

They all looked out of the windows, searching for the facility, wondering what it would look like.

I couldn't begin to think what it would be like to live in isolation for this long, thought Alex.

Cruising for a further five minutes, Brad banked to the left. It was then they all spotted a landing strip in the distance. Suddenly, Brad's radio came to life; he was ordered to move away from the area, immediately, or they would be shot down.

'Young man,' shouted the senator down the hand-held microphone, 'my name is Senator Gerry Helleman, and I, along with my friends are passengers on this jet, and we have reason to believe that you are keeping prisoners, passengers and crew from Flight 77 to be precise, which supposedly crashed into the Pentagon. I don't know if you and the rest of your colleagues have seen the television recently, or read any newspapers lately, but there are a growing number of articles and disclosures about the events surrounding 9/11. So I would strongly suggest you give us the authority to land.'

To their astonishment, they all noticed row after row of single-story buildings, all surrounded by what seemed to be barbed wire, some of which looked as though it might be electrified. Alex also noticed that there were a number of towers strategically placed around the perimeter of the facility, reminding him of the prisoner-of-war camps the Germans used during the Second World War.

'Well it appears that Harry's note, along with the email was correct all along,' declared the Senator, glancing out of the small Learjet's window. The rest of them nodded their heads in agreement, staring at the unimaginable image before them.

'We'll wait a few minutes, then I'm going to land over by those bushes to the left. The tarmac looks reasonably sound from this distance,' suggested Brad, nodding to his left

317

They didn't have long to wait before permission was given for them to land, with Brad being informed which runway to use, and within minutes the sleek Learjet was taxiing to a remote part of the base. After Brad had cut the jet's engines, they all climbed out, and waited anxiously on the tarmac. In the distance, through the shimmering heat, they noticed a line of large black limousines, their darkened windows reflecting in the sun. The imposing cars came to an abrupt stop, inches from the nervous visitors.

All of a sudden, they all felt threatened. They knew they couldn't go back to the jet and fly away. Harry had an awful feeling that they could all be held here. But the more he thought about it, the more he realized he was becoming paranoid. At least they had the good sense to leave the details of the base with the senator's personal secretary.

The cars' engines were killed, yet there was no sign of any movement coming from any of them.

'There're only trying to frighten us, don't worry,' whispered the senator.

'They don't have to try too hard, I'm already shaking in my boots,' replied Sally.

Without any warning, the car doors suddenly opened, revealing six very muscular gentlemen. Harry moved his eyes from one to another, weighing them up. They all looked as though they worked out, and they all wore the same black suits and mirrored sunglasses.

Harry had to smile to himself even though he was frightened – they all looked as though they were extras in the next sequel to The Matrix.

Taking off his sunglasses, one of the men made his way over to the group. He introduced himself to them all.

'Good afternoon, gentlemen ... sorry, and lady. My name is General Andrew Rainford, I'm responsible for the running of this government complex. You were fortunate that you weren't shot down when we first monitored you on the radar. This base is out of bounds to everyone – even the President would require special authorization before he'd be allowed to enter. I can inform you that I have been given direct orders from the highest authority to escort you within the complex, and off the record I, along with my fellow officers, have been waiting for this day to arrive for a long time. We have never been comfortable with the incarceration of these good men and women ... I have instructed all of the "detainees" – that's what we call them – to meet us in the main recreation hall, and Senator, I would like you to address them, give them the good news that they will soon be reunited with their loved ones.'

Harry's shoulders lifted. He was elated that he was at last going to meet Nat, also somewhat surprised that they were being received without any kind of threat.

The General led them to the waiting cars, and once they were seated, they made their way towards the line of buildings, first having to pass through the two sets of security posts, unheeded.

The General had mentioned to them on the way over that he had informed the 'detainees' that they were going to be given some unexpected good news. After pulling up outside the main building, they all made their way into the bustling hall, with Harry hurriedly entering through the large wooden double doors, his head moving from left to right, seeking out the face of his friend Nat.

There were a large number of people wandering around the floor, all looking bewildered, not knowing what to expect. Harry even noticed a few women with babies. 'Well,' he whispered, 'life goes on regardless of the circumstances.'

He stealthily moved around the room, acknowledging with a smile anyone who glanced at him. It was after heading towards the front of the hall, near the stage, when he noticed Nat. He had a smile on his face, stretching from one ear to the other; tears running down his cheeks.

'You certainly took your time . . . call yourself a detective?' sobbed Nat, grinning.

'Sorry partner,' murmured Harry, realizing he was also crying.

Slowly walking towards each other with open arms, they came together, embracing each other tightly. Both of them, not feeling at all embarrassed, burst into uncontrollable tears of joy.

When they finally parted, the rest of the crowd in the hall started to cheer and clap, shouting out their own feelings. The atmosphere was ecstatic, with both men and women hugging each other, all with tears streaming down their faces. They all had an idea they were going home.

During all the excitement, Sally had produced a notebook from her pocket so she could capture the response in words for her next story. But on reflection she decided to put it away, as she felt the image before her would be something she would treasure for the rest of her life.

When the senator felt it was the right time to address them, he made his way onto the stage, gesturing to the crowd for silence. The tension in the room was electric, the atmosphere wonderful. Certain he had their undivided attention; he started to inform them why he was with them today.

'I know you have already been told that you will be given some good news. Well, ladies and gentlemen, the good news is by this time tomorrow you will all be back with your families.'

The senator knew there was no need to say any more for the time being – that was all the news they wanted to hear. Once the crowd had settled down, the senator quickly asked them to pack whatever they needed for the flight, informing them they were to be flown out on two aircraft around lunchtime the following day.

'And not to worry,' he reassured them, 'this time you will arrive safely at the correct destination.' Again the response to his 'witticism' was rapturous and joyous. Yet there were a few angry words aimed at the General and his aides, demanding answers. The General kept constantly apologizing to them all, saying he was just following orders, and he was truly sorry for keeping them locked away all this time. Eventually, the crowd accepted his apology and dispersed, knowing that their nightmare was nearly coming to an end.

With everyone starting to make their way to their apartments to organize themselves for the following day, Harry quickly briefed Nat about his involvement with the group, also the other disclosures which had come to light over the last few days, which didn't come as no surprise to Nat, especially after what he'd been through over the last six years, yet he was eager to find out what was happening out there in the big wide world. He told Harry that all the time they had been held at the facility they had never been given a newspaper or allowed a television. Nat also insisted on introducing Harry to Jack, the 'janitor' who had organized the sending of the letter.

Jack wrapped his hands around Harry's, pumping them up and down in an excited manner, apologizing for keeping his friend in isolation for so long.

'Jack, it wasn't your fault. But I would like to thank you for looking after my friend.'

'No problem. I don't know if Nat has told you everything, Harry, but I'm also a government agent.'

Harry wasn't surprised, but he was relieved to know that Nat had had a caring person to watch over him.

The senator asked the general if he could use a landline, so he could contact his secretary back at his New York apartment.

'Come this way Senator, this office is private – the phone is over there on the desk. Corporal, please guard the door – no one is to enter whilst the senator is on the phone.'

'Sir, yes, sir,' replied the soldier, saluting them both.

The senator spent ten minutes describing the scenes he had just witnessed to his secretary, before checking to make sure that the collection of the passengers and crew were in hand.

He was assured that everything had been organized, and he wasn't to worry.

Before leaving for the base, the senator had instructed his secretary to contact the two Airlines who had lost planes on 9/11; United Airlines, and American Airlines, and warn them of the possible rescue of the passengers and crew from Flight 77, and for each of them to organize an aircraft to fly them all back to JFK airport the following day. Both Airlines said that wouldn't be a problem, adding that this was the least they could do.

For the passengers and crew of Flight 77, the next few hours would feel like years. The emotions going through the men and women were mixed. Had their husbands and wives remarried? Were their mothers and fathers still alive? How would they react? Hundreds of thoughts were running around in their heads.

'THE PLANE FACTS'

August 6 2001: Suspicious trading of companies affected by 9/11 may begin by this date

Insider trading based on advanced knowledge of the 9/11 attacks may have begun on this date, if not earlier. Investigators later discover that a large number of 'put option purchases' (a speculation that the stock will go down) that expire on September 30 at the Chicago Board Options Exchange are bought on this date. If exercised, these options would have led to large profits. One analyst later says, 'From what I'm hearing, it's more than coincidence.'

(Reuters, 20/9/01) Paul Thompson, The Terror Timeline

April 29 2004: Bush and Cheney Privately Meet with 9/11 Commission; Decline to Provide Testimony under Oath

President Bush and Vice-President Cheney appear for three hours of private questioning before 9/11 Commission. (Former President Clinton and former Vice-President Al Gore met privately and separately with the commission earlier in the month.) (Washington Post, 30/4/04; *New York Times*, 30/4/04)

The commission permits Bush and Cheney to appear together, in private, and not under oath. The testimony is not recorded. Commissioners can take notes, but the notes are censored by the White House.

(Newsweek,2/4/04; Knight Ridder, 31/3/04; New York Times, 3/4/04) The commission drew most of their questions from a list submitted to the White House before the interviews, but few details about the questions or the answers given are available. (Washington Post, 29/4/04) Two commissioners, Lee Hamilton and Bob Kerrey, leave the session early for other engagements. They claim they had not expected the interview to last more than the previously agreed upon two-hour length. (*New York Times*, 1/5/04) Paul Thompson, The Terror Timeline

January 29 2002: Bush Sees an 'Axis of Evil'
President Bush's State of the Union speech describes an 'Axis of Evil' consisting of Iraq, Iran, and North Korea. Adviser Richard Perle cautioned against these same three countries a month before 9/11. Bin Laden is not mentioned in the speech. (CNN, 29/1/02) The speech is followed by a new public focus on Iraq and a downplaying of bin Laden.

Huffman Aviation flight school, where Mohamed Atta and other alleged hijackers trained, had a Learjet seized by the DEA with '43 pounds of heroin' on board. No one was ever prosecuted in connection with the 'biggest drug seizure in central Florida history'. (9/11 cover-up)

Chapter Twenty-Three

'The Lord watch between me and thee, when we are absent one from another.'

Bible

SEPTEMBER 17 2007, BIGGS AIR FORCE BASE, El Paso Texas

The day the surviving passengers and crew from Flight 77 had thought would never arrive, had arrived.

They, along with the senator and the group, stood side by side on the apron of the runway, basking in the warmth of the morning sun, focusing on the miracle unfurling before them.

'Harry,' murmured Nat, 'what will happen now to the president and his advisors. Do you know if he's addressed the American people yet?'

'I've no idea, I haven't bothered with the news recently, I've been too busy, but I'll check it out, once we've landed. When I come to think about it, I have noticed over the past few days that the president has been conspicuous by his absence, so what does that tell you?'

'Interesting,' remarked Nat, as he began to make his way over to one of the waiting aircraft.

The sudden realization of the events that were about to be played out suddenly alarmed Nat, which made him stop in his tracks. 'Harry, I'm frightened – there'll be all those reporters with their cameras stuck in my face, screaming out for some kind of statement. It's not just me who will be unnerved – the others will be frightened and overawed as well.'

'Nat, don't worry, the senator has already made arrangements for a VIP suite to be made available for the reunion, as far away from the rest of the main terminal building as possible. He has also informed the press that there will be a statement issued to them all, once everyone has been secretly taken away from the airport. He drafted it out last night; so you will all have time to read and digest it, once we are on board and safely on our way.'

After thirty tense minutes all the passengers were on board the two aircraft, safely strapped in their seats. The cabin's atmosphere was serene, with everyone sitting still, all gazing through the windows, waiting nervously for take-off.

Nat began thinking of what he would say to his mother, especially after all these years; also, the thought of his father not being there to greet him caused him some heartache. I'll take it as it comes, he thought.

The deafening rumble of the enormous engines indicated that they had been given clearance for take-off. The two aircraft taxied towards the runway, and without too much of a delay the pilots opened the throttles, making them judder, taking them effortlessly down the runway, and finally take off. The second aircraft departed minutes after the first one.

Once both aircraft were in the air, with the seat belt light extinguished, the senator brought out the champagne. Larry emulated the senator in the other aircraft. Larry had insisted that they split up, ensuring that ALL the passengers were looked after during the tense flight to JFK airport.

'There are going to be a lot of tears when we meet our families,' said Nat to Harry, clinking their glasses of bubbly to the people closest to them.

'Yes, but in this case the tears will be tears of joy,' answered Harry.

JFK AIRPORT

Once word had got out to the media and the public about the return of the passengers and crew from Flight 77, a multitude of interested people, along with hundreds of reporters from all over the world, were all waiting patiently around the perimeter of the airport, and inside the arrivals hall.

There were also the families and friends of the passengers and crew of Flight 77, waiting nervously in a private room in the terminal building.

The main terminal building at JFK airport was buzzing with anticipated newspaper reporters and camera crews, all vying for that all-important interview with the passengers and crew, most of them unaware that they had no chance of that.

Most of the airport had been taken over by the world's media, TV trucks with giant antennae extended to their maximum height dominating the scene. Among them were thick, overlapping cables and news commentators with their microphones at the ready for their live feeds to the newsrooms around the world.

Air traffic control at JFK Airport had arranged with the other Airlines earlier that morning asking them to delay all their incoming and outgoing flights once the two aircraft carrying the returning passengers were nearing the airport. All emphatically agreed.

It was around noon when the two aircraft appeared from the East; the sun reflecting off the planes wings. Once everyone positioned around airport was certain it was them, the shouting and cheering erupted from thousands of happy, anxious onlookers. The packed crowd of reporters and newspaper camera men were jostling one another, all eager to take that important picture.

After a pleasant and event-free flight, they began to make their final approach towards JFK airport. When they were nearing the terminal buildings, peering out of the windows, the passengers were shocked to see the vast number of spectators and news reporters waiting for their return.

'This monumental day will be remembered by every law-abiding citizen of the free world,' the senator declared to the now excited passengers. 'We must all remember these events, and keep reminding our children and grandchildren of the mistakes and terrible decisions this American administration have made.'

Everyone on board nodded, agreeing loudly with his sentiments.

Once the two planes had landed safely, they were instructed to taxi towards the main VIP arrivals hall. On exiting the aircraft, the flight crew wished everyone a good day and the best of luck for the rest of their lives. Hugs and tears were the order of the day as they left. The passengers tentatively made their way towards the VIP room, knowing that their loved ones would be waiting. They had to be brave, not just for their sakes, but for everyone else's around them; the automatic doors opening to a silence you could cut with a knife.

It was only when they entered the room that the atmosphere completely changed, the air becoming charged with emotion, men, women and children running across the room shouting, crying and hugging their loved ones.

The group, along with the senator, stood by the entrance, soaking up the euphoric reactions of the families.

There are no words that could define the momentous spectacle in front of me, thought Alex, lost in the atmosphere radiating around him.

Nat then appeared in front of them, stopping to shake their hands, and once again thanking them for all their help and determination, tears welling up in his eyes. After taking a deep breath, Nat slowly entered the room, scanning the faces of the exuberant crowd around him, his eyes darting in all directions, searching for his mother, then spotting her, all alone, sat on a chair by one of the large viewing windows, seeming to be in a daze, probably assuming her son was never coming home. Then holding back the tears; trying to suppress the lump swelling up in his throat, he cautiously made his way towards her, not wanting to frighten her. Then kneeling down, he gently reached out and tenderly cupped her hands in his, stroking them. 'Ma, it's me, Nat. I've finally come home.'

Looking up into his watery eyes, she smiled, and fell into his welcoming arms, sobbing her eyes out.

Harry, Alex, Larry and Sally, plus the senator, took one last look at the happiness radiating around the room before walking away, leaving the automatic doors to close behind them.

'A good job well done, Senator. Now we can begin to question the President and his accomplices,' remarked Sally.

At that moment they all felt relieved, and elated. Tears were in all of their eyes, and Alex had a lump in his throat, which he was trying to swallow down, knowing he wouldn't be able to. With their arms wrapped around each other's shoulders, in a group, they made their way to the waiting car which would eventually take them all back to the senator's safe, warm apartment.

'THE PLANE FACTS'

A Short History of Impeachment

The right to impeach public officials is secured by the US Constitution in Article 1, Sections 2 and 3, which discuss the procedure, and in Article 11, Section 4, which indicates the grounds for impeachment: 'the President, Vice President, and all civil officers of the United States shall be removed from office on impeachment for, and conviction of, treason, bribery, or other high crimes'.

Removing an official from office requires two steps: (1) a formal accusation, or impeachment, by the House of Representatives, and (2) a trial and conviction by the Senate. Impeachment requires a majority vote of the House; conviction is more difficult, requiring a two-thirds vote by the Senate. The Vice-President presides over the Senate proceedings in the case of all officials except the President, whose trial is presided over by the Chief Justice of the Supreme Court. This is because the Vice-President can hardly be considered a disinterested party – if his or her boss is forced out of office he or she is next in line for the top job!

What are 'High Crimes and Misdemeanors'?

Bribery, perjury and treason are among the least ambiguous offenses meriting impeachment, but the ocean of wrongdoing encompassed by the Constitution's stipulation of 'high crimes and misdemeanors' is vast. Abuse of power and serious misconduct in office fit this category, but one act that is definitely not grounds for impeachment is partisan discord. Several impeachment cases have confused political animosity with genuine crimes. Since Congress, the vortex of partisanship, is responsible for indicting, trying and convicting public officials, it is necessary for the legislative branch to temporarily cast aside its factional nature and adopt a judicial role.

The Fifth Amendment

'No person shall be held to answer for a capital, or otherwise infamous crime, unless on a presentment or indictment of a Grand Jury, except in cases arising in the land or naval forces, or in the Militia, when in actual service in time of War or public danger; nor shall any person be subject for the same offense to be twice put in jeopardy of life or limb; nor shall be compelled in any criminal case to be a witness against himself, nor be deprived of life, liberty, or property, without due process of law; nor shall private property be taken for public use, without just compensation.'

Chapter Twenty-Four

'The only thing we have to fear is fear itself.'

Franklin D. Roosevelt (1882–1945)

SEPTEMBER 17 2007, CAMP DAVID

Camp David is located seventy miles from the White House in the Catoctin Mountains of Maryland.

It was established in 1942 as a place for the President to relax and entertain. President Franklin Delano Roosevelt wanted to escape the summer heat of Washington, DC, and the higher altitude of the Camp provided cool breezes and good security.

President Roosevelt called the Camp 'Shangri-La' after the mountain kingdom in James Hilton's book Lost Horizon.

It was renamed Camp David in 1953 by President Eisenhower in honor of his grandson.

The President had just turned off the TV after watching the passengers and crew land safely at JFK airport. He didn't want to prolong the pain and suffering any longer than necessary.

'Things are moving too quickly for my liking, sir,' was the first thing the Secretary of Defense said as he entered the president's office.

'I can see what the hell's happening, you dumb shit,' screamed the president, 'and where the hell did Senator Helleman get all his information from? For Christ's sake, we've being paying out millions of dollars over these last six years ensuring everyone kept their mouths shut. We've even had to silence a few of those who were giving us some concerns.'

The president started pacing around the room, keeping a watch-ful eye on his Secretary of Defense, becoming worried that he might panic, deciding to divulge everything to the press.

'Where are the rest of them? They should have been here by now,' shouted the president.

'The Vice-President and Secretary of State are in the next room on the phone to their families. The last time I saw the others was in the Situation Room at the White House yesterday. I would presume they're on their way over here ...'

The conversation was interrupted by the ringing of the phone on the president's desk. He picked it up and listened to the voice on the other end; his expression and obvious agitation didn't give the SoD much confidence.

After listening for maybe a couple of minutes, the president slammed the phone down, and collapsed into the chair behind the desk. He leant back, and did a fair imitation of a church steeple with his hands, stroking the underside of his chin with the tips of his fingers. He began to stare out of the window, watching the innocent wild birds flying from tree to tree, wishing he was one of them. He didn't turn around; he just spoke quietly, his voice quivering slightly.

'It looks like we are the fortunate ones. . . the rest of them have been arrested. They didn't even manage to get their bags packed... Secret Service Agents were waiting for them when they arrived home last night ...'

They were interrupted by a knock at the door.

'Enter,' shouted out a nervous and worried president.

In walked the president's personal secretary looking pale and distressed.

'Mr President, there are a number of government agents at the main gate insisting they be allowed to enter. They are here at the behest of the Speaker of the House; with direct orders to arrest you, and escort you all back to the White House for questioning, Sir.'

The president had come to the conclusion that the game was finally over. No, it's not, he thought, lifting himself of the chair.

Looking across at a frightened Secretary of Defense, the president ordered him to go and summon the Vice-President and Secretary of State, and pointing to his personal secretary, instructed him to contact the pilot and have him prepare Marine 1, and to get in touch with the crew of Air Force One, as that would be required very soon, and also to ensure that the fuel tanks were filled to their maximum.

'We are going to Andrews airfield, and on to Saudi Arabia, but earlier than planned,' said the president, hastily throwing a number of documents into his leather briefcase.

After a quick phone call to the pilot, the president was advised by his secretary that Marine 1 would be ready to leave in two minutes.

At that moment the SoD's cell phone rang. He looked down to see Nash's name come up on the ID screen. He hesitantly answered it.

'Not now, Nash, I'm busy at the moment.'

'Yes, I know, I'm one of the agents down by the main gate,' whispered Nash, covering the mouthpiece with his hand. 'We're here to arrest you all. If you let me through, I may be able to stall the others for a while, then at least you'll have some time to decide what your next move will be,' he suggested.

'We've already made that decision. We're taking Marine 1 to Andrews, and from there we are flying to Saudi Arabia on Air Force One, so goodbye Nash.'

'In that case, unless you want me to spill the beans, you'd better take me with you,' pleaded Nash.

'Wait a minute, I'll have to ask the president.'

Putting the phone down by his side, he conveyed Nash's proposal.

The president nodded, still staring out of the window. He wasn't too bothered; he just wanted to get away from there as quickly as possible.

'Wait there, Nash, I'll send someone down to escort you back here,' snapped the SoD.

As Nash was making his way into the main hall, the President, along with the SoD, VP and SoS, were hurriedly leaving, heading straight for the helicopter which was waiting for them on the carefully manicured lawn, the blades slowly beginning to rotate. Nash didn't utter a word, he just followed them out, his head down, not wishing for anyone in the vicinity to recognize him.

Marine 1 had lifted off before the doors were safely closed.

'Never mind the fucking door, just make sure you're strapped in,' bellowed the president, panicking.

With the door securely closed, the five of them sat back, hoping they would make it to Andrews Air Force Base before anyone realized what they were up to.

The president once again contacted Air Force One's pilot and crew, insisting that they be ready to take off as soon as they arrived.

In a storm of flying dust, and a deafening roar from the engines, Marine 1 touched down just feet from the gantry leading up to the aircraft.

The president had already opened the door to the helicopter, and was attempting to jump out before the rotor blades had stopped. Ducking beneath still-churning rotors, three fleeing men, and one woman, raced over towards AFO, with the distinctive wail of police sirens in the background.

Yet one lonely figure stayed back in the helicopter, deciding they no longer wanted to be associated with the President.

Hoping everyone was focused on the spectacle enveloping around the president, the shadowy figure stealthily emerged from the helicopter's open door, and glancing left and right, satisfied there was nobody in sight, casually headed towards the gate in the perimeter fence, slowly blending in with its surroundings ...

Andrews Air Force Base is a United States Air Force base in Prince George's County, Maryland. Located near Washington, DC, it is the home base of the US presidential aircraft, Air Force One.

Air Force One is the air traffic control call sign of any US Air Force aircraft carrying the President of the United States.

Hastily making his way into the cockpit, the president ordered all the crew, including the two pilots, to leave the aircraft immediately.

'All of you out now,' screamed the president, herding the frightened looking crew members through the exit and down the stairs as quickly as possible. The president praying that they were all off the aircraft before any of the pursuing vehicles arrived.

'We can't possibly fly the plane by ourselves,' shouted one of the fugitives.

'Don't worry, I haven't been wasting my time whilst I've been traveling around the world on presidential duties. I had an idea one day this situation may arise, so I cleverly used the time to my advantage. Unbeknown to the pilots, they have been innocently giving me instructions on how to operate and fly this aircraft, and to put all your minds at ease; flying Air Force One has become so automated that once the plane's onboard computers are programmed with the flight's data - destination and cruising altitude, the aircraft will literally fly itself, so just go back there and sit down. Strap yourself in and make yourselves as comfortable as possible, it's going to be a long flight.'

Once the gantry steps had been disengaged from their holding position and the doors securely closed, the president informed the passengers over the intercom that he was preparing for take-off. The three fugitives were so preoccupied with finding seats and buckling up for the flight, that they hadn't noticed that one of the group – who had entered Marine One, had mysteriously disappeared during the time they were making their escape.

AFO slowly eased away from Marine 1, with the president trying very hard to skirt around the dozens of police cars who were attempting to block their path, barely avoiding colliding with several of them as they locked their brakes, leaving clouds of thick black smoke to pour from their tires. 'What the hell are they doing?' the president cried out. 'They're going to kill us.'

The president began to concentrate, carefully going through the preflight checklist, ensuring the onboard computers were all activated and ready for take off, also feeling confident that they had managed to escape; when suddenly, gazing up through the cockpit window, he was alarmed to see a large number of police cars and fire-tenders, headlights blazing, forming a barrier one hundred metres in front of the aircraft, preventing it from taking off.

'Listen up back there. Make sure you're all strapped in properly, it's going to get bumpy,' called out the president.

The roar of the engines increased, causing the behemoth to glide smoothly down the apron, leaving dozens of emergency vehicles to swerve out of the way, desperately trying to avoid being crushed by the enormous wheels of the Boeing 747. The crunching bangs of collisions piercing the thunderous noise of the aircraft.

AFO was just a few metres away from colliding with the vehicles which were trying to block their path, when unexpectantly, the aircraft veered to the left, causing the nervous passengers to scream out in fright, all three of them being thrown about in their seats.

Advancing down the now congested runway, one of the aircraft's large wheels clipped the rear bumper on one of the police cars, forcing it to one side, then smashing into the back of another pursuing vehicle, causing it to flip over and crash down on its roof, the passenger compartment pounded flat in an explosive halo of shattered glass. Other vehicles were hastily swerving out of the way, tires screeching and exploding, the smell of burnt rubber drifting in the afternoon air.

AFO finally accelerated down the runway towards the open countryside, and freedom, leaving the pursuing vehicles, along with their occupants staring in disbelief, the look of disappointment showing in all their faces. After a further nervous sixty seconds of accelerating, Air Force One was eventually airborne; the sounds of sirens growing fainter and fainter behind them.

The passengers in the private presidential lounge breathed a sigh of relief, rubbing their sides, checking one another for any sprains or bruises. Certain that no one was seriously injured, they all settled back in their seats, preparing themselves for a long flight.

During the time the president and his accomplices were making their escape, the Speaker of the House had taken over as President; assuming responsibility for running the country, as stipulated in the American Constitution.

Orders had been given for F-16s to be scrambled from Langley Air Force Base. Ironically, two of the pilots were Gary and Ray. They didn't hesitate to jump into their jets and chase after the president. There were a total of ten F-16s in the air monitoring AFO. Air traffic control instructed the pilots to report back when they had clear sight of the cockpit of AFO.

It didn't take long for them to reach AFO. With a maximum speed of 1,500 mph, the F-16's were nearly three times as fast.

'Control, this is Delta One, we have visual contact, over,' reported Gary.

'Delta One, keep a safe distance, we are trying to persuade the President to return to Andrews, over,' replied control.

'Roger that, control,' was his reply.

The Speaker of the House had taken over all of the negotiations with the fleeing President.

'Mr President, you and the rest of your senior advisers must return to face your punishment. The whole nation is watching and listening. There is no way we can let you leave the country.'

'Don't waste your breath; we are not turning back, so just get on with electing a new government and a new President. You know what? I did all of this for America, for the country I love. I always had the best intentions for my people. We needed to be the predominant country in the world, and return it to the great nation it once was. We were losing the fight on terrorism, something had to be done about it, and I DID IT!' The president was laughing in a high-pitched hysterical laugh, a hair's breath from being out of control.

'For the last time, Mr President, please turn the plane around,' pleaded the Speaker.

'Go to hell,' cried the president.

For five tense minutes, AFO, along with its escort of ten F-16's soared thousands of feet above the dark blue waters of the Atlantic Ocean. Millions of people throughout America, and around the world were glued to their television screens, either at home, in offices and department stores, or witnessing the unthinkable event on the two large screens in Time's Square, as it was being broadcasted live from a camera mounted on the nose cone on one of the F-16's.

'Mr President, this will be my last appeal I am going to make before I order Air Force One to be blown out of the sky; I cannot, I repeat, cannot let you leave the country, please return to Andrew's,' implored the Speaker of the House.

'You haven't got the balls,' yelled the president, as he was closely monitoring the F-16's through the cockpit window.

'Delta One, this is the Speaker of the House, take them down, that's a direct order.'

'Roger that Madam Speaker,' replied Gary, and instructing the other pilots to move away from AFO.

Gary felt he needed to talk to the Vice President first; he presumed he was on board. 'Mr Vice-President, I hope you can hear me over the intercom, this is Delta One, the pilot you ordered to shoot down United Airlines Flight 93 over Pennsylvania, and in one of the other F-16s is the pilot who escorted Flight 77 to the secret base. So you see, ladies and gentlemen, you can all go to hell.'

Two Astra BVRAAM air-to-air, heat-seeking missiles left Gary's F-16 at Mach 2, which took less than five seconds to strike Air Force

One's engines on both wings. The flames and debris shot out from all sides of the plane. Bright bursts of fire illuminated the sky. What was left of Air Force One plunged into the sea, resulting in enormous plumes of spray and steam to soar skywards.

Gary had made sure that AFO was well clear of any signs of civilization before firing his missiles, as he didn't want any more innocent deaths on his conscience.

The group were all sitting down in the front room of the senator's New York apartment when they witnessed the destruction of AFO on the television screen. No one spoke, leaving the silence to stretch for ten minutes. The atmosphere in the room was subdued. At last, the 'group' had been vindicated after all the abuse and hurtful comments they had endured over the past six years.

It was Alex who broke the sullen silence. 'Well, I suppose I can go home now. But to be honest, I am going to miss you all. Thanks for your help and support over the last few days. Wow, what a story I'm going to tell my mates down at the local pub when I get home.' It was now a time for celebrating.

'A new start for our country begins today,' stated the senator. 'No doubt there will be dozens of other officials being arrested and questioned about their involvement. It's going to take years to sort this mess out.

'Alex, we need to sort out a flight for you, your family must be sick with worry … I have a phone in the next room. Go ahead and ring your sons, I think they will be happy to hear from you.'

Alex stood up and shook the senator's hand, thanking him once again.

Settling down by the desk, Alex eventually reached Michael at home.

Alex said he didn't want to say too much over the phone, but he did say he was fine and he was looking forward to coming home. Alex then rang Andrew, repeating the conversation he'd had with Michael.

When he had finished he sat back, reflecting over what had happened to him over the past few days, also feeling drained, and happy to be going home.

Returning to the rest of the group, there wasn't any more cheering or backslapping going on. They were all saying that they would be interested in hearing all the relevant facts surrounding the events of 9/11.

The senator's secretary walked into the room with a sheet of paper in his hand, which he passed on to Alex.

'You have been booked first class on tomorrow evening's flight to London's Heathrow airport. From there you will catch a transfer flight to Manchester. A car has been arranged with the British government to collect your sons from Leeds, from where they will be chauffeured across to Manchester airport to meet you. You will all be chauffeured home from there. Your sons have been notified, so there is no need for you to ring them again.'

Alex's eyes were filmed with tears. He thanked the senator and his secretary, and took the itinerary to study it quietly in the corner.

'You will need some space and privacy with your family once you arrive home. You've been through a lot recently,' remarked the senator.

Glancing over once again, Alex whispered to him, 'Thank you,' and carried on reading.

The rest of the afternoon was just a daze for them all.

They gradually left for their own homes, and insisting on accompanying Alex to the airport the following day.

'Don't argue,' said Larry, 'we will be there for you, you are one of the Plane Facts group now, we always stick together. And rather than hanging about for most of the day, waiting for your flight, why don't we all take you down to see the Statue of Liberty, and before that we can all call in at my favorite eating place for a typical American breakfast. It's the least we can do after all you've been through, and you did say you would have liked to have seen Lady Liberty.'

Alex was stunned by the love oozing out from the group.

'Thanks, Larry, that would make my day, or should I say … my holiday.'

'That's settled then. We will collect you at eight a.m. from the hotel. Hopefully the senator may arrange to have four VIP tickets waiting for us at the ferry ticket office; you know how difficult it is to get tickets at such short notice?' chuckled Larry.

'Very funny Larry and yes, I think I may be able to sort that out for you.' The senator laughed, which made them all start laughing.

Alex once again thanked them all for their kindness, and wished them all goodnight, and ending by saying as usual, 'See you later.'

And as usual, the rest of them just stood and stared, trying to work out the meaning of what Alex had just said. Larry said he would explain it to them later, once Alex had left.

The senator had offered to have his driver take him back to his hotel, but Alex declined, saying he wanted to be alone for a while.

After a leisurely sixty minute walk, welcoming the fact that he was not having to be always glancing over his shoulder, also reliving the last few hectic and frightening days, he decided to hail a cab to take him back to the hotel; he also needed to collect the possessions he had left behind in Larry's apartment.

Alex walked in through the main entrance of the hotel with mixed feelings.

His thoughts drifted back to the night he'd arrived, all that excitement, not knowing what would be in store for him whilst visiting New York – little did he know at the time what trouble he would end up in.

The desk clerk gave Alex a puzzled look, and without comment passed over his room key. 'Thank you, and have a nice day.' Alex smiled.

On reaching his room, Alex was shocked to see the damage that had been inflicted on the woodwork to the door frame; fortunately the hotel's management had re-fitted a new door. 'Well they certainly don't do things by half in America. They could at least have asked for a spare key,' laughed Alex as he was entering his room; and to his pleasant surprise, Larry had already organized for his belongings to be moved to Alex's room. He must have returned earlier in the afternoon, Alex presumed.

It didn't take him long to sort out the clothes he'd left, plus his books, which he carefully packed away in his suitcase and small shoulder bag.

'Well, at least I'll have something to take back from my holiday. Shit, that reminds me, I said I would bring something tacky back for the boys. I'll ask Larry's advice on that tomorrow, I'm sure he'll have some suggestions.'

The past few days had completely worn Alex out, and all his muscles were starting to ache.

He decided he would have a long soak in the bath before retiring to bed.

Leaning back in the bath, Alex wondered what it would have been like if Marie had been here with him, all that running about…

It was the coldness of the bath water which brought Alex out of his slumber.

'Jeez, it's c-c-c-c-cold, what time is it? B-b-b-b-loody hell, I've been in here two hours, no wonder the waters c-c-c-cold.'

Jumping out of the bath, Alex quickly rubbed himself down with a big fluffy towel, hoping to generate some warmth around his cold shivering body.

Once he was warm and dry and in his pajamas, he placed his suitcase over by the door, ready for the morning.

He then slipped into bed, hoping he would have an undisturbed sleep for once.

'THE PLANE FACTS'

July 26 2001: Ashcroft Stops Flying Commercial Airlines; Refuses to Explain WHY!

CBS News reports that Attorney General Ashcroft has stopped flying in commercial airlines owing to a threat assessment, but 'neither the FBI not the Justice Department ... would identify (to CBS) what the threat was, when it was detected or who made it'. (CBS News, 12/7/01) Ashcroft demonstrated an amazing lack of curiosity when asked if he knew anything about the threat. 'Frankly, I don't,' he told reporters. (San Francisco Chronicle, 3/6/02)

It is later reported that he stopped flying in July based on threat assessments made on 8 May and 19 June. In May 2002, it is claimed the threat assessment had nothing to do with al-Qaeda, but Ashcroft walked out of his office rather than answer questions about it. (Associated Press, 16/5/02)

The San Francisco Chronicle concludes, 'The FBI obviously knew something was in the wind ... The FBI did advise Ashcroft to stay off commercial aircraft. The rest of us just had to take our chances.'

(San Francisco Chronicle, 3/6/02) CBS's Dan Rather later asks of this warning: 'Why wasn't it shared with the public at large?' (Washington Post, 27/5/02) Paul Thompson, The Terror Timeline

Chapter Twenty-Five

'Adversity does teach who your real friends are.'

Lois McMaster Bujold

SEPTEMBER 18 2007, Chelsea Hotel

For the first time in ages, Alex had managed to have a good night's sleep.

He woke up at 7 a.m. and he was washed, dressed and heading down the creaky lift with his cases by 8 a.m. He dropped his keys off at reception, wishing the desk clerk to 'have a nice day', and exited the entrance expecting to see Larry waiting for him on the sidewalk. 'I guess he's still in bed; lazybones,' remarked Alex, giggling to himself.

Alex was still overawed by the lobby in the hotel. If I do come back to visit New York, he thought, I will make sure I come back here.

He had noticed over the last few days, during the time he had been on the run, the endless number of stretch limousines.

'Wow,' he cried out in surprise, 'here comes one now.'

'Hell fire,' Alex shouted, noticing Larry's cheeky face peeping out of the open back window of the limo.

'Your carriage awaits you sir,' said Larry, opening one of the doors for Alex.

'Where did you get this from?' asked Alex. 'You haven't stolen it, have you?'

'Compliments of the senator. He said we must all relax in style for the day, so we are … Applejack's Diner at 1725 Broadway and

55th Street, please driver, we're going for breakfast, in comfort,' announced Larry.

The diner was situated near the corner of Broadway, so it wasn't much of a problem for the driver to park the exceptionally long car outside.

The glances from the pedestrians, along with the customers already seated in the diner, made them all start to giggle like children as they left the car.

'Grow up, guys and gals, this is serious,' said Harry, laughing out aloud himself.

When they had all composed themselves, they made their way inside.

Once again, Alex was impressed by what he saw. The booths were made of wood and glass, and dotted around the room were shelves which held framed pictures of famous celebrities.

The place was clean, and it had a friendly atmosphere, which Alex was now becoming used to. They all ordered American breakfasts, with Alex deciding to be brave, ordering pancakes with maple syrup. He could never understand how you could eat something so sweet with bacon and eggs. A bit like sweet and sour chicken at the Chinese, he then thought.

They were all delighted with the food, and as expected there was a constant supply of black coffee served throughout the course of the meal.

After paying the bill, they all climbed back into the limo, and politely asked the driver to take them to the ferry for Ellis Island.

The conversation in the drive over eventually came back to the previous day's exploits and the shooting down of Air Force One.

'Why do you think the President didn't return to the airfield, Harry, and what will happen to the rest of his so-called accomplices?' asked Alex.

'I can't answer that, Alex,' replied Harry. 'The only consolation is that we as a nation won't have to go through a long trial, hearing witness accounts day after day, with hundreds of so-called whistleblowers claiming they were terrorized into perpetrating the acts of violence after they and their families were threatened. I think I can say this for all of us Americans in the car, we have had enough bad publicity for one decade. It's something the rest of the world will remember about The United States America – we're not infallible, as we think. Do you all agree?'

There was universal agreement from them all, even from Alex.

'I have heard that constitutional lawyers representing those involved are claiming their clients are completely innocent, saying it was the president and his closest advisers who instigated the whole thing,' commented Larry.

'I can't believe that. They must have known what was going to happen – you can't choreograph something so meticulous without the help of the CIA, the FBI and the FAA,' stated Sally.

'No doubt we'll never find out, I can imagine most of what happened will be kept out of the public domain … I'm so sorry, in all the excitement of the past few days, I haven't asked you how Tony is. Is he any better?' asked Larry.

'You don't have to apologize, Larry, in actual fact, I forgot about him at one point. Yes, he's fine, thanks. The doctor said he actually opened his eyes yesterday, and he should be on the mend now. The problem I've got is having to tell Mom that Tony's alive. I'm going to have to think of a way of breaking the news, gently.'

'If you need any support, and help, we're here, right, Harry?' said Larry.

'Too right,' shouted Harry.

'Whatever happened to Nash, Harry?' asked Alex.

'We're not certain, the security cameras at Camp David show him, along with three other men and one woman, heading for Marine 1, yet the CCTV cameras at Andrews Air Force Base only picked up four shadowy figures entering Air Force One. The senator has asked airport security to check all the tapes, then hopefully they may be able to make a positive ID of them all.'

The mood in the car became suddenly depressed and solemn.

'Hey, come on, we are supposed to be enjoying ourselves, let's all cheer up. Alex will be on his way home soon, so let's send him home feeling happy. OK?'

They all agreed, giving each other 'high fives'.

THE STATUE OF LIBERTY

The statue has guarded the entrance to lower Manhattan since 1886, hoisting her torch high overhead in a salute to personal independence, and casting a censorious gaze east towards Europe, an 'unenlightened' entity to the original builders when it came to individual freedoms.

Sculptor Frédéric Auguste Bartholdi built the 305-foot-tall, 225-ton statue, but Gustave Eiffel contributed the skeleton.

'Liberty Enlightening the World', a gift from the people of France, was unveiled in 1886.

The limo driver sedately parked the car by the side of the road, as near to the ferry terminal as possible.

The weather was ideal for cruising around the island, Larry announced. Alex wasn't too sure – he could see a few swells, making the contents of his stomach react to the motion.

'Come on, you softies, the cold breeze will blow the cobwebs away,' shouted Larry.

'I think the breeze will blow away more than cobwebs, Larry,' cried Alex. 'Make sure you're all downwind of me if I become ill, and if you see me run for the side, duck.'

The rest of the group looked towards Alex, concern on their faces, as they didn't want to be near him in those circumstances.

They all eventually made it safely on board, and thanks to the first-class tickets the senator had managed to bribe from one of the ferry's main shareholders, they were able to relax in the luxury suite, overlooking the front of the boat.

'Relax and enjoy the view, you may never see it again, Alex,' remarked Sally.

'I hope to return someday,' answered Alex, handing over the envelope he'd posted to Larry's sister. 'Here, you may as well have these now, Larry said I could keep them as a reminder of my visit, but I'm sure they'll be of some use to you if you decide to write a full account about Tony and Nat.'

'Thanks Alex, but I think it would be best if I handed them over to the senator, I'm sure he'll know what to do with them,' replied Sally, and planting a kiss on his cheek.

I could get used to this, thought Alex, a big smile on his face. He sat back, and to his surprise the movement of the ferry wasn't as bad as he had thought it would be.

The mood of the nation was sombre. People were shocked by the revelation of the President of the United States and his closest advisers being party to the most horrendous acts of terrorism on American soil.

The ferry made its way slowly around the island, ensuring that the many tourists on board had enough time to snap hundreds of photos to take back home.

By the time it was on its return journey the wind had increased, causing a heavy spray to come across the boat. This was a good excuse for Alex to go back inside into the warmth of the cabin.

When the seventy-five-minute trip was over, they all visited the restroom to wipe away the spray from their clothes, as they didn't want to dirty the seats in the car.

It was time to drive Alex to the airport. He had mentioned early on in the day that he would like to be there at least two hours before the flight left, so he would have time to relax before leaving America, and his new-found friends.

JFK Airport, New York

Fog was starting to descend over the runway, which made Alex think he might be in America a while longer.

'Don't look so worried, Alex,' remarked Harry, 'I've just checked with the information desk, they said they don't expect any delays. The fog should be lifting soon; it doesn't hang around this airport for too long. So that's it, Alex, you will soon be on your way.'

'Yes, and thanks again for letting me stay at your apartment the other night. I hope you can now start living your life to the full again, now you know Nat's safe and well.'

'It's going to take him, and the rest of the passengers and crew, some time to get used to being in crowds; also having to catch up on the events of the past six years … now that is a lot of reading, Alex.'

'Shit, I promised to buy the boys something tacky from New York. Any suggestions, people?' He looked around the group for help.

'You'd be best waiting until you get through to the duty-free side of the gate, there is bound to be a souvenir shop selling those kinds of things,' suggested Larry.

'Thanks, I suppose I'll have to,' replied Alex.

Looking up, he noticed that the screen was now showing that his flight would soon be boarding.

Checking to make sure he had his shoulder bag with him, Alex turned around to face the familiar, friendly faces.

He shook their hands in turn, and hugged them tightly, informing them individually that he hoped to come back soon, to visit them. He also invited them to come over and visit him in the UK if they wanted to. He gave each of them a note containing his address and telephone number, hoping they would keep in touch.

Tears were starting to flow down his cheeks, and the rest of the group found it hard not to show their own feelings.

When all the goodbyes had been said, Alex headed towards the departure doors, waving over his shoulder, leaving them to stare at his back.

'Alex,' they all called out in unison, 'SEE YOU LATER!'

'THE PLANE FACTS'

United Flight 23 Hijacking Averted?
Shortly after 9 a.m. United Airlines Flight 23 receives a warning from flight dispatcher Ed Ballinger. Flight 23 is still on a Newark, New Jersey, runway, about to take off for Los Angeles. Apparently in response to Ballinger's message, the crew tells the passengers there has been a mechanical problem and returns to the departure gate. A number of Middle Eastern men (one account says three, others say six) argue with the flight crew and refuse to get off the plane. Security is called, but they flee before it arrives. (CBS News, 14/9/01; Chicago Daily Herald, 14/4/04) Later, authorities check their luggage and find copies of the Koran and al-Qaeda instruction sheets. Ballinger suspects they got away. A NORAD deputy commander later says,
'From our perception, we think our reaction on that day was sufficient that we may well have precluded at least one other hijacking. We may not have. We don't know for sure.' (Globe and Mail, 06/13/02)

September 19 2001: Unverified Reports of Additional Flights to Be Hijacked
The FBI claims on this day that there were six hijacking teams on the morning of 9/11. (*New York Times*, 19/9/01; Guardian, 13/10/01)
On 14 September, two knives were found on an Air Canada flight that would have flown to New York on 9/11 if not for the air ban. (CNN, 15/10/01)

Chapter Twenty-Six

'Beginning is easy – continuing is harder.'

__Japanese proverb__

United Kingdom

After a tearful reunion with his sons at Manchester Airport, being constantly bombarded with questions about his ordeal in New York, Alex led them over to the waiting chauffeur-driven car, and in comfort, headed back across the Pennines, to the safe sanctuary of his home.

Since returning from New York, Alex had been spending most of his time reminiscing about the past few hectic and frightening days, both with his sons and with his mates down at the local pub.

Alex's fifteen minutes of fame became more like fifteen hours, and counting, with everyone wanting to talk to 'The Englishman' who was party to bringing down the American government.

He had become an overnight celebrity, which Alex wasn't too keen on.

Forty-eight hours later

Relaxing in his chair by the fire, Alex was just about to start reading one of the books he'd bought on his trip when the hall phone rang.

Dropping the book on the coffee table, making his way across the room to answer it, there was an impatient loud knocking on the front door. 'Just hold on a moment will you please?' shouted Alex, glancing across at the distorted figure, silhouetted through the frosted glass of the door.   On reaching the phone, Alex answered it.

'Hello, Alex Monroe speaking.'

'Alex, it's Larry.'

'Hell fire Larry, missing me already . . . ?'

'Alex, the senator finally received the findings of the CCTV footage from the security firm at Andrews,' interrupted Larry. 'You're not going to believe this Alex ... the four figures running up the steps into Air Force One ... Nash wasn't one of them. He's still out there somewhere . . .'

ACKNOWLEDGEMENTS

I wouldn't have been able to compile the facts and statistics for this novel without the aid of the following publications:-

The New Pearl Harbor, David Ray Griffin (Arris Books)

The 9/11 Commission Report – Omissions and Distortions, David Ray Griffin (Arris Books)

9/11 Contradictions, David Ray Griffin (Arris Books)

The Terror Timeline, Paul Thompson (Harper)

Dude, Where's My Country, Michael Moore (Penguin Books)

The Terror Conspiracy, Jim Marrs (The Disinformation Company)

The Uncensored History of the 9/11 Commission Investigation, Philip Shenon (Little, Brown)

9/11: The New Evidence, Ian Henshall (Robinson)

Also I wouldn't have been able to write this novel without the help and patience of my wife, June and all my family.

TO THE READER

As I have already stated at the beginning of this novel, the story is based on my imagination.

YET:- 'The Plane Facts' statements that appear before each chapter, plus the details listed on the 'leaflet' and statements in the news articles, have been taken from the above publications and the media.

There are hundreds of publications, along with thousands of details in the media, and on the Internet, listing the facts and eyewitness accounts of the tragic events of 9/11.

It was when I was reading about all the lies, distortions and contradictions given out by the American government and the 9/11 Commissions Report, that I knew I had to get across some of the appalling facts to a wider reading audience.

Unless you, as an avid reader, know about the availability of these publications, you won't go out and buy them. These books tend to be located either on the lower ground floor or hidden somewhere in the political section of bookshops.

I hope you have enjoyed this novel.

If you want to find out more information, I would strongly recommend that you purchase at least one of the above publications.

Thank You

Lightning Source UK Ltd.
Milton Keynes UK
04 March 2010

150898UK00001B/62/P